WORD OF HONOR

Visit us at www.boldstrokesbooks.com

What Reviewers Say About Radclyffe's Books

A Matter of Trust is a "...sexy, powerful love story filled with angst, discovery and passion that captures the uncertainty of first love and its discovery." – *Just About Write*

Shield of Justice is a "...well-plotted...lovely romance...I couldn't turn the pages fast enough!" – Ann Bannon, author of *The Beebo Brinker Chronicles*

"The author's brisk mix of political intrigue, fast-paced action, and frequent interludes of lesbian sex and love...in *Honor Reclaimed*...sure does make for great escapist reading." – *Q Syndicate*

Change of Pace is "...contemporary, yet timeless, not only about sex, but also about love, longing, lust, surprises, chance meetings, planned meetings, fulfilling wild fantasies, and trust." – *Midwest Book Review*

"Radclyffe has once again pulled together all the ingredients of a genuine page-turner, this time adding some new spices into the mix. *shadowland* is sure to please—in part because Radclyffe never loses sight of the fact that she is telling a love story, and a compelling one at that." – Cameron Abbott, author of *To The Edge* and *An Inexpressible State of Grace*

Lammy winner "...*Stolen Moments* is a collection of steamy stories about women who just couldn't wait. It's sex when desire overrides reason, and it's incredibly hot!" – *On Our Backs*

"With ample angst, realistic and exciting medical emergencies, winsome secondary characters, and a sprinkling of humor, *Fated Love* turns out to be a terrific romance. It's one of the best I have read in the last three years." – *Midwest Book Review*

"*Innocent Hearts*...illustrates that our struggles for acceptance of women loving women is as old as time—only the setting changes. The romance is sweet, sensual, and touching." – *Just About Write*

Lammy winner "...*Distant Shores, Silent Thunder* weaves an intricate tapestry about passion and commitment between lovers. The story explores the fragile nature of trust and the sanctuary provided by loving relationships." – *Sapphic Reader*

In *When Dreams Tremble* the "...focus on character development is meticulous and comprehensive, filled with angst, regret, and longing, building to the ultimate climax." – *Just About Write*

By the Author

Romances

Innocent Hearts

Love's Melody Lost

Love's Tender Warriors

Tomorrow's Promise

Passion's Bright Fury

Love's Masquerade

shadowland

Fated Love

Turn Back Time

Promising Hearts

When Dreams Tremble

The Lonely Hearts Club

The Provincetown Tales

Safe Harbor

Beyond the Breakwater

Distant Shores, Silent Thunder

Storms of Change

Winds of Fortune

Honor Series

Above All, Honor

Honor Bound

Love & Honor

Honor Guards

Honor Reclaimed

Honor Under Siege

Word of Honor

Justice Series

A Matter of Trust (prequel)

Shield of Justice

In Pursuit of Justice

Justice in the Shadows

Justice Served

Erotic Interludes: *Change Of Pace*
(A Short Story Collection)

Erotic Interludes 2: *Stolen Moments*
Stacia Seaman and Radclyffe, eds.

Erotic Interludes 3: *Lessons in Love*
Stacia Seaman and Radclyffe, eds.

Erotic Interludes 4: *Extreme Passions*
Stacia Seaman and Radclyffe, eds.

Erotic Interludes 5: *Road Games*
Stacia Seaman and Radclyffe, eds.

WORD OF HONOR

by

RADCLY*f*FE

2008

WORD OF HONOR

ISBN 10: 1-60282-018-X
ISBN 13: 978-1-60282-018-0

THIS TRADE PAPERBACK ORIGINAL IS PUBLISHED BY
BOLD STROKES BOOKS, INC.
NEW YORK, USA

FIRST EDITION: JUNE 2008

CREDITS
EDITORS: RUTH STERNGLANTZ AND STACIA SEAMAN
PRODUCTION DESIGN: STACIA SEAMAN
COVER DESIGN BY SHERI (GRAPHICARTIST2020@HOTMAIL.COM)

Acknowledgments

The Honor series has spanned nearly the entire length of my professional writing career. *Above All, Honor* has had multiple publishing "homes," had even more covers, and has been translated into French and Spanish. Blair Powell, Cameron Roberts, and the world they inhabit are as real to me as the room I sit in now. In the more than ten years that I have written the story of their first tumultuous year together, my life has undergone almost as many changes. I discovered the Internet, found *X-Files* fanfic, posted my novels online, published my first book, started a publishing company, retired from surgery, and with *Word of Honor*, will have published my twenty-ninth novel. Cam and Blair's story is not the first story I told, but it has been the most enduring, and as to whether they will return, as a good friend of mine has written, "*Never Say Never.*"

My thanks go to my first readers Connie, Diane, Eva, Paula, and RB, as well as to my editors, Ruth Sternglantz and Stacia Seaman, and to the generous proofreaders at Bold Strokes Books for making this a better book. All the credit goes to these dedicated individuals and the responsibility for any shortcomings to me.

Sheri, with gratitude, for divining my thoughts and creating magical images for our covers.

To Lee, for patience, good humor, understanding, and the best of all stories. *Amo te.*

Radclyffe 2008

Dedication

For Lee
Every word

CHAPTER ONE

Thursday

I'm going to kill whoever is pounding on the ceiling downstairs," Blair Powell muttered, stretching across the naked body of her lover to squint at the alarm clock. "It's five fifteen. I'm not just going to kill them, I'm going to dismember them."

"Baby, hang on for a minute." Cameron Roberts pulled Blair down against her chest and stroked her back. Threading her fingers through Blair's tousled, curly blond hair, she kissed her. She bypassed the playful first-of-the-day *good morning, I love you* kisses and moved right along to the deep, possessive *you belong to me* kisses that would distract Blair from the activities going on in the command center below them.

"Mmm." Blair relaxed on top of Cam and fit her hips to the hollow of Cam's pelvis. "Don't think I don't know what you're doing."

Cam chuckled and skimmed her hands up and down Blair's back, ending at her firm backside. She massaged Blair's ass and kissed her again. When Blair gasped and tipped her head back, Cam trailed the tip of her tongue down Blair's neck to the base of her throat. "If you don't know by now, I've been doing something wrong for almost a year."

"I know you think this will buy whoever's down there a few more minutes of safety."

"Is it working?"

"What do you think?" Blair braced her arms on either side of Cam's shoulders and watched Cam's face as she slowly rocked between her legs. In mid-November, dawn was still an hour away, and she had only the glow of the streetlights bordering Gramercy Park to see by, but it didn't matter. She would have known Cam's scent, her touch, the carved angles and planes of her face in total darkness. Her heart beat to the rhythm of Cam's heart, and she knew with quiet and unrepentant certainty that were Cam's heart to stop beating, hers would too. Cam's heart beat quickly now, strong and full, as Cam lifted her hips to meet Blair's. Cam's jaw tightened and her dark eyes focused with fierce intensity on Blair's face.

"I think you've started something you're going to have to finish," Cam said.

Blair smiled, her breath coming faster as she felt the teasing anticipation swirl in the pit of her stomach. "Oh really?"

Cam reached between them and cradled Blair's breast. She rubbed the pad of her thumb over Blair's nipple until Blair caught her lower lip between her teeth and moaned softly. "Yes, really."

"If you keep doing that," Blair murmured, leaning down to lick Cam's lower lip, "I'm going to *finish* first." She closed her eyes and bore down harder with each rolling thrust, letting the pleasure Cam was igniting in her nipple flame the excitement between her legs. So easy, so easy to let everything go, to lose herself for just a few minutes in Cam. "God, that feels good."

A loud thumping filled the room and the bed vibrated, the legs rattling against the polished wood planks.

Blair's eyes snapped open. "What the—"

"Ignore them," Cam ordered, covering Blair's other breast. Rapidly, she squeezed and released her nipples. "Weren't you just about to—"

"Yes."

"Yes, what?"

"I'm going to come," Blair whispered, her lips parted in pleasure.

"That's what I thought." Cam drank in the sight of Blair trembling above her, the muscles in her neck standing out in sharp relief as she climbed toward climax.

"Oh that's…Cam, I'm…" Blair whimpered softly and shuddered into orgasm.

Cam caught her as she slumped down and cradled her face against the curve of her neck. She kissed Blair's forehead as Blair snuggled into her and sighed contentedly. "The alarm doesn't go off until six. Go back to sleep."

"What about you?" Blair said drowsily.

"You can join me in the shower."

Blair murmured something that sounded like *goody* and dropped off.

Cam sifted Blair's hair through her fingers and watched the patterns of light flicker on the ceiling as sunlight penetrated the fall sky. The sound of hammering and the occasional screech of nails pulling free from wood filtered up from the floor below. The renovations on the command center used by the Secret Service agents who guarded Blair should be finished in a day or so. The same morning as the terrorist attacks on the World Trade Center, four heavily armed men had invaded Blair's penthouse apartment in a building bordering Manhattan's Gramercy Park and nearly succeeded in killing her. Blair's loft—code-named the Aerie—had largely escaped damage during the assault, but her Secret Service operations center one floor down had taken heavy fire. Blair hadn't been able to return to Manhattan until just a few days ago when her protection detail could resume on-site monitoring as well as coordinate the security for her day-to-day activities. In addition to personal protection, her eight-person security team coordinated advance reconnaissance for her many public appearances and assessed the myriad reports complied daily by the National Intelligence Program from sixteen or so intelligence organizations.

Unfortunately, although the command center was functional, some construction remained to be finished, and Blair's tolerance for noise and disruption was wearing thin. Everyone's patience, not just Blair's, was honed to the bone. The lives of the men and women who provided vital security for the first daughter, as well as those who had been assigned to Cam's special OHS counterterrorism team, had been irrevocably altered on the morning of September 11. For those who dedicated their lives to preserving the security of the nation and its most important representatives, the desperate search for answers and the heightened pressure to prevent further tragedy were a constant strain.

Cam considered her new team—the best of the best—culled from other security agencies when the Office of Homeland Security was hastily put together and she was named a deputy director. Renée Savard, former FBI; Felicia Davis, former Secret Service; Ricky Sanchez, her newest recruit from the ATF; and one other, a deep CIA operative who might still be the target of a domestic terrorism cell and those in power who aided them. All highly trained, all seasoned agents. None of them were sleeping well. All of them struggled with guilt over their inability to foresee or prevent the terrible events of that fateful Tuesday in September. And now they lived with the unspoken fear that it could happen again unless they did something.

Two months after the attacks, the nation remained at red alert and Blair's security status at Priority One. Blair was never without a security detail, not even when she was home. The only reason there wasn't an agent in her apartment at that moment was because Cam had been Blair's security chief for most of the previous year and could stand in for an agent when necessary. Still, Blair chafed at the restrictions, and as much as Cam understood and sympathized with her lover's reluctance to have her freedom so severely restricted, she wholeheartedly embraced the necessity of safeguarding the president's daughter. Blair was not just the president's only child, she was an important public figure in her own right. She often represented the White House at public functions and acted as an international diplomat in her father's stead. She was a symbol of the United States, and as such, her security was nearly as critical as the president's.

Cam shifted carefully and tightened her hold on the woman who slumbered in her arms. Blair had already been a target of a sniper's bullet and the skillfully orchestrated full-on tactical assault that had nearly succeeded in assassinating her in her own home. Cam had been in charge of Blair's security detail then, and she would never forgive herself for allowing the infiltration of her team by a traitor who nearly managed to gun down her lover. She'd been cleared of any dereliction of duty, but no report exonerating her from responsibility for the assault could assuage the knowledge that she had failed. She could not afford to fail again. None of them could.

"You're not sleeping," Blair said, smoothing her palm over Cam's chest. "And you're not relaxed. Your heart is pounding like you're running a marathon."

"That's what instant replays of the good parts do to me," Cam replied lightly.

"Cameron."

Cam sighed. "Sorry. I don't know why I haven't figured out that you can read my mind."

"I can't read your mind. But I know what your body's telling me. What are you worrying about?"

"Nothing." Cam kissed Blair before she could protest. "I mean it. I was just thinking."

"And…" Blair leaned up on an elbow and traced a finger along the edge of Cam's jaw. "Don't make me pull it out of you, Cam. That will only piss me off."

"Being back here—it's hard not to think about what happened."

Blair caressed Cam's face. "I suppose it would be foolish of me to think you're ever going to forgive yourself."

"It's not about forgiveness," Cam said. "I need to understand what went wrong, so it doesn't happen again."

"I get that part," Blair said. "But I also know you're blaming yourself."

Cam laughed sharply. "Since I was in charge, that seems appropriate."

"See? You're starting to piss me off."

"I know. I'm sorry." Cam ran her hands through Blair's hair and cradled her face in her palms. She traced her thumbs over the arch of Blair's cheekbones. "I love you. It doesn't matter to me who your father is or what claim the world has on you. You're the woman I love, and that means I need to keep you safe."

"Oh, Cam." Blair kissed her softly, then shook her head. "I love you for exactly the things about you that drive me crazy."

Cam grinned. "I think that works in my favor."

"I think you're right."

"Is it time for that shower?"

Blair bit Cam gently on the chin. "You think if you cloud my brain with sex I'll forget that you're beating yourself up over something that wasn't your fault?"

"I know you won't let me get away with feeling guilty for long." Cam wrapped her arms around Blair and turned them over in bed until she was lying on top of her. "I know you love me and you want to protect me."

"That seems silly, doesn't it," Blair said. "Me protecting you."

"No, not at all." Cam rested her forehead against Blair's. "It makes me feel safe. The only place in the world I feel safe is with you."

"Don't make me cry, Cam." Blair's voice was hoarse and her hand trembled as she ran her fingers through Cam's thick dark hair. "You've been hurt too—almost killed more than once. I can't stop seeing every single bruise and scar, even when I close my eyes."

"Blair, baby," Cam said soothingly.

"No. Don't tell me about facts and figures and how it's a one in a million thing you'll ever be hurt again." Blair's smile softened the harsh edge to her words. "I understand the risks. It's a new world now, and I know there's no looking back. I understand that we all have to do what we can to make it a safe one."

Cam was quiet a long moment. "I was thinking one of the first things we need to do is get married."

Blair laughed, some of the heaviness in her heart lifting. "Well, I'm glad that's on your agenda, because we have a date to do just that in just about ten days."

❖

Diane Bleeker bolted upright in the center of the king-sized bed in her Upper East Side condo overlooking Central Park. The space beside her was empty, and with a gasp, she threw back the covers and swung her legs to the floor. She was nude except for a pale peach camisole, and she shivered although the apartment was warm. She grasped a navy silk robe from the bottom of the bed and pulled it on as she rushed down the darkened hall. She didn't bother turning on lights. The early gray light filtering through the double glass doors from the living room balcony was enough for what she needed to see. Valerie.

Heart sinking, she surveyed the empty living room before yanking open the closet next to the front door. Valerie's coat was there, but the last time Valerie had vanished in the middle of the night, she had taken nothing with her.

"Diane, I'm here."

"Oh!" Diane clutched her robe closed and spun around. Valerie stepped inside from the balcony and closed the doors behind her. She wore an oversized cotton shirt closed with a few buttons between her breasts. Her legs were bare. "God, darling, you must be freezing."

"I'm fine," Valerie said.

When she gripped Diane's shoulders carefully and kissed her, her hands were cold but her lips were invitingly warm. "I can't seem to stop frightening you. I'm sorry."

"You didn't frighten me." Diane rubbed Valerie's forearms, wishing that she could warm the cold place inside her. She'd never been more aware that love was not always enough, and she alternated between feeling angry and helpless. "Couldn't sleep?"

"Just restless." Valerie forced a smile, which she expected Diane could see right through. In the four weeks since she had almost been killed by the same fanatical "patriot" who had tried to assassinate Blair, she'd been haunted not by the near-death experience, but by the fifteen years of her life she had blindly devoted to an organization she could no longer trust. Recruited into the Company right out of high school, she had assumed an identity that had been painstakingly created for her, and over the years she had been many people. So many people that she wasn't certain there was anything of *her* left at all. When she awakened in the night from her never quite sleeping state to find Diane slumbering innocently beside her, she was tormented with the absolute certainty that she did not deserve this woman's trust or her love. Cameron Roberts might have orchestrated both her death in an explosion in the Atlantic as well as her subsequent rebirth as an OHS agent, but that didn't mean the Company hadn't targeted her for elimination. Even someone as powerful as Cameron Roberts could not protect her from a shot in the dark on a deserted street or an ice pick slipped between her ribs in a crowded subway. In some part of her mind, she had always expected death to come that way, swiftly and unexpectedly. She didn't fear her own death, but she was terrified that her mere presence in Diane's life placed her in harm's way.

"If you tell me what's wrong, I can help you," Diane said quietly.

Valerie caressed Diane's cheek and kissed her again. "I'm not certain I should be here. It might be better if I stayed in a hotel for a while."

"Because?"

"Someone may be looking for me."

Diane drew a shaky breath. "Someone may be trying to kill you."

"Diane," Valerie said gently.

"There's no point pretending otherwise. I know you might still be in danger." Diane took Valerie's hand. "Come back to bed."

"I can't. I need to get ready for the briefing."

"I keep forgetting how ridiculously early you people start your day." Diane forced a note of levity into her voice. "Then come into the kitchen while I make coffee."

Valerie followed her, and in comfortable silence they ground coffee, filled the coffeepot, and took down cups while waiting for the coffee to brew. She had never shared such simple domestic moments with anyone in her life. She had never lived with anyone, never had a long-term relationship, never been in love. She had loved another woman, one woman, and loved her still, but not with the consuming need that she felt for Diane.

Valerie leaned back against the counter and Diane put her arms around her waist.

"You told me that Cam hasn't been able to uncover any evidence that the Company or anyone else is looking for you," Diane said. "You said the cover story of you being killed in the boat explosion would be enough. Especially with your handler gone."

"All of that is probably true. Henry was the link between me and whoever he reported to up the company food chain, and with him dead and the cover story Cam put out about my death, I might just be a line item on someone's tally sheet." Valerie knew the hole in the argument was that her handler might have given her identity away, but she wasn't going to frighten Diane over things she couldn't change. "So with everyone in the intelligence community focused on finding who was behind 9/11, I'm probably not on anyone's to-do list."

"But you don't believe it?"

Valerie looked away.

"I know it's hard for you to trust me—"

"No," Valerie said immediately. "I do trust you. It's just that—*listen* to yourself. You're standing in your kitchen talking about handlers and targets and cover stories." Frustrated and angry, hating the weakness that kept her in Diane's life when she knew, she *knew*, it was wrong, Valerie plunged a hand through her short, thick red-blond curls. She'd cut her hair, she'd changed the color, she was wearing green contact lenses to cover her blue irises—another new identity, another new history. But at heart, she remained a cipher, even to herself. "Is this really what you want in your life?"

"Is that a rhetorical question?" Diane snapped. "Because I'm tired of answering it." She gave Valerie a small shake and forced her to meet her gaze. "I love you," she said with slow emphasis on each word. "What part of that don't you understand?"

"Any of it." Valerie closed her eyes and pulled Diane close. They were very nearly the same height, and she rested her cheek against Diane's. The scent of Diane's perfume lingered ever so faintly along her hairline. She'd gone to sleep countless nights dreaming of that fragrance. "I don't have a clue why you love me."

"Well, I'm tired of telling you." Diane kissed Valerie's mouth, then moved to her neck. "So I'll have to work harder at showing you. Come back to bed. The coffee will keep."

Valerie laughed softly and abandoned good judgment, letting Diane tease her into surrendering, for the moment.

❖

A stocky young redhead sipped coffee from a tall paper cup as he stood at the window of his rental unit watching Blair Powell's building. Directly across the gated park that occupied a square city block, the lights came on in Blair Powell's loft. Shadows flickered behind the drawn curtains of what must be the bedroom. To the casual observer on the street, her windows appeared to be like all the others in the building, but he knew they were constructed of bulletproof glass. The doorman who stood inside the double doors in a topcoat and uniform was also a private security agent. A Secret Service agent would be stationed behind the desk. Secret Service Agent Cynthia Parker had been at that post when his brothers-in-arms had burst through those doors a little over two months before, firing automatic weapons. According to intelligence reports, the female Secret Service agent had killed one of his compatriots before she'd been gunned down. They had expected casualties upon entry, and one death was excellent. They *hadn't* anticipated that Cameron Roberts would fire on her own agent without a moment's hesitation. They had always planned for Secret Service Agent Foster to die during the assault, but not before he had assassinated Blair Powell. They had underestimated Cameron Roberts not once, but twice. That could not happen again.

His cell phone rang, and without taking his eyes off the first daughter's bedroom, he answered it.

"Yes sir?"

"Good morning, Colonel," General Thomas Jefferson Matheson said cheerily. "Enjoying the view?"

"Yes sir, very much, sir."

"I'm happy to report you'll have the afternoon off."

Colonel Jonathan Perry frowned. "I'm not due to be relieved until eighteen hundred hours, sir."

"I've been advised that our bird will be flying this afternoon. We'll pick her up when she lands."

"Sir, I would prefer to follow her my—"

"Patience, Colonel," Matheson said, his deep baritone oddly soothing, "our time is very nearly at hand. I have something special planned for you."

"Yes sir, whatever you say, sir."

"You might use the time off to buy some new winter clothing. It's cold in Colorado this time of year."

"Yes sir," Perry said with a slow smile. "I'll do that."

CHAPTER TWO

Paula Stark halted just inside the reinforced steel door of the command center and surveyed the long rectangular room. Opposite her, floor-to-ceiling windows faced Gramercy Park. The glass was reinforced, shatterproof, and impregnated with filters to block UV and infrared penetration, making video surveillance from external sources impossible. The filters also distorted the view through a high-powered laser rifle scope.

A semicircular monitoring station covered with equipment—satellite receivers, radio transmitters, computers, and every other form of electronic hardware required for communication and intelligence assessment—took up the far end of the room. In addition, separate high-speed computer and surface lines maintained direct links to the NYPD and the New York City Transit Authority in case another 9/11 event necessitated the evacuation of Blair Powell—code name Egret—from the city. Just now, at a little before seven a.m., Secret Service agents from the night shift occupied rolling desk chairs in front of the bank of monitors displaying continuous feeds from the video cameras mounted above the entrance to the building, in the lobby, over the rear exit, and in the underground parking garage.

"Looks like they're about done." Renée Savard gestured to two workmen who stood on tall wooden ladders in the center of the room, riveting bulletproof shields to the subfloor of the loft apartment above. Should a bomb detonate in the command center, Blair's apartment would be partially buffered from the direct effects of the blast. "Finally."

"Can't be too soon for me." Paula was very aware of Renée's shoulder almost brushing hers, and she needed to remind herself not to touch her. An hour before they had been lying naked in bed together, which made the transition to being just colleagues a challenge. But what made maintaining her professional distance from Renée even harder was that Renée had come close to dying when the South Tower came down, and not much later had been wounded in the gun battle to apprehend the man believed to be partially responsible for the terrorist attack. Paula had a hard time not constantly touching Renée to reassure herself she was alive and well. Although only slightly taller than Paula's 5'7", Renée gave the impression of more height because she'd lost weight, and what had once been a naturally trim, athletic figure was now honed down to taut muscle and bone. Her coffee and cream complexion was as flawless as ever, but her blue eyes had lost their sparkle. In fact, Renée rarely smiled, and Paula missed not just her radiance, but her joy. She forced a smile and tried to keep her tone light. "After an hour of listening to this racket, I have a headache."

"You shouldn't complain." Renée gave her boyishly handsome dark-haired lover a playful arm bump. "You security guys get the room with a view and we're stuck in the back with no windows."

Paula lowered her voice and teased, "Spooks are supposed to be hidden away in dark corners."

"You wouldn't say that if the commander were here."

"Damn right I wouldn't." Despite the fact that Paula was now the chief of Blair's security detail, she and the other team members who had worked under Cameron Roberts before Cam moved over to the OHS still considered her their leader. Paula was just getting used to hearing people call her Chief, and although she didn't let anyone know, she was also just beginning to believe that she didn't have to fill Cam's shoes to do the job right. She squeezed Renée's hand for a millisecond, then released it. "I'll catch up with you later."

"Be careful," Renée said, as she always did when they parted.

"You too," Paula replied. They didn't talk about it, but she knew that Renée felt the same way she did. They loved their jobs, they loved their country, they loved each other. Danger was an inherent part of their work, and not something anyone in their position dwelled on. But the unfathomable events of 9/11 had taught them and everyone who worked to secure the safety of the nation that death waited around the next corner. To forget was to invite disaster. None of them would ever forget.

❖

Renée stopped in the small kitchenette midway between the Secret Service command center and the new regional office of the OHS. She wasn't sure how the commander had gotten the team out of DC and onto the same floor as Blair's security ops, but she was glad not to have to worry that someone was tapping their lines or hacking their files. Here they could fly under the radar, which was just the way they all liked it.

She fished her coffee cup out of a precariously stacked pile on the drain board and filled it. She heard voices coming from the conference room as she walked down the hall cautiously sipping her coffee. It was fresh and strong. She was willing to bet the commander had made it. It didn't matter what time Renée arrived for work, Cam was always there first. So too, it seemed, was Valerie. Cam and Valerie sat at one end of a long conference table, cups of coffee and open file folders in front of them. Cam tapped her pen on a tabletop as they talked.

"Morning," Renée said as she sat down opposite Cam.

Both women returned her greeting, then Cam said to her, "We'll wait for the others to brief formally, but I'm glad you're here. I'm going to be out of pocket a fair amount for the next week or so, and you'll be in charge here."

"Yes ma'am," Renée said. Six weeks ago she had thought her career was over. She'd taken a bullet in the knee during the raid on Matheson's mountain compound, and the injury was the kind to put her out of the running for any kind of field duty in the FBI despite the fact that she'd made almost a total recovery. Then Cam had offered her something better. Not just a place on her newly formed OHS team, but responsibility for the antiterrorism arm of their operation.

"You and the rest of the team need to focus on finding Matheson," Cam went on, "while I…" She grinned ruefully and shook her head. "While I am busy doing the marriage stuff."

"Wedding planning," Valerie said in her low, husky voice. "It's called wedding planning, Cameron. I know, since it's all Diane talks about these days. I think she's enjoying your wedding a lot more than you are at the moment."

"It couldn't be a worse time to be getting married," Cam said.

"With all respect, Commander," Renée said, "I think it's a perfect time."

Cam raised an eyebrow.

"Personally, of course, I think it's great. But it's more than that. You and Blair are sending a message. You're telling the world that life goes on, that we're not afraid, that we won't be beaten. That we won't live our lives in fear. You're making a statement for all of us."

"Ah hell," Cam muttered. "The last thing I want is to be a symbol of anything."

"Blair has always been a symbol, and never more than now," Valerie said, sounding oddly gentle. "Standing beside her in this is another way of telling the world she's not touchable."

Renée wasn't surprised that Valerie was the one to point out the one thing that would mean more to the commander than anything else. Blair's safety. Valerie and the commander had a history, and as much as the rest of them admired Cam and would give their lives for her, they weren't her friends—not in the way that Valerie was. No one other than Blair and Valerie ever really spoke to the commander without a certain degree of reservation and respect. The boundaries were necessary to enable the team to function, and although Valerie was officially part of the team, she would always be a little bit apart. Just as she was a little bit apart from all of them.

"Making Blair a target hardly seems a great way to keep her safe," Cam said, almost to herself.

Valerie extended her hand as if she were going to touch the commander's forearm, and then pulled it back. "The more visible she is, the tighter her security will be. She'll be safer in Colorado than she might be walking down the street here in New York. I know it will be difficult, but try to enjoy the next week or so."

"I agree," Renée said. "Blair has great security. Mac and Ellen are doing the advance groundwork at the lodge, and you know they're the best at it."

Ellen Marks, a seasoned agent, had been on sick leave for almost three months following an injury sustained in a bomb blast. She and Mac Phillips were already at the Rocky Mountain ski resort where the wedding would take place. Part of their advance work included coordinating plans with local authorities for security along Blair's anticipated travel routes, detailing evacuation plans in case of injury or imminent threat, and liaising with representatives from the local media.

Cam nodded. "It's good to have Ellen back on the team."

"And we're close to getting this bastard, Cam," Valerie said with quiet vehemence. "We know who he is, we know where he came from, and we know where his last base of operations was. Felicia is cross-referencing his known contacts—family, ex-Army associates, military school graduates—against names Ricky is pulling from the ATF and FBI patriot watch lists. We'll find him through his friends." Her gaze became distant and her voice dropped to a whisper. "The friends are always the weak links."

Renée wondered if that was why Valerie seemed to have no friends, no family, no connections to anyone except the commander, and now, Diane. The Company discouraged its field operatives from forming intimate relationships, even friendships, because friends could be compromised. Unless of course the relationship itself provided cover. Valerie had been alone for years except for her handler, whom Cam had ordered killed just weeks before. Renée tried to imagine what it would be like to be violently cut off from the only real relationship one had ever had, even if it was a manipulative one. The loneliness had to be devastating, but Valerie never seemed anything except calm and cool. And she had Diane now. Sometimes it seemed love was all that kept any of them going. Renée allowed herself a brief moment to think about Paula and to be thankful for having found her, before refocusing on the hunt for the man who had helped destroy so many lives.

"We have to dig under rocks and sift through a quagmire of disconnected bits of information to get even a whiff of Matheson's trail," Cam said bitterly, "but all *he* has to do is listen to the news or read the daily paper—or better yet, check the goddamn White House Web site—to know exactly where Blair is." Cam stood abruptly, surprising Renée with the barely constrained tension in her body and the rage in her voice. The commander never lost control. "While we keep her locked down, he's walking around free. It's wrong."

Renée caught the look of concern that flashed across Valerie's face for a fraction of a second before her usual impenetrable expression returned. They all tended to forget that the commander was human, because they looked to her as their foundation. Her sense of duty was absolute, the clarity of her belief never cloudy, and her certainty of the right course never in doubt. She epitomized what every young agent dreamed of being—brave, honorable, and just. And for those who'd seen battle, like Renée, her strength of purpose helped them cast aside their own disillusionment and disappointment. Cam helped them believe that justice would triumph. And in all of this, she stood alone, and that, Renée realized, was unfair. Sometimes they all needed to let her be human.

"I'm going to get the morning reports together for the briefing," Renée said as she rose. "See you in a few minutes."

She closed the door gently on her way out.

❖

Cam stared at the closed door for a moment, then sank into her seat. She rubbed the bridge of her nose and tilted her head back to stare at the ceiling. "Sorry."

Valerie moved her chair closer until her stocking-clad knees just barely touched Cam's dark blended silk trousers. She rested her fingertips on Cam's thigh. "You needn't apologize to me."

"What are the chances that he'll give up?"

Valerie considered lying, because Cam looked tired. More than just tired, she looked soul-weary. At one time, Cameron had escaped her pain and loneliness by taking refuge in Valerie's arms. She had comforted Cam then, and by doing so had found her own solace. She had nothing as simple to give now, because that door were closed for both of them. So she gave her what she knew Cam needed most. The truth. "He won't give up. He might have had some rational plan before September—some reason, at least in *his* mind, for what he was doing. I don't think that's the case now. He's a fanatic, and Blair is a symbol of everything he seeks to destroy."

"Why go after her and not her father?" Cam asked, as if there were some reason to insanity.

"I don't know," Valerie said. "Perhaps because she's more real than her father. The presidency is an institution as much as a person, but Blair is a living, breathing woman. Her loss would strike at the heart of people."

The pain in Cam's chest at the thought of Blair hurt was real, as acute as the bullet that had torn into her flesh and spilled her blood out onto the sidewalk in front of this very building. When she looked at Valerie, agony swam in her eyes. "If I find him, I'll kill him. No questions asked."

"Yes," Valerie said calmly. "If you do, and it comes to that, I'll make sure it appears totally justifiable."

"Just like that? Your total support, even if I'm wrong?"

"You're not wrong. We both know he's guilty. He's a murderer and a traitor."

"What about the law? What about justice?"

"Justice," Valerie said contemplatively. "Justice is often so much simpler than the laws we create to define it. There isn't a member of this team or Blair's security detail who would question the rightness of eliminating him."

"That makes us vigilantes."

"No, that makes us soldiers, and make no mistake, Cameron, this is war."

Cam placed her hand over Valerie's. "I don't want you or any of the others to jeopardize yourselves for me."

"That's an order you can't give." She smiled as she threaded her fingers through Cam's. "Or I should say, you can give it, but I doubt that any of us will listen."

"Some leader I am," Cam muttered.

"That's exactly right."

The door opened and Felicia Davis, a statuesque African American woman who looked as if she should be gracing the pages of a fashion magazine rather than hacking into databases, said, "The team's assembled and there's a message for you, Commander." Her gaze flickered down to their joined hands and then away, her expression never changing. "Do you two want more coffee?"

"No, thanks," Cam said, continuing to clasp Valerie's hand lightly. "We'll be right there."

"Good enough."

Valerie waited until they were alone again, then asked, "Does Blair know just how badly you need her to stay out of the public eye right now?"

"No. And I'm not going to tell her."

"Why not? If she knew what this was doing to you—"

"No. Everyone who has ever loved her has asked her to give up something, and I'm not going to be another one."

"Well then, we'll just have to find him and make sure he's not a problem."

Cam smiled grimly. "I have a feeling if we don't, he'll find us."

CHAPTER THREE

R icky, why don't you bring us up to speed on your frontrunners,"
Cam said, addressing the newest member of her team. Ricky
Sanchez, a thirty-year-old with curly, dark hair, an olive complexion,
and bedroom eyes, had most recently been stationed in the Southwest
with the ATF. He'd run a number of operations with the DEA when their
territories overlapped. Drugs and firearms often went hand in hand, and
both were popular commodities with the paramilitary groups for use in
financing their operations. The patriot organizations served as conduits
between drug runners from Mexico and South America and dealers in
the States, and the money they made brokering the goods went for guns.
The guns were valuable assets when negotiating with foreign terrorists,
who very often had money but no ready access to weaponry. Sanchez
was as close to an expert on the patriot organizations as could be found,
and when Cam offered him the opportunity to come over to her team,
he jumped at it. Married with two kids, he'd been urged by his wife to
get out of the field, and every agent knew that antiterrorism was the hot
place to be now.

"The patriots have no central organization—no ruling hierarchy,"
Ricky said, lounging back in his chair. He wore boot cut jeans, a wide
leather belt with a hammered silver buckle, and scuffed hand-tooled
Tony Lamas. "These guys have too much ego to actually work together.
They all want to be in charge."

He leaned forward enough to push several keys on a small laptop
computer and an image projected on a wall-mounted monitor. Head
shots of three men, ranging in age from late twenties to early fifties,

appeared. All were clean-shaven, with short, military-style haircuts and flinty stares.

"From left to right—John Jamieson, Robert Douglas, and Randolph Hogan. The White Aryan Brotherhood, the Soldiers of God, and the Homeland Liberation Front. These three are the most radical of the patriot leaders—they like to make noise about taking back America for the Americans, meaning white men—but we haven't been able to put them anywhere close to the guys who took down the Towers."

"What about Matheson?" Cam asked. "Any connection to him?"

"We're looking for one." Ricky shrugged. "These guys are camera shy, and they rarely communicate by anything other than disposable phones or face-to-face meetings. Even then, they usually send their second or third in command."

Savard cut in. "On the other hand, the hijackers weren't particularly careful about covering their movements after they entered this country. The FBI has a fairly complete picture of where they lived, where and when they took their flight training, and the routes they took to get to the airports. Somewhere along the way, they crossed paths with the team that hit the Aerie. There's no way it could have been coordinated the way it was without someone organizing it here. We just need to find the intersection point."

Cam nodded. "I agree. We know Matheson sent that team to Manhattan to hit Blair. They were his hand-picked boys. Which means he knew the timetable for the hijacking. I can't believe he would have let anyone else orchestrate this thing. We need to backtrack his movements." She looked to Felicia. "Somewhere, he left a bit of paper. He used a credit card for gas, paid for dinner, spent the night in a Motel Six. Got a parking ticket. He might be elusive, but he's not invisible. Find out where he's been in the last four months and put him with one of Ricky's guys. Or one of the hijackers."

"I'm on it, Commander," Felicia said. "If he so much as took money out of an ATM, I'll find out when and where."

Cam swept her hand toward the screen. "All of these guys. We need to know everything there is to know about them. Yesterday."

A knock on the door caught everyone's attention, and Cam walked over to open it. Stark stood in the hallway.

"Sorry to interrupt, Commander, but I just got a call from Egret. She informed us she's going to DC."

Cam frowned. "First I've heard of it."

"Lucinda Washburn was mentioned."

"Ah, that explains it," Cam said with a sigh. Lucinda Washburn was Andrew Powell's chief of staff and also a close, longtime friend of Blair's family. When Lucinda called, everyone jumped. "When?"

"We have a flight scheduled in two hours, so I thought you'd want to know. I assume you'll be accompanying her, and we're leaving for the airport in forty-five minutes."

"Thanks, Chief. Let me finish up here, and I'll be with you."

"Yes ma'am."

Cam closed the door, thinking the dog-and-pony show was about to begin. She would have minded the public exposure a lot more if she wasn't looking forward to getting married. Love had a funny way of changing one's outlook on things. She turned back to her team. "So, let's go over it again. What do we know, and what do we need to know. And how are we going to find it out."

❖

Cam found Blair in the studio section of the loft where Blair painted. The 4x5 foot canvas on the easel in front of her was a riot of bright red, glaring purples, and garish yellows. Blair had applied the paint thickly, in wide swirling swaths, and Cam felt almost dizzy from the motion as her gaze tracked over the surface. Blair didn't usually paint abstracts, but she had been for the last few weeks. As Cam took this one in, she realized it wasn't as abstract as she'd first thought. She recognized what she was looking at. A fireball. She'd seen something like it time and time again in the replays of the jetliners crashing into the North and South Towers. She wondered if Blair had consciously depicted the inferno that had resulted, and didn't know if she should ask. After growing up with a mother who was a world-renowned painter and being surrounded by her mother's friends, Cam had learned that artists drew from deeply personal, often painful emotions to infuse their art with power and passion. Perhaps this was Blair's way of exorcising the horror, and Cam wouldn't take a chance of hurting her by asking.

In her usual work attire of paint-streaked jeans and T-shirt, with her hair tied back by a red bandanna, Blair looked young and vulnerable. Cam's heart swelled and she wished with everything she was that

Blair's life could be as simple as other people's seemed to be—that her days could be filled with friendship, and with the work she craved, and with the love they shared. Jazz played on the stereo in the corner, and Blair didn't turn as Cam approached.

"Baby," Cam called softly.

Blair looked back, a question formed in her eyes. "What is it?"

Cam smiled. "Nothing."

"No. You sighed. What's bothering you?"

"You're scary, you know that?" Gently, Cam kissed Blair and put her arms around her waist.

"Cam, I'm covered with paint," Blair said, trying to pull away. "Your suit."

"Forget my suit," Cam murmured. "I love you."

Blair stilled and her eyes softened. She looped her arms around Cam's neck and kissed her back. "I'm all right."

"I know." Cam held her, running her hands lightly up and down her back. "Stark told me Lucinda requested our presence."

"She called after you left for the briefing. I told her we were both too busy, but she insisted we talk face-to-face." Blair rolled her eyes. "At least this time she didn't play the national security card."

Cam grinned. "She's probably holding that in reserve."

"Lucinda never holds anything in reserve. She doesn't need to. She's always got plenty of ammunition."

"True." Cam released Blair and checked her watch. "Do I need to pack? Are we staying overnight?"

"I think it's an in-and-out thing. Besides, I'm not staying in DC. We just got home."

Cam glanced around the loft. It *was* home. At least one of them, she thought with satisfaction. They had just completed the purchase of the house on Whitley Point where they'd been staying intermittently for the last two months. That house above the windswept dunes was their refuge, and at least a dozen times a day, she wished she could just send Blair there with a security detail until some kind of sanity was restored to the world. Except that wasn't likely to happen soon, if ever, and Blair would never submit to being sequestered. Even for her own safety.

"Let me get some work together for the flight, then," Cam said.

"I need to shower and change." Blair brushed her fingers over

Cam's cheek. "I expect this will be about the wedding, and I know how much you have on your mind right now. Thank you for doing this."

Cam caught Blair's wrist and brushed her lips over Blair's fingertips. "I'm doing this for me too. I'm fine."

"Say that in a week." Blair kissed Cam's cheek and walked away. Cam watched her go, thinking that a lot could happen in a week.

❖

The West Wing of the White House was never quiet, but since 9/11, the activity level had escalated to the point that there was very little difference between noon and midnight. Aides worked eighteen hours straight and staffers slept on couches. Even the White House chief of staff catnapped on her sofa, which was where Blair and Cam discovered Lucinda Washburn when her assistant Emilio bade them to enter her hallowed quarters.

"Sorry," Blair said as Lucinda lifted the arm that had been covering her eyes and glanced toward the door.

"Good, you're here." Instantly alert and looking completely fresh, Lucinda shifted her stocking-clad feet to the floor and slid into her pumps without looking. She walked to the credenza and poured coffee. Looking over her shoulder, she asked, "Some for you?"

"No, thanks," Blair said. She and Cam took their usual seats side by side on the sofa. "How are things?"

Lucinda lifted her brows as she settled into the wingback chair across from them and sipped her coffee. "We're making progress. Being able to identify the hijackers has helped things tremendously." She shifted her gaze to Cam. "How are we doing on identifying the domestic cell?"

"We have a lot of threads, but no connecting factors yet."

"It's frustrating that we can identify a terrorist leader thousands of miles away but we can't use our surveillance to find a traitor in our own backyard."

"I think we call that preserving civil rights," Cam said dryly.

"Of course," Lucinda agreed. "But it's damned inconvenient when we're under attack from our own people."

"We'll get them," Cam said.

"No doubt." Lucinda set her cup aside. "You're here for another reason."

"I can't imagine what," Blair said.

Lucinda half smiled. "We tried to quietly slide an announcement of your upcoming nuptials into the press briefing this morning."

Blair snorted.

"Yes. Suddenly, global terrorism is no longer everyone's top priority." She fixed Blair with a piercing stare. "You are."

Blair stiffened, and Cam took her hand.

"So far, we've had calls from the Christian Morality Coalition, Family First, the chairman of the reelection campaign, several of our largest donors, and the National Organization for Gay Rights." Lucinda shook her head. "Congratulations, Blair. You're a celebrity."

"That wasn't my intention," Blair snapped. She rose abruptly and took one step toward the floor-to-ceiling windows that fronted the Esplanade before realizing that she'd made that trip across Lucinda's office in anger or frustration a dozen times before. Not once had the journey ever helped her understand why her private life was of such interest to so many, and it never changed the outcome of whatever Lucinda had decided to do about it. She regarded Lucinda. "How's my father taking it?"

"We haven't drafted his official statement—"

"I don't care about the party line." Blair hoped Cam couldn't see her shaking. She hated that her life was something that required her father to consult with his advisers before commenting.

"I'm sorry," Lucinda said gently. "Your father feels exactly the same way today as he did when you first told him. He supports you, and he plans on attending."

"That's a very bad idea," Cam said immediately.

"As is usually the case, Commander," Lucinda said wryly, "I agree with you. However, you may have noticed that it's a Powell family trait to do exactly as they please regardless of what their advisers recommend."

Blair sank down beside Cam. "I'll ask him not to come."

"You certainly can," Lucinda said, "but I don't think it will change his mind."

"We haven't factored a presidential presence into our advance planning," Cam said. "Stark's team hasn't—"

"Tom Turner sent his people to Colorado several days ago. I suspect they'll liaise with Mac Phillips and Ellen Marks today."

"And Stark hasn't been informed?" Cam said incredulously. "That's a complete breach of protocol."

"These are unusual times," Lucinda said. "The president's security adviser wanted it done this way. While in Colorado, President Powell's security chief will command the total operation."

"I don't like it," Cam said flatly.

"No, I didn't think you would, and I imagine that Agent Stark will agree with you." Lucinda lifted her hands. "On the other hand, it's not negotiable."

"Tom is a good man," Cam went on as if Lucinda hadn't spoken, "but he isn't used to the kind of personal security that Blair requires. No one gets as close to the president as they do to Blair."

"Agent Stark will remain in charge of Blair's personal detail, unless there is an emergent situation."

"Which is exactly when Blair would need the best coverage." Cam shifted on the sofa and took Blair's hands. "Blair, I know what this means to you. It means a lot to me too. But I think we should postpone."

Blair studied their joined hands, then met Cam's gaze. "All right."

Lucinda crossed her legs and folded her hands in her lap. "A month ago you would have made me very happy. Unfortunately, we can't back out now because too many eyes are watching. Plus, we can't have it appear as if your father is capitulating to the vocal right."

"You can't force us to get married," Blair objected. She ran a hand through her hair. "This is unreal. All of a sudden, you *want* me to get married."

"Don't you?"

"Yes!"

"Good." Lucinda rose, walked to her desk, and called her assistant. "Emilio? Is Dana Barnett here yet? Send her in, would you?"

"Dana Barnett," Blair said. "Isn't she—"

"A reporter for the *Washington Chronicle*. Yes," Lucinda replied as Emilio held the door open for a woman of average height and build in wrinkled tan chinos, a white T-shirt, and a shapeless black V-neck sweater. She wore mud-encrusted combat boots and needed a haircut.

Her collar-length chestnut hair was shaggy and her deep brown eyes shadowed with fatigue. Despite her casual attire, she moved briskly and swept the room with sharp eyes that appeared to take in everything with one glance.

"Ms. Barnett," Lucinda said. "Thank you so much for coming."

Dana's eyebrows lifted almost imperceptibly. "You're welcome," she said in a resonant alto. "I just got off a plane, so forgive my informal attire." She nodded in Blair and Cam's direction. "Good morning, Ms. Powell. Deputy Director Roberts."

"Good to meet you," Blair said. She and Cam stood, and Blair held out her hand. "Where are you in from?"

"The Middle East," Dana said somewhat evasively. She glanced at Lucinda. "I didn't get much of a briefing, just that you wanted to see me."

"I told the people at the paper I'd fill you in," Lucinda said. She gestured to the seating area. "You must be tired."

"No, actually, I spent the last six hours sleeping on the floor in the hold of a military transport plane. I'd rather stand, if you don't mind."

Blair thought what Dana Barnett hadn't said was that she'd rather be anywhere else but there. She could almost feel her bristling. From what she knew of Dana's reputation, she was a hard-hitting investigative reporter who covered controversial topics in every corner of the globe. She didn't doubt that Dana's assignment in the Middle East had to do with terrorism.

"Since you've been out of the country," Lucinda said smoothly, apparently oblivious to the edge in Dana Barnett's manner, "you may not have heard that Ms. Powell and the deputy director are getting married next week."

"Congratulations," Dana said, her eyes wary.

"As you can imagine," Lucinda said, "there is a great deal of media interest in the entire event. To facilitate information flow and spare Ms. Powell and the deputy director undue attention, we've decided to allow one reporter total access to the first daughter for the duration of the event. Exclusive coverage commencing with the preplanning stages."

Dana slid her hands into the pockets of her chinos and glanced from Lucinda to Blair. "I can recommend several excellent lifestyle reporters who would—"

"That won't be necessary. You've got the job." Lucinda smiled.

"Luce," Blair said, "can we talk for a minute, please?" The last thing Blair wanted was a reporter in her face twenty-four hours a day. It was bad enough to have twice a day press conferences.

"I think it's an excellent idea," Cam said.

Blair stared at her. "What?"

"It will limit your exposure if the members of the press realize that you're not available to make impromptu comments, and it will allow *us* to determine when and how you're interviewed." She nodded. "It's a good idea."

"It's a lousy idea," Blair retorted.

Dana Barnett folded her arms, an amused expression on her face.

"I realize you've just come off an arduous assignment, Dana," Lucinda said. "We'll arrange transportation for you to Manhattan tomorrow. You can start then."

The smile on Dana's face disappeared. "I'm afraid I really can't—"

"I haven't agreed—" Blair interrupted.

Lucinda glanced at her watch. "And I'm late for a meeting with the budget committee. Thank you all so much for coming." She reached across her desk, grabbed a stack of folders, and walked out.

Blair and Dana stared after her.

"Son of a bitch!" Dana and Blair exclaimed simultaneously.

Cam, wisely, said nothing.

CHAPTER FOUR

Dana took a deep breath and smiled ruefully at the first daughter. She'd seen her in photographs and on television before, of course, but she'd never met her in person. Dressed casually, with her hair loose and her temper showing, Blair Powell was even more beautiful than her media image projected. Dana had always admired her for her subtle disdain for political games and her tendency to be outspoken regardless of the party line. And the fact that she had become more candid about her sexual orientation in the last year had earned Dana's respect. As a reporter, Dana had a healthy regard for the power of the press to make or break careers as well as sway public opinion. It was refreshing to meet someone so close to the seats of power who didn't seem to care, although handling her press relations must be a nightmare for the White House.

"Nothing personal, Ms. Powell," Dana said, "but I'm not the right reporter for this assignment."

"Nothing personal, Ms. Barnett," Blair said, "but this assignment doesn't work for me either."

Dana laughed, then caught the steely expression on Deputy Director Roberts's face. Dana wasn't naïve, and even if she hadn't just come back from the Middle East, she would have had a very good idea of just how precarious the state of national security was at the moment. Anyone who paid attention to the political scene, and Dana did, knew that Blair Powell had dropped from sight immediately after 9/11 and the White House had been very vague as to why. Now she was emerging in the midst of controversy. So much for maintaining a low profile, which Dana was willing to bet the White House and the deputy director would have preferred. She didn't envy Roberts's position in all of this, and she definitely didn't want to piss her off.

"I agree with your take on controlling the press by setting up exclusive coverage, Deputy Director," Dana said. "It's a good idea. My only point is—"

"I think you've made your position clear," Cam said flatly. "You apparently find contributing to Ms. Powell's security beneath you."

Dana flushed. She knew, as did every other reporter in the United States—in the world, most likely—that Cameron Roberts had nearly died from a sniper's bullet intended for the first daughter. Roberts might have taken the bullet because she was protecting her lover, but no one doubted she would have done it for anyone under her protection. She was a genuine hero, and one who hadn't capitalized on her notoriety in any way. For just a second, Dana felt petty in her desire not to be cast as a celebrity reporter, and the discomfort stoked her temper. "There are half a dozen reporters the *Chronicle* could assign who would fit in better than me and who have more experience with this kind of thing. I'm a field reporter, for Christ's sake."

"It doesn't matter," Blair interjected, "because it's not happening." She looped her left arm through Cam's and held her right hand out to Dana. "Like I said, nothing personal. It was nice meeting you."

"Same here," Dana said.

When the first daughter and the deputy director started out of the office, Dana hurried after them. It would have been nice to think the matter closed, but she knew things were never that simple where politics were concerned.

❖

"You were kind of hard on her, weren't you?" Blair asked lightly as she and Cam left the West Wing.

"She's cocky," Cam said.

"And?"

"And nothing." Cam pulled her cell phone off her belt and punched in Paula Stark's number on speed dial. "We're coming out, Chief." She glanced at Blair. "Ready to go home?"

"More than ready." Blair slowed in the lobby just inside the entrance to the West Wing and pulled Cam around to face her. "You don't usually give up so easily."

Cam grinned. "Who said I was giving up?"

Blair rolled her eyes. "That's exactly what I was afraid of." She looked around to make sure no one was listening, but everyone seemed to be rushing to get to their destination and paid them no mind. Nevertheless, she lowered her voice out of habit. "I'm not having a stranger follow me around, recording my every thought and feeling, during one of the most important times of my life. God, Cam, I don't even do that for a routine public appearance."

Cam settled her hands on Blair's shoulders. "Nothing is routine anymore, baby."

"This is ours," Blair said vehemently. She pressed her hand to Cam's chest. "Ours. I'm not letting anyone take it away from us, not even Lucinda and my father."

"No one will. I promise." Cam kissed her softly while a uniformed Marine guard standing nearby stared straight ahead, seemingly oblivious to them. "But the press are going to be all over us, and that makes Stark's job ten times more difficult. Lucinda is right on this one, Blair. It's the best way to control the flow of information *and* keep some distance between you and the reporters."

"No," Blair said. "As far as I'm concerned, the matter is closed."

Cam said nothing, but her eyes took on the shuttered appearance they always did when she was holding in her temper.

"And don't think about pulling rank on me, either," Blair snapped, the effort it took to keep her voice down making her tremble.

When it came right down to it, Blair knew that what *she* wanted didn't carry as much weight as what others decided was best for her. And one of those *other people* who had that kind of power over her was her own lover. She resented being made a bystander to her own life, and her solution to that in the past had been to assert her independence any way she could. Sometimes in ways that weren't particularly smart, or safe. But now she had something that mattered as much as her own personal freedom, and that was her relationship with Cam. When the two things that mattered most to her were at odds, like now, Blair's better judgment sometimes suffered in the wake of impotent fury. "I don't want to fight about this."

"Neither do I." Cam tensed as they stepped outside under the portico.

Blair noticed Cam automatically scan the grounds. Despite the fact that they were in one of the most secure locations in the world, Cam didn't let down her guard. She never let down her guard. Blair wasn't sure she would recognize her if she ever truly relaxed. Even as she thought it, Blair knew there was one time when Cam wasn't thinking about danger, wasn't thinking about guarding her, wasn't thinking about anything at all. When they made love, when Cam gave herself to Blair, the only thing in her mind—the only thing that mattered—was what existed between the two of them. Blair was certain of it, because that was the way she felt too, and she desperately wanted to have that feeling for more than just the moments when they made love. Not just for herself, but for Cam. And if she had to stand up to Lucinda and her father and the whole goddamn world to get it, she would.

❖

"Dana! You're back!"

"Hiya, gorgeous." Dana stepped around behind an old-fashioned gunmetal gray desk with dented file cabinets built into either end and kissed the silky-soft skin of the white-haired woman who guarded the door to editor-in-chief Clive Russell's office with the ferocity of a gorgon. Rumor had it that Amanda Smith held more shares in the paper than half the board members, but preferred her role as secretary to sitting in meetings. Dana had a feeling Amanda had more power right where she was. "Thanks for arranging my ride back."

Amanda merely smiled as her gaze swept over Dana. "Bad over there?"

"Bad and getting worse," Dana said grimly. She had a feeling she hadn't seen the last of Afghanistan, and considering what she'd been piecing together from her sources in the military and on Capitol Hill, Iraq was about to be added to the nasty mix.

"Those pieces you sent back were horrifying." Amanda touched Dana's arm fleetingly. "And brilliant. As always."

Dana flushed at the compliment. Amanda had been known to skim a reporter's copy and hand it back to be rewritten, declaring it a waste of Clive's time. Only a rookie would ever argue with her. Dana eyed the closed door to Clive's office. The lights were on but the blinds in the two huge glass windows facing into the newsroom were drawn, meaning he was unavailable. "I need to see the man."

Still smiling, Amanda shook her head. "Not now, you don't. It's budget time. Try him tomorrow around nine twenty. He'll have a few minutes then."

"It's important."

Amanda regarded her steadily and Dana held her breath.

Dana never pulled rank, even though she was one of the senior investigative reporters and could pretty much call her own shots as to what she worked on and when. She was as much a team player as she could be, given that her nature was to be solitary. She'd gotten used to being alone as a child. She had no siblings and didn't fit in with the other kids in her working-class neighborhood. After a certain age, the boys wouldn't play with her and she had no idea how to play with the girls, whose games didn't interest her. She couldn't fathom the fun in playing house and pretending that she wanted to grow up to be something that felt completely foreign to her. She didn't want to be someone's wife or mother. She wanted adventures like those in the books she loved to read. She wanted to explore the world like the characters she pretended to be. And most of all, she wanted to know *why*—why the world worked the way it did. And the more she learned, the more she questioned. Her love of words and her endless curiosity led her into journalism, and here she was. Traveling the world and asking why.

"You know I can't do this," Dana said, hearing the plea in her own voice.

"Five minutes," Amanda said gently. "Don't make me come and get you."

Dana kissed her cheek again. "Thanks. I owe you."

Amanda chuckled. "Of course you do. Go on now."

As Dana walked to the door, she heard Amanda pick up the phone and murmur something. She knocked and a deep rumble that she took to mean *come in* emanated from the other side.

"Hi, Clive," Dana said as she entered the cluttered office. The evening edition of the *Chronicle* sat in the center of the huge oak desk. Stacks of papers covered just about every surface in the room that wasn't already occupied with the computer, fax machine, television, phones, and other equipment that kept Clive connected to the world of information. "Sorry to bother you."

"Then why are you?" the big man behind the desk asked impatiently.

Despite the hundreds of times she'd seen him, Dana was still taken aback by not just his size, but his presence. Clive filled the room even when he was sitting behind his desk. His close-cropped red hair was sprinkled with gray, but he looked younger than his fifty-odd years by a decade. The ex-college football player's neck was almost as wide as his head and his shoulders bigger than her refrigerator. She'd known him long enough not to be intimidated by his appearance, but she never liked being on the receiving end of his formidable temper. Fortunately, since she never missed deadlines and always gave him more than he asked for, his ire was rarely directed at her.

"I need a favor," Dana said, hoping the fact that she never asked for one would make up for her going outside channels. "Some idiot pulled my name out of a hat and assigned me to do a celebrity personal for the next couple of weeks. I need you to get me out of it. Things are really heating up over—"

"I'm the idiot," Clive growled.

Dana stared. "You? Why? Why would you do this to me? You know I'm not—"

"The White House called, Barnett. You know, the place on Pennsylvania Avenue where the president of the United States lives?"

She gritted her teeth. "I've seen it."

"Then you probably also know that we try to be accommodating when the chief of staff over there asks us for a favor," Clive said sarcastically.

"I get that part," Dana said. "I understand politics, even though it's not my favorite game." She ran her hand through her hair. "But Jesus Christ, Clive. Me?"

He regarded her impassively.

Dana narrowed her eyes, searching her mind for what she was missing. Then she shook her head in disgust. "Obviously sleeping on the floor of a transport plane jarred something loose between my ears. It's about me being a lesbian, right?"

"That wasn't mentioned."

"It didn't need to be." She jammed her hands in her pockets and turned in a tight circle, wishing there were room to pace. She should be more bothered that she'd been chosen for an assignment for no other reason than the fact she slept with women. Then she thought of the society reporters and couldn't help but laugh despite her irritation. "Wouldn't Priscilla Reynolds just love this assignment."

The corner of Clive's mouth twitched, as if he were actually about to smile. Priscilla prided herself on being the first to know everything that was newsworthy about everyone on the Hill. Rumor had it a lot of her information came from pillow talk, and she was unabashedly outspoken about her aversion to gays and lesbians. On the rare occasions when Dana and Priscilla ran into each other, Priscilla acted as if Dana had a contagious disease.

"A newspaper doesn't turn down an offer for exclusive coverage, especially not when it's something this big." Clive passed a sheet of paper across the desk. "This is a preliminary guest list."

Dana scanned it. It was shorter than she might have expected, but despite the public announcements regarding the event, she suspected that the president's daughter wanted as much privacy as possible. She recognized quite a few of the names. One stood out and she raised an eyebrow. "Emory Constantine? The stem cell researcher?"

Clive nodded. "The *elusive* Dr. Constantine. The one who doesn't give interviews and has almost as many security guards as Blair Powell. Since the attack on her in Boston last month, the Johnson Foundation has been locked up tighter than Fort Knox. There's a story there, and I want you to get it."

"There's talk that the foundation is doing more than just basic biological research." Dana handed the list back to Clive. "As in biological warfare."

"If they are, no one's talking about it. Maybe you can change that." He rolled his massive shoulders. "Dr. Constantine apparently likes the ladies."

Dana snorted. "Well then, I sure as hell don't qualify." She folded her arms. "And I *don't* get my stories in the bedroom."

"I don't care how you get the story. Just get it." He pointed to the door. "Now get out. I'm busy trying to figure out how to pay your salary next year."

"Have you factored in a raise?" When Clive placed both hands flat on the desk as if he were about to get up, Dana backed toward the door. "I'm going."

"Make sure you get your ass on a plane to Manhattan."

"Yes, boss," Dana muttered as she let the door close on her last hope of reprieve. "Crap."

"Here you are, dear," Amanda said, holding out an envelope. "Your itinerary and tickets. You're expected at Ms. Powell's in the morning."

"Pretty sure I'd be going, weren't you?"

Amanda smiled beatifically. "Of course. You were my first choice."

Crap.

❖

Matheson walked carefully along the narrow rows between the plain white headstones, leaving his son's grave behind. When he reached the banks of the Potomac, the hallowed ground of Arlington Cemetery stretching out behind him, he stared across the water. The Lincoln Memorial and the White House stood opposite him just beyond the river. Symbols of freedom and national pride, now tarnished by those who had forgotten what had made the country great. The most powerful nation on Earth made impotent by laws enacted to protect the unworthy, financially and morally bankrupted from supporting the weak, the ignorant, and the debauched. It was time to return to power those who rightfully deserved it, to reward the sons of those who had built this great land. When he showed the people the mockery their leaders had made of their heritage, when the pretenders were unveiled as nothing more than puppets for perverts and thieves, the true patriots would rise again. And he would have justice.

CHAPTER FIVE

As the plane touched down at Teterboro Airport across the river from Manhattan in New Jersey, Cam noted the two hulking black shapes with bright halogen eyes idling on the tarmac. She couldn't see beyond the tinted windows of the Suburbans, and she considered how easy it would be for someone to intercept the assigned vehicles on their way to the airport and replace them with identical vehicles filled with hostiles. That would, of course, assume a break in communication had gone unnoticed somewhere along the approach route. How long would it take to make the switch? Thirty seconds? Would a burst of static and less than a minute of patchy radio communications signal to anyone back at the command center that something had gone wrong? Could Blair walk unsuspectingly down the stairway from the plane and directly into a fusillade of bullets?

"Just sit tight for a second," Cam murmured to Blair and unbuckled her seat belt.

"Cam?" Blair called after her, but Cam had already edged her way up the aisle.

"Who do you have on the ground?" Cam asked as she dropped into the seat next to Paula Stark.

Stark folded the week's itinerary she'd been studying and slid it into the inside pocket of her navy blue blazer. Without the slightest hesitation, she replied, "Phelps, Edwards, Ramsey, and Wozinski. Problem, Commander?"

"I don't want Blair to disembark until you've verified the identities of everyone in both vehicles."

Stark regarded Cam steadily. "That's standard procedure."

"I know." Cam blew out a breath and looked past Stark out the window. The runway lights created sharp, flat circles of white interspersed with inky blackness, like so many pearls on an ebony chain. "And I know that you know it. I just—" She lifted her shoulder. "I'm sorry."

When Cam started to rise, Stark, in a wholly uncharacteristic move, restrained her with a hand on her arm. Cam could count on one hand the times Stark had touched her, so she sat back down and waited for Stark to speak.

"I don't think I've ever said this to you, but I've always believed it," Stark said, holding Cam's gaze. "You're the best Secret Service agent I've ever seen. None of our training prepared us for what happened in September, but you made the right calls and probably saved all of us. If you ever have a feeling something's not right, I want to know about it."

"Even if it's just nerves?" Cam said self-critically.

"It's not nerves, Commander. It's instinct."

Cam smiled faintly. "I don't think I've ever said this to you, but I believe it. You're the right person to head Blair's detail."

Stark blushed and, for the first time, looked down. "Thank you."

"There are some things you need to know about Colorado. Let's talk when we get back to base."

"Yes ma'am."

❖

"What was that all about back there in the plane?" Blair asked once she and Cam were settled in the back of the Suburban. Greg Wozinski, six-five and two hundred fifty pounds of blond-haired, blue-eyed beefsteak, managed to appear invisible as he occupied the facing seat in the rear of the armor-plated SUV. His expression was impassive and he might have been deaf for all the reaction he gave to their conversation. Nevertheless, she kept her voice low. She leaned into Cam's body and kept one hand on Cam's thigh. "What happened?"

"Nothing important," Cam said.

"Stark doesn't usually keep me strapped in that long after landing. Did you tell her to do that?"

"I don't tell Stark what to do."

"You're hedging."

Cam took Blair's hand and held it against her middle. "I would have asked her to do it, if she hadn't been planning to already. Your security is going to be doubled until after the wedding."

"It could hardly be any heavier," Blair said tightly. "I've got people with me all the time. And let's not forget, soon I'll have my very own personal reporter."

"That hasn't been confirmed."

"Oh, please. Lucinda has decreed it." Blair leaned her cheek against Cam's shoulder. "I love her. I really do. But I can't believe I let her use me the way she does. Is nothing sacred?"

"For Lucinda? Yes. The presidency." Cam kissed Blair's temple. "But she loves you too."

"That doesn't stop her from manipulating my private life."

"She doesn't see any difference between the personal and professional."

"I used to think that about you," Blair said.

"For most of my life that's been true." Cam shrugged. "It's that way for most agents."

"If you had to choose between me and your duty…" Blair shook her head. "Never mind."

"You. I'd choose you."

"I'm sorry. I shouldn't have asked you that. I'm just tired."

Cam released Blair's hand and slipped her arm around her shoulder, pulling her closer. "We're all tired. But you can ask me anything you need to know, anytime."

"I don't want Dana Barnett inside my life."

"You'll be safer this way."

Blair pulled away. "I've already got all the security I need. You said so yourself."

"That's not what I—"

"Forget it. Let's just forget it. I already know how you feel. You agree with Lucinda."

"Yes," Cam said, feeling a barrier settle between them. On this one issue, Blair's safety, she would never compromise, no matter how much Blair needed her to. Not even when it drove a wedge between them.

❖

Diane held open her apartment door and peered at Blair, who'd arrived unannounced. Seeing Blair in tight jeans and a tighter black sweater, with her hair down and a wild look in her eyes, Diane was reminded of old times. Old times when Blair was unhappy and looking for trouble to take her mind off her troubles. What was different was that Patrice Hara, one of Blair's Secret Service agents, stood just to the left of the door with her back to the wall in a position that gave her a view up and down the hallway to the elevator and the stairwells. In the pre-Cam days, Blair would have given her spookies the slip. "Hello, darling. You do know it's after midnight?"

"The night is young." Blair tossed her leather jacket on the chair as she crossed Diane's living room to the minibar tucked into one corner. She pulled a bottle of wine and a corkscrew from underneath and set about opening it. Diane's platinum blond hair fell loose to her shoulders and, barefoot and wearing pale blue silk pajamas, she looked ready for bed. "Am I keeping you awake?"

"Of course not—I was reading. I still keep New York hours." Diane settled onto the arm of the sofa, watching Blair curiously. "Since you've gone domestic with Cam, you're the one on a DC schedule. Up at an ungodly hour and no carousing until dawn anymore."

Blair paused, the wine bottle suspended in one hand as she looked around the apartment. "I didn't even think to ask if Valerie was here. I can't get used to you living with someone."

"She's not here. And I'm not living with her."

"Uh-huh."

"She's still…at work hardly seems to cover it." Diane walked over to the bar, picked up an empty wineglass, and held it out. "And even if I were cohabitating, you can drop by anytime. What's going on?"

"Cam is working late too."

"That's nothing new."

Blair filled their glasses and sipped from hers. "We have a new member of the wedding party."

"Really? I was about to tell you the same thing."

"You tell first. I think your news is probably better than mine."

Blair flopped onto the couch and propped her scuffed brown boots on the gleaming wood coffee table.

Diane curled up beside her on the deep red sofa, drawing her legs up beneath her and turning sideways to face Blair. "I got an e-mail from Emory. She's coming into the city tomorrow for some kind of grant meeting and she mentioned she was going to spend a few days here before heading out to Colorado. I invited her to get together with us while we put the finishing touches on the wedding plans. Do you mind?"

"No, that's great. I like Emory." Blair stared moodily into her wine. "I'd offer for her to stay at my place, but who would want to stay there? I don't even want to stay there."

"I already told her she could stay with me, but she said she was fine at the hotel." Diane tapped a polished fingernail on Blair's knee. "What's Cam done, sweetie?"

"What makes you think it's her?"

"You're fretting. Lucinda annoys you. Nosy reporters make you swear. I have even been known to irritate you now and then. But only Cam makes you fret and pine."

"I'm not pining. I'm pissed off."

"Okay." Diane stroked Blair's leg, then patted it. "So. Tell."

"Lucinda had the bright idea of assigning a reporter to cover the wedding, and Cam agrees."

Diane frowned. "You knew you were going to create a buzz. After the press announcement this morning, I'm surprised you don't already have a news van parked in front of your building."

"I do. Three of them." Blair grimaced. "Fortunately, they can't come within thirty feet of the entrance, so all they can do is yell questions. This situation is different."

"What, Lucinda promised some reporter a one-on-one? You've done plenty of interviews before."

"We're not talking an interview," Blair said glumly. "We're talking a member of the wedding. She's showing up tomorrow and she's going to be with us all day, every day, until this is over."

"You're kidding."

"I'm not."

"And you agreed?" Diane got up to refill their glasses. "Why?"

"*I* didn't agree. Lucinda ordered it and Cam backed her." Blair waved Diane and the wine away. She hadn't even finished half a glass yet. She hated being at odds with Cam. For so many years, anger had fueled her life. Her resistance to the restrictions imposed by her father's career had actually invigorated her. Certainly, her rage had inspired some of her best paintings. Since Cam, she had learned to compromise, and the new balance in her life had led her in surprising new directions in her art. She didn't resent the changes, but there were times, like now, when she needed Cam to take her part. And it hurt when she didn't. "You know what it's like saying no to Lucinda."

"But that's not what has you drinking wine on my sofa in the middle of the night."

"It's silly, but I want Cam to care about the wedding like I do."

Diane wrapped her arm around Blair's shoulders and hugged her. "Congratulations. I don't think I've ever actually heard you say that you wanted something from a lover before. Other than hot sex, that is."

Blair laughed. "That's one thing I never have to request from Cam."

"Don't gloat."

"You should talk," Blair teased. "If wanting something from her is such a good thing, why does it feel lousy?"

"Just because we want something doesn't mean we're going to get it, or even that we should. But we rarely want things from people we don't care about, and you never let yourself care before."

"You already know I'm crazy about her."

"I know," Diane said, "but that's not the same thing." Diane rubbed Blair's shoulder. "But she probably can't read your mind, so you'll have to tell her what you need."

"It sounds silly when I say it out loud."

"No it doesn't."

Blair sighed. "Besides, she's not going to change her mind about the reporter."

"Cam doesn't strike me as the type who likes publicity any more than you do. Why is she going along with it?"

Blair said nothing.

"Aha. What aren't you telling me?"

"Cam thinks it will make security easier because we'll be able to limit my exposure. Fewer press conferences, fewer interviews. You know the drill."

Diane laughed. "You don't really expect Cam to say no to anything that's going to keep you safe?"

"I am safe," Blair said vehemently. "Have you looked outside your door? Hara will be there until I come out. And there are more downstairs, outside the building and in the car."

"Well, I happen to be glad about that. I wish Valerie had people following her everywhere she went." Abruptly, Diane stood and strode to the balcony doors. She wrapped her arms around her body as if she were cold. "I know the lack of privacy is horrible for you." She spun around, her eyes fierce. "But you have a team of experts to keep you safe. No one is protecting her."

"I'm sorry," Blair said softly. "I should be grateful, and I'm not. And you must be sick with worry over her."

Diane pushed her fingers through her hair and heaved a deep breath. "I want to believe that no one cares about her or about what she might know any longer, but it's hard. I know that agents like her have very little connection to one another, and almost no one except their handlers even know who they are. But every time she walks out the door…"

"You're afraid she won't come back," Blair said, voicing their shared nightmare.

"I can't tell her because she already thinks I'll be better off without her."

"God, they don't get it, do they?" Blair said in exasperation.

Diane laughed. "Which part? That if we'd be better off without them, we wouldn't be so terrified of losing them?"

"For starters." Blair held out her hand and Diane took it, settling beside her on the couch once again.

"So," Diane said. "Tell me about this reporter."

"The only good thing about this," Blair said, "is that she's not any happier about it than I am. Dana Barnett. She's—"

"The investigative reporter? I've seen her on television. God, she's gorgeous."

Blair leaned back and regarded Diane through narrowed lids. "I thought you were off the market?"

"Off the market, yes. Dead and buried, no."

Blair laughed. "She's very good looking. She also seems tough and smart and doesn't want this assignment. So maybe she won't bother us very much."

"She can bother me all she wants," Diane muttered.

"Well, don't expect me to run interference. I'm out of practice." Blair nudged her. "And don't forget that Valerie is armed."

Diane smiled. "I never thought I'd say this, but I really can't imagine being with anyone except her. God, that is terrifying."

Blair leaned her head back and closed her eyes. "Tell me about it."

❖

Paula Stark rubbed her eyes and picked up the most recent stack of intelligence reports in one hand and a cold cup of coffee in the other. She sipped absently while scanning the memos from that day's summaries, focusing on the sections that had been highlighted by Iggie Jackson, the acting communications coordinator while Mac was in Colorado. She paid particular attention to anything mentioning Andrew Powell, New York City, the Midwest, patriot organizations, or Blair. Five of the twenty pages were devoted to excerpts from newspaper articles, Web posts, speeches, or other responses to the official White House press release regarding the upcoming wedding. All of the usual suspects were represented—fundamentalist Christians, the Roman Catholic Assembly of Archbishops, the Anglicans, and any number of other religious institutions opposed to gay marriage—but what interested her most were several statements from patriot organization leaders. She circled one from Randolph Hogan.

"Something interesting?" Cam asked as she dropped into a swivel chair next to Paula.

"One of the right-wing paramilitary guys posted a blog blaming Blair for the decline of…just about everything. The family, the church, and the state of the nation."

Cam frowned and held out her hand. She read the excerpt and handed it back. "He's on our list of possible Matheson contacts."

"I know. I got the update from Renée while we were in Washington." Stark set the stack of papers aside. "Coincidence?"

"What do you think?"

"I think all these guys are in bed together. On the other hand, if he's got ties to Matheson, he'd be pretty stupid to make a public statement like this."

"Ego often trumps judgment," Cam noted.

"It would be nice to have someone inside his camp."

"Maybe we do, but the FBI has not been forthcoming about their sources." A muscle bunched along the edge of Cam's jaw. "And apparently they didn't get the directive about interagency cooperation."

"It's going to take a while for everyone to adjust to this new hierarchy," Paula said. "I'm not even sure who I work for anymore."

Cam regarded her steadily.

Stark grinned. "Well, I know who I report to, Commander."

"Nice save." Cam laughed briefly, then her eyes grew serious. "We're going to have serious chain of command issues in Colorado. You know about Tom Turner?"

Paula frowned. "I do now. He called this afternoon to tell me his people were on the ground out there. *Coordinating* with Mac and Ellen. He was very friendly and made it sound like we'd all be one big happy family."

"Tom's priority is POTUS, and it should be," Cam said. "My concern is Blair."

"So is mine." Paula sensed Cam waiting, and she had no problem replying to the unspoken question. "My job is to secure the welfare of the first daughter. Nothing takes priority over that."

"Thanks, Chief."

"No problem, Commander."

"I take it you've been briefed on the new member of the team joining us tomorrow?" Cam checked the plain-faced clock on the wall. One a.m. "Today, I should say."

Paula pointed to a folder. "Dana Barnett." She hesitated, judging her next words. She did not want to tread into personal territory with the commander, but she needed to know what kind of trouble she was looking at. "I don't imagine Egret is pleased."

Cam smiled wryly. "I didn't know you were given to understatement, Chief."

"We'll handle it," Paula said confidently.

"I imagine you will." Cam stood, her eyes weary. "Probably better than I have. Good night, Chief."

Paula watched her go, wishing she knew how to ease her burden. Then she reached for the last of the security bulletins, because they all had their parts to play even if they didn't understand this new stage they'd been thrust upon.

CHAPTER SIX

Friday

A little after six, Cam got up from the sofa where she'd fallen asleep a few hours earlier and walked into the kitchen. She had slept in a T-shirt and a pair of flannel boxers, and the apartment felt cold. Cold and empty. She contemplated making coffee, but sat at the breakfast bar instead and read the note that she'd read three times when she had returned from the command center the night before.

Cam, I've gone to Diane's. I'll probably spend the night. I love you, Blair.

Cam touched the lower right hand corner of the slip of paper with the tip of her index finger and slowly turned the note clockwise until the words blurred, although the message remained starkly clear. Blair was angry. Upset and angry. She'd gone to a safe place, not onto the streets or to a club or into a stranger's bed. She had done that more than once—taken refuge in sex when the invisible bars of her very real cage had become too oppressive and she'd finally broken free. Even before Cam had fallen in love with her, she'd hated to see Blair waste herself on women who couldn't begin to appreciate what it meant to touch her. Now, the idea of anyone else putting that hazy look of desire in Blair's eyes, bringing that tremble to her lips, causing that quick catch of excitement in her breath was enough to make Cam lose any semblance of civilized reason. She became animal, primitive, driven by the instinct to guard what was hers. She slowed the revolution of the notepaper and read it again.

I love you, Blair.

Cam smiled dryly. They'd made an agreement not that long ago that neither of them would leave if they were angry. Blair had adhered to the letter of the law. Even though she'd left, she'd told Cam where she was going.

I love you too, Cam thought. She left the note on the counter and went to the bathroom, stripped, and showered. After she pulled on jeans and a workout T-shirt, she called Renée Savard.

"Good morning, Commander," Renée said, sounding as if she'd been awake for hours.

"I'm going to be a little late this morning. I need you to handle the briefing and find out where they transferred the detainees from Matheson's compound. I want to question them."

"We've got some of their statements in the FBI reports, such as they are."

"You mean we have what someone else thinks we should know," Cam corrected. "Time to gather our own intel."

"Yes ma'am. Shall I make flight arrangements?"

"Yes." Cam paused. "For both of us. Today."

"Yes ma'am," Renée said, her excitement apparent even over the phone.

"Thanks." Cam disconnected and contemplated her next call. It wasn't difficult to find Blair. Her whereabouts were known to at least half a dozen people at any given moment. All she needed to do was call the shift leader in the command center and ask. She dialed a number and waited.

"Hello?"

"Diane, it's Cam. Is Blair there?"

"Good morning, Cam. No, I'm afraid you've missed her. She left a while ago."

Cam's stomach tightened. Why hadn't she come home? Did Stark's team have her or had she slipped out on them? For an instant she came close to disconnecting the call to roust Stark and demand a status check. Instead she closed her eyes and remembered the note. *I love you.* "Did she say where she was going?"

"Forgive me," Diane replied with a note of disbelief in her voice, "but don't you have ways of finding out where she is?"

"I do. But she wouldn't like it."

Diane laughed, the sound of bells pealing on an impossibly clear, bracingly brisk spring morning. "Oh, you are very good."

"Apparently not."

"Well, I shall have to play my part as well. As her best friend, of course, my only concern is her best interests. So I'm not inclined to help you."

"I know," Cam said completely seriously.

"Are you appropriately sorry for upsetting her?"

"Completely."

"Do you have any idea what you're apologizing for?" Diane asked gently.

"Not entirely, but it doesn't matter. She's upset, that's all I care about."

"She said she was going to the gym."

"Thank you," Cam said. "You could've drawn that out quite a bit longer, you know."

"I know, but there's no pleasure in it when I know that she needs you to find her as much as you do."

"I don't think I've mentioned it," Cam said, "but I appreciate everything you're doing for the wedding."

"I'm doing it because I love Blair, and you make her happy. And I'm really quite fond of you too." Diane drew a breath that sounded shaky. "And you saved Valerie's life."

"No thanks are needed for that."

"But I thank you nevertheless," Diane whispered. "Now go see to Blair."

"I will." Cam disconnected, collected her keys and wallet and gym bag from the closet, and headed out the door.

❖

The first thing Cam saw when she turned down the narrow alley off Houston was the Suburban in the middle of the block, parked halfway up on the sidewalk to allow delivery trucks and the occasional cab to get past. She was certain the agents in the vehicle took note of her, but there was no outward indication that they saw her. She didn't acknowledge them either as she pushed through the unmarked windowless door sandwiched between a shoe repair shop that had been closed for two decades—a few unclaimed shoes coated with a thick layer of dust lay on the counter behind the smeared front window—and a bodega with iron grates drawn down to the sidewalk. The instant she stepped into the dimly lit hallway and began climbing the steep narrow stairs, she smelled mold, sweat, and testosterone. The third floor reverberated with the rumble of male voices and bodies falling, and heavy equipment thudding onto the floor. The warehouse-sized space was lit at intervals with fluorescent lights dangling unevenly on chains and whatever light filtered through the grimy windows set high in the wall along the roof line. Two roped-off boxing rings with stained canvas mats stood center stage, surrounded by a haphazard array of weightlifting equipment, speed bags, and hanging heavy bags. As was often the case, Blair was the only woman in a sea of bulked-up men covered with tattoos and scars. One of the new members of Blair's team, Cliff Vaughn, a muscular African American looking out of place in his tailored slacks and double-breasted blazer, stood with his arms folded over his chest on the far side of the boxing ring where Blair was sparring with a young white guy with a shaved head and prison tats on his neck. Patrice Hara, flanking the ring on the side closest to Cam, nodded a greeting without taking her eyes off Blair as Cam slipped up beside her.

"Morning, Commander," Hara said.

"Hara. How's she doing?"

"She's playing with him."

"Ah." That was not good news. When Blair was spoiling for a real fight, she never instigated it. Being smaller and more agile than all of her opponents, she frustrated them by refusing to engage—slipping or blocking their punches and then sneaking in for a quick jab. Men who weren't used to her very quickly forgot that they weren't supposed to hit a woman, and after each impotent blow they threw, they came back harder. Blair couldn't avoid every punch indefinitely, and ultimately, one landed hard enough to knock her down. Then she came out swinging, and they swung back. She usually managed to fight off her pent-up fury, but unfortunately, she ended up taking a beating too. This morning, Cam just wasn't in the mood to see Blair get hammered by this young guy's hard right hand.

Quickly, she skirted around the ring to the tiny women's changing room. A single bench stood before three rickety steel lockers without locks. She pulled open a locker, stripped down to her sports bra, and tossed in her clothes. Then she yanked on long, loose blood-red Thai fighting shorts and kicked into her loafers for the walk back to the ring. A few heads turned but she stared straight ahead, wrapping her hands with fight tape on her way. When she reached the ring she slid an arm under the lower rope and slapped the mat hard to get the fighters' attention. As soon as both Blair and her opponent turned in her direction, Cam vaulted the ropes into the ring, barefoot.

"Thanks for warming her up," Cam said in a friendly tone as she tapped her fist lightly against the young guy's shoulder. "You mind if I get in a few rounds?" Her tone of voice indicated it wasn't a request.

The guy shrugged. "Sure. She's slippery."

"I noticed."

"Don't you have a briefing?" Blair said as she danced from foot to foot. She'd tied her hair back with a rolled black bandanna and she wore her usual sparring outfit—a cut off T-shirt that left her midriff bare and gray cotton gym shorts. A strip of tape covered her navel ring to prevent it from being torn out inadvertently.

"Savard's handling it." Cam bowed slightly. "Freestyle?"

Blair grinned and tilted her head. "Sounds good."

Cam's fighting style was a mixture of Thai kickboxing and the hand-to-hand combat techniques employed by federal agents. Blair had adapted her formal martial arts training to street fighting. They were equally matched. Cam raised her hands to face level, her fists loosely clenched, and circled. Blair, pumped from having been sparring a while, didn't hesitate. She feinted a punch and swept Cam's legs out from under her. Cam hit the canvas and rolled backward, rising to her feet just in time to block the follow-up jab she knew was coming. They traded kicks and blows for ten minutes until they were both drenched in sweat, then Cam sidestepped a snap kick aimed at her chin that could have broken her jaw if it had landed. She swung around behind Blair, clamped her forearm across Blair's throat, and planted her knee in the center of Blair's back. Then she lifted in a move designed to snap an opponent's neck or break their spine. She modulated the force of both the choke and the backbend so she wouldn't injure Blair, but it was a painful hold nonetheless. Blair resisted for a few seconds, then rapidly slapped Cam's arm twice to signal submission.

Immediately, Cam released her and stepped back.

"You okay?" Cam asked, panting lightly.

Blair nodded, also breathing quickly. "Nice move. I always forget that when you fight, you fight to kill."

"These guys at Ernie's aren't the right partners for you. We should set you up with Stark or Hara so you can learn to fight the way you need to on the street."

"Why not Wozinski?" Blair grinned.

"You might hurt him."

"I didn't hurt you." Blair gripped the ropes, swung over onto the floor in one fluid motion, and headed off.

Cam quickly followed her to the locker room.

"So," Blair said as she pulled off her T-shirt and dropped it on the bench. She peeled her shorts off and faced Cam nude, the width of the narrow bench all that separated them. "You think I need to learn to fight to kill?"

Cam skimmed her finger down the center of Blair's chest, gathering a drop of sweat on her fingertip. Holding Blair's gaze, she touched the tip of her tongue to the tiny droplet. "I do."

Blair's eyes darkened and her skin flushed. "We managed to fuck in here once with no one noticing. Care to try for twice?"

"I want," Cam said with a grin. "But I think not."

"We're getting old."

"We have a comfortable bed twenty minutes away."

Blair leaned over the bench and braced both hands on Cam's shoulders. Then she kissed her, a long, probing kiss designed to make them both needy. It worked. She pulled away, breathing hard. "I missed sleeping with you last night."

Cam stripped, aware of Blair's eyes raking over her body. "I missed you too."

"Are you mad?"

Cam stepped over the bench and pulled Blair into her arms. She coursed her hands up and down Blair's back, caressing the hard pumped muscles beneath her satin skin. Blair parted her thighs in a movement as innate as drawing breath, and just as naturally, Cam slid her leg between them. Cam kissed Blair's mouth, her neck, the base of her throat. She whispered against her skin, "I'm sorry."

Blair drove her fingers into Cam's thick dark hair and pulled her head back to cover her mouth with another bruising kiss. Their bodies, slick with sweat from the workout and the heat of rising passion, fused. Blair traced her lips over the rim of Cam's ear. "I love you so much it hurts."

"I never want to hurt you," Cam murmured, her eyes black with need. She brought her hand between them and cupped Blair's breast.

"Enough," Blair groaned, covering Cam's hand with hers. "I'll bet you any amount of money Cliff is right outside that curtain."

"I wouldn't care except I don't share." Cam forced herself to step back. "Thanks for letting me know you went to Diane's last night."

"I just needed to vent," Blair said, reaching for a clean T-shirt with shaking hands. She laughed unsteadily. "God, I'm a mess." She glanced at Cam, her mouth curling into a half-smile. "What I really need is for you to fuck me."

"I'll make a note of it." Cam pulled on briefs and then her jeans, never taking her eyes from Blair. "It's mutual, by the way."

Blair raised an eyebrow. "Which part?"

"All of it. I need you inside me right now. I want to marry you. I want our wedding to be as special as what we share."

"Damn you, Cameron," Blair whispered, tears brimming on her lashes. "I'm not done being pissed off yet."

Cam brushed her thumb beneath Blair's eye, catching her tears. "Okay."

"Finish dressing. I don't trust myself." Blair grabbed Cam's wrist and gently bit her thumb. "And your note? Mark down I want it more than once."

Cam laughed. "Got it."

A few minutes later, they were ready to leave. Cam gripped her gym bag and wrapped an arm around Blair's waist, stopping her just before they left the locker room. "I may be flying out later today."

"Until when?"

"Hopefully just tonight. Possibly until tomorrow."

Blair searched Cam's face. "Is it anything I need to be worried about?"

"Absolutely not. Just some routine information gathering."

"That requires the deputy director to do it personally," Blair said sarcastically.

"There are some things I need to do myself," Cam replied.

"I'm being an ass." Blair gave Cam a quick kiss. "I know you should be at a briefing right now instead of chasing down here after me—"

"I'm exactly where I want to be." Cam took Blair's hand. "I needed to kick a little butt to get my day off to a good start."

Blair snorted. "Dream on."

Cam flashed her grin. "I'll be too busy making those notes."

CHAPTER SEVEN

L et me out on the far side of the park," Dana instructed the cabbie as she extracted money from her wallet.

The taciturn driver swerved to the curb and she handed him a handful of bills. "Got a receipt?"

Wordlessly, he tore off a blank square from a coffee-stained pad and handed it through the divide between the front and rear seats. She pocketed it, grabbed her duffel, and stepped out into a cold misty rain a little before eight a.m. Hunching her shoulders in her too light nylon windbreaker, she hiked to the corner, dodging early morning pedestrians, and stopped on the corner to study Blair Powell's apartment building across the way. She'd spent most of the previous evening scouring online sources for information on her new subject. She never undertook any assignment without doing the background work herself. A lot of reporters used assistants to prepare profiles and gather data, or didn't bother at all, but she did the legwork. She never knew what little nugget of information might spark a story, and she trusted her instincts more than anyone else's. If she was going to spend the next ten days with the first daughter of the United States, she wasn't going to be writing about Blair Powell's fashion sense. She was going to write about what she had discovered was surprisingly absent in the media. An in-depth look at the woman behind the glamorous façade. Thumbnail sketches abounded—wealthy only child, glamorous and sophisticated first daughter, notorious bad girl. All too easy and all supported only by superficial glimpses, as fleeting as a reflection in the surface of a fast-running stream.

Who was Blair Powell? That's what Dana planned to find out.

The apartment building was a typical New York City building—plain-faced stone façade, short green awning above double glass doors with the shadow of a doorman just inside. The exact location of the first daughter's apartment was not public knowledge, but a quick search of the reverse directories indicated that most of the units in the building were held as corporate rentals, and she was willing to bet they were empty or used intermittently for vetted government officials and visiting dignitaries needing temporary housing in the city. She was also willing to lay money that she would never find out. She crossed to the wrought iron fence that enclosed Gramercy Park and peered through the gray drizzle into the impeccably maintained postage-stamp park. Not surprisingly, it was empty. With a practiced eye, she swept the streets looking for anything suspicious. She might be back on American soil, but the habits she'd developed in combat zones around the world were permanently ingrained. Never take anything for granted and always question the unusual.

Dana didn't see anything she hadn't expected to see. A news van was parked diagonally across the street from the entrance to Blair Powell's apartment building and another down the block. Security cameras swiveled lazily above the front door and high up on the corners of the building. A black Suburban with dark tinted windows and a short, subtle satellite antenna bookended the van on the opposite side of the entrance. Two opposing forces—the media and those devoted to secrecy.

"It's going to be a fun week or so," Dana muttered as she slung the strap of her duffel over her shoulder, jammed her hands in the pockets of her black chinos, and headed off to start her new assignment.

Dana hadn't quite reached Blair Powell's front door when it swung open. She couldn't make out the features of the person just inside, but she got the impression of big. When she stepped into the lobby, she saw that she was right. Tank would have been a good nickname for the clean-shaven, square-jawed man with the inscrutable dark eyes. The flesh-toned curlicue wire leading from his right ear down his neck and disappearing under the collar of his nice white dress shirt spelled Fed.

"Good morning, Ms. Barnett," he said in a pleasant baritone. "I'm Agent Ramsey. If you'd step over to the desk for a moment, please."

A bank of elevators made up the wall to her left, and the last one was keyed. To her right a freestanding waist-high counter stood out from the wall. Dana hefted her duffel on top and walked to the end of the desk. She preferred not to be frisked in full view of the front door. Agent Ramsey joined her, his expression still pleasant, and quickly and efficiently patted her down. He wanded her and the duffel. "Would you open the bag, please."

"Sure." Dana unzipped and opened the duffel to reveal her clothes neatly rolled and stacked inside.

Ramsey methodically sorted through the contents, then stepped away. "Thank you."

While Dana secured her clothes, he murmured into a wrist unit.

"If you'll wait here for a moment," he said.

"Right." Dana stared at him while he divided his attention between the front sidewalk and her.

Five minutes later, one of the two unkeyed elevators opened and an athletic woman a few years younger than Dana stepped out. Her dark collar-length hair was plainly styled and her brown eyes sharp despite the faint shadows beneath them. She approached quickly with her hand outstretched. "Morning. I am Agent Stark."

Dana shook her hand. "Dana Barnett. I take it you know why I'm here."

"Yes." For a brief second, a smile flickered across the agent's face. "I'll let Ms. Powell know that you've arrived. Before you meet with her, there are some things we should review."

"Fine," Dana said, annoyed by the red tape even though she had expected it. Security types were notoriously anal, even worse than their military counterparts in her opinion. Somehow, she found the overt military hierarchy easier to tolerate than the secrecy and paranoia that often seemed to permeate the civilian security agencies. As she stepped into the elevator, she wondered what it must be like to be immersed in that atmosphere day in and day out for months and years at a time. The doors glided closed and they were alone. Time to send out a test probe. "Is Cameron Roberts still heading up Ms. Powell's security?"

"No," Stark replied.

Dana didn't consider the response any particular indication of cooperation, since it was public knowledge that the celebrated agent had been replaced. She was encouraged, though, since most of the Feds she knew wouldn't agree it was raining if they were standing in a downpour. "So who has the job now?"

"Here we are," Stark said as the elevator door opened.

So much for two-way communication. Dana followed her out into an unadorned foyer with hallways extending to each side. They turned right and immediately entered a small conference room. Four chairs flanked a scratched wooden table. Otherwise the room was empty. Obviously, they didn't get many visitors. Dana waited until the agent indicated a chair, then pulled one out, dropped her duffel, and sat down. Agent Stark sat across from her.

"I will provide you with Ms. Powell's daily social schedule so you can decide which events you'd like to cover," Stark said. "Along with that, we'll arrange your transportation."

"Thank you." Dana contemplated the best approach and then decided there was no way to diplomatically handle things. "I don't suppose you're any happier about me being here than I am."

Stark said nothing but again, that flicker of a smile.

Dana grinned. "Okay, maybe you're even more unhappy than me."

"We enjoy a challenge."

Dana laughed. "So do I." She leaned forward and her laughter died away. "I'm very serious about my work. I respect what the first daughter is doing and I consider it a privilege to be able to tell her story. I'm going to want unrestricted access to her twenty-four hours a day. That was the deal."

"That will be up to her."

"Then I should be talking to her."

Stark leaned forward too, her hands loosely clasped on the tabletop, her eyes boring into Dana's. "While in the first daughter's presence, you will be subject to the jurisdiction of the Secret Service. We will tell you where to move, when to move, and how quickly. If at any time the security of the first daughter is threatened, your safety will not be a priority."

"I understand." Dana actually felt relieved. She liked this woman. She understood that even though the assignment might be a soft one, the circumstances were not. Anyone who thought that the world was going to return to the way it had been before September was fooling themselves. Getting an inside look at the first daughter's security was a story in itself. "I'm pretty steady under fire, Agent Stark."

"I'm aware of that." Stark knew a great deal about Dana Barnett in addition to the fact that she was thirty years old, the daughter of a steelworker, and an Ivy League graduate with a full merit scholarship. She knew where Barnett had been for the last six weeks and just how much heavy bombardment and small weapons fire she had endured. Stark was also aware that the year before, the reporter had been isolated with a group of Red Cross volunteers during an uprising in Africa and had carried a wounded nurse on a makeshift litter for twenty miles through the jungle. All things considered, if they had to deal with a reporter inside their perimeter, Dana Barnett was an excellent choice. Stark doubted that Egret would agree, but that had little to do with Barnett personally. "I don't think you'll find this assignment as exciting as your last one."

"Believe me, I won't mind."

Dana had no doubt that Stark or someone on her team—and it was apparent to her now that Stark was in charge—had investigated her far more thoroughly than she had been able to investigate any of them. There had to be a file on her somewhere, but if anyone really wanted to know about her all they needed to do was read her articles. While the news was based on fact, the truth a reporter chose to bring to the public was always colored by their own perceptions, prejudices, and beliefs. She prided herself on digging out the real story, despite its popularity, or lack of it.

Stark stood. "If you'll wait here, I'll advise Ms. Powell that you'll be joining her later. She is not scheduled for anything until this afternoon. Then I believe she and a friend are conferring with the caterers."

Dana winced and quickly smothered it. "I would very much like to meet with her before her formal day begins. If you could relay my request."

"I'll tell her," Stark said, feeling very very glad she didn't have Dana Barnett's job.

❖

Blair lay on her stomach, her eyes closed and her head pillowed on her folded arms. She focused every ounce of her concentration on not having an orgasm. The ride back from the gym in the rear seat of the Suburban had been intolerable. She kept seeing Cam in the ring, the muscles in her abdomen bunching and stretching as Cam blocked her kicks and parried her punches. All she could feel was the hot slide of Cam's fingertip between her breasts and the slick tease of Cam's tongue inside her mouth. She'd wanted her right there in the locker room, and she hadn't cared if Cliff or Hara or every man in the gym had heard them fucking. The only reason she let Cam put her off was because she knew it would be even better when she finally got Cam inside her.

Where she was now.

Cam brushed her mouth over Blair's ear and pushed a little deeper. "You're holding back."

"No, I'm not." Blair trembled, opening her legs a little wider. Cam's knuckles brushed the underside of her clitoris and she bit her lip as whispers of pleasure swirled through her belly. "But you can…go ahead and come if you want to."

"Why, thank you," Cam murmured, half laughing, half groaning. She lay partially on Blair's back, her weight braced on one arm, slowly rocking against her ass while she thrust her hand between Blair's legs. She kissed the back of Blair's neck, then the edge of her jaw, and leaned farther over and found her mouth.

Blair arched her back and sucked on Cam's tongue. When she felt Cam's thumb press and circle between her buttocks, she moaned. Breaking the kiss, she panted and clenched her thighs, trying to hold back the tide. "Oh God."

"You're so tight on my fingers right now," Cam groaned, resting her face in the curve of Blair's neck. Her breath wafted hot across Blair's face. "You're going to come."

"Yes," Blair whispered. "You. Wait."

Cam held her breath as Blair flowed beneath and around her. "Oh yes."

Before the last tendrils of her orgasm had spun themselves out, Blair raised her hips and, despite Cam's protests, dislodged her. Then she pushed Cam over onto her back and slid down between her legs. Cam was just as hot and hard as Blair had known she would be, and Blair moaned with pleasure as she took her into her mouth.

"What happened to more than once?" Cam groaned. "Oh, God, baby."

"I'll be back for seconds," Blair said, quickly taking her in again. As Cam pulsed between her lips, she reached up to caress her breasts and abdomen, judging how close she was to coming by the heaving of her chest and the quivering of her muscles.

"Blair," Cam warned, half sitting as she clutched Blair's head. She jerked once, then curled forward, trembling violently. "I'm coming, baby."

This was the moment Blair loved, when her strong, brave lover was completely, totally hers. When Cam fell onto her side, her limbs twitching helplessly, Blair stretched out beside her and kissed her. "I love you."

"Same," Cam croaked.

"Catch your breath, and I'll be ready for round—" Blair stiffened as the phone rang. She ignored it and it stopped ringing. "I'm going to have that disconnected."

"Good idea."

Blair cradled Cam's head against her breasts and stroked her hair. "You're going to need another shower."

Cam opened her eyes. They were hazy and satisfied. "Take one with me?"

"What time are you leaving?"

"Nine."

Blair tried to keep her voice even. "We don't have much time."

"Sure we do." Cam eased Blair onto her back and caressed between her legs.

Blair caught her breath. "Okay. We've got enough time."

Grinning, Cam sucked a nipple into her mouth and massaged Blair's clitoris with her thumb.

"Time's up," Blair cried, letting the inevitable claim her. When she couldn't take another second of pleasure, she clamped her hand over Cam's. "Stop."

"Not a chance." Cam laughed.

"Okay. Revise that. Desist momentarily."

Cam dropped onto her back and pulled Blair into her arms. She kissed her and sighed. "On second thought, maybe you working out with Stark or Hara isn't such a good idea."

"You're not serious."

"They're going to be frustrated enough when you beat the hell out of them. Adding sexual torment on top—"

Blair slapped Cam's stomach. "Not everyone finds me irresistible."

Cam tilted Blair's head up with a finger beneath her chin. "You're wrong about that."

"You're not worried, are you?" Blair asked, frown lines forming between her brows.

"No." Cam kissed her gently. "Don't you think you should check who called?"

"No. I don't care who called."

"Okay."

"Just like that?" Blair murmured. When Cam didn't answer, Blair heaved a sigh and reached across her for the phone. She checked Caller ID, then pushed Call. "It was Stark."

"Mmm."

"Paula? It's Blair. Who?" Blair sat up, continuing to stroke Cam, who regarded her intently. She covered the mouthpiece. "Barnett."

"I want to speak to her before I leave today," Cam said.

Blair rolled her eyes. "All right. Half an hour." She tossed the phone aside and glared at Cam. "This is all your fault, you know."

"I know."

"It's a good thing you're so good in bed."

"Ah, is there any safe answer to that?" Cam asked.

Blair shook her head, her gaze dropping to Cam's mouth. "But there is a very good reply of another sort."

"How much time do we have?" Cam moved down the bed.

Blair spread her fingers through Cam's hair. "Enough."

CHAPTER EIGHT

S ir?"
"Good morning, Colonel." Matheson held the phone in one hand and balanced his coffee mug on the knee of his crisply creased trousers with the other as he sat in a comfortable chair in front of a huge stone fireplace. He'd played on that hearth with his best friend as a child. Charlie was dead now, a martyr in the battle to secure the American way of life. But his memory remained, and his son, unlike Matheson's, also lived on to fight for the cause.

"I received some intelligence that I thought I should bring to your attention."

"Go ahead, Colonel."

"A reporter has been assigned to cover the target's upcoming… uh…event. Full access."

"Anyone we can use?" Matheson watched the logs shift, sending showers of sparks onto the stones.

"Doubtful, sir, but we're running background checks now."

"How reliable is your source?"

"Very, sir. She's an assistant in the office of the White House Deputy Press—"

"That will do." Matheson didn't trust even the most secure of lines. He smiled at the thought of a patriot in the West Wing. A woman, whom no one would suspect. It wasn't true that only men could serve, it was simply a matter of recognizing a woman's unique skills. While not having the mental fortitude or physical constitution for combat, women were a natural for communications work. "I like the press angle. Get me a list of names. We'll want someone out there right away to establish connections before the target arrives."

"Yes sir. Are you comfortable, sir? Everything you need there?"

"Perfectly, Colonel. Thank you and carry on."

"Sir."

Matheson disconnected and settled back in the chair, crossing his long legs at the ankle. Information was easy to come by. Until recently, access to potential targets—people and places—had been relatively simple as well. Getting close to Blair Powell might be more difficult now, but it was far from impossible. He smiled. A challenge merely made the hunt more satisfying.

The outcome was not in question. After all, he had God on his side.

Dana stepped off the elevator into a foyer that could have been in any luxury apartment building in the city. The eight by ten foot space was dimly lit by wall sconces, the marble floor nearly hidden beneath a thick oriental carpet, and the walls papered in some muted classic pattern above dark wood wainscoting. The surroundings spoke of money and taste and elegance. Even the cameras discreetly tucked into several corners weren't that unusual in a security-conscious city, nor was the fact that the elevator required a special key, which Agent Stark had produced when they were ready to ride up. The man standing with his back to the wall next to the only door in the foyer was different, though. A blond-haired, blue-eyed clone of the one who had greeted her in the lobby downstairs scrutinized her and Stark with unapologetic intensity. Agent Stark handed him Dana's ID, which Dana had surrendered upon request when Stark had informed her that the first daughter would see her.

"This is Dana Barnett," Agent Stark said, handing the ID to the agent guarding the door.

The man studied Dana's face, then the ID, then Dana once more. He held out her ID and she took it.

"Why the ID check? Doesn't he believe you?" Dana asked Agent Stark. She didn't get an answer, and she wasn't entirely surprised. Thus far she'd been told three times in slightly different fashions that the

Secret Service does not discuss protocol. "If I don't know, I may have to make things up."

"Perhaps you just shouldn't report on topics that haven't been cleared," Stark replied mildly.

"Is anything ever going to be cleared?"

"I'm sure Ms. Powell's wardrobe...no, actually, I'm not certain of that either."

Dana grinned ruefully. She had a feeling that Agent Stark wasn't making a joke. "All right, tell me if I'm hot or cold. He won't take your word for it because I could have coerced you into bringing me up here. However, since I wouldn't know to give you my ID to give to him, that's a signal that you brought me here intentionally. It's a code."

"I doubt that Ms. Powell has much time allotted for you," Stark said. "We probably shouldn't waste any."

"You're right." Dana waited while Stark knocked on the door. "But I was hot, wasn't I?"

As she spoke, the door swung open and Blair Powell regarded them with interest. "Something new and exciting I should know about?"

Stark blushed. "No ma'am. Dana Barnett to see you."

Blair looked Barnett over. She appeared slightly more rested than the day before, but obviously wasn't concerned about the image she projected. Her chinos and white button-down collar shirt were clean but not pressed, the black leather belt cinched above narrow hips was dull with age, and her boots similarly worn. Her casual disregard for her appearance and her lack of desire to make a good impression were refreshing.

"I gather you couldn't convince anyone there'd been a terrible mistake?" Blair asked.

Dana couldn't help but smile. "Apparently, Lucinda Washburn doesn't make mistakes." She raised a hopeful eyebrow. "What about you? Any luck?"

"Apparently not," Blair said dryly, appreciating Barnett's disregard for her position. Usually the press tended to be obsequious or obnoxious, but rarely unimpressed. "You're here."

Cam stepped up next to Blair. "I only have a few more minutes."

"I know." Blair slipped an arm around Cam's waist. "Come in, Ms. Barnett."

"Please, call me Dana." Dana followed the first daughter and the deputy director as they crossed to a seating area in the center of the loft. She had caught the flash of discomfort that streaked across Blair Powell's face an instant before she hid it behind the beautiful façade the world was used to seeing. The first daughter was unhappy about something. The deputy director looked as impassive as a stone statue. Except. Except when her eyes moved ever so briefly to Blair Powell's face. Then her charcoal eyes sparked with tenderness and heat. The wave of raw desire emanating from Cameron Roberts washed over Dana so unexpectedly she had no time to prepare. She broke out into a sweat and her heart rate soared. *Jesus. These two should come with a warning sign.*

Roberts turned to Dana and Dana stiffened under the unwavering gaze.

"Sit down, Ms. Barnett," Roberts said, taking Blair Powell's hand as the two sat on a leather sofa in a seating area with a fireplace on one wall, huge windows on the other and open space. The hammered tin ceilings had to be twenty feet high.

Dana forced her tense muscles to relax as she settled onto a matching sofa with a sleek dark coffee table the same color as the floor between them. "I appreciate you seeing me this morning, Ms. Powell."

Blair smiled. "I have a feeling you would have made Stark's morning unpleasant if I hadn't."

"I make it a point not to misrepresent myself, so I won't disagree." Dana fixed on the deputy director. "You wanted to talk to me?"

"I supported Lucinda Washburn's position on you having exclusive access to Ms. Powell for the next week or so," Roberts said, "because I feel that it benefits the first daughter. If that should no longer be the case, we'll sever your contact with her."

"Are you trying to offer me a loophole to slip out of this assignment, Deputy Director?"

"Is that what you want?" Roberts replied.

Dana thought about the two women sitting across from her. Blair Powell was publicly one of the most important women in the United States by virtue of her position as well as her popularity. Cameron Roberts held a critical position vital to the security of the United States and yet remained a cipher, virtually unrecognizable to the man on the street. They were about to become the focus of intense media scrutiny and much debate. They were news, no question. But they were more than reluctant celebrities—they were the public and not so public faces of power, and she had the opportunity to be closer to them than anyone in her position ever had. "No. I'm not looking for an out."

"Why not?" Cam asked. "Twenty-four hours ago you didn't think this assignment was very important."

Dana took a deep breath. "I apologize for that." She looked at Blair. "Ms. Powell, I hope you forgive my arrogance. I'm honored to be able to take part in what I know must be a very important event in your life."

Blair laughed. "What part interests you the most? My trousseau? The menu? The floral arrangements?"

"Uh." Dana felt the blood drain from her face and scrambled for an answer. She frowned. "How do you decide what to wear? I mean, for the majority of couples it's a tux and a dress. So what will it be for you two? Dresses?" As she looked from one to the other, she had the satisfaction of seeing Cameron Roberts's face blanch.

"Ignore her, darling," Blair murmured, loud enough for Dana to hear, "she's baiting you."

"It's working," Roberts muttered. She stared at Dana. "Whatever story you think you're going to get, you will not be allowed to compromise her security."

"Agent Stark made that very clear," Dana said without rancor.

"We don't anticipate any trouble." Roberts clasped the first daughter's hand as she spoke. "But in the event of an emergency, you'll be expected to follow orders. If not—"

"I'm a reporter, Deputy Director, and I've been to the front. I understand chain of command, and I understand that in the heat of battle not everyone is created equal." She didn't expect anyone to look out for her if something untoward happened. "I have no problem with that."

"Well, I do," Blair said, standing abruptly and walking away.

Surprised, Dana stared after her, then said to Roberts, "I'm sorry."

Roberts nodded, looking as if she wanted go after the president's daughter, but she didn't. "Anything you may see or hear regarding her security is strictly classified. If one word about procedure makes its way into your article, I will personally—"

"It won't," Dana said sharply. "I know my job and my responsibility."

"Good. Having you around isn't going to be easy for her. Don't make it any harder."

"What about you? You're in this too."

"I'm not noteworthy." Roberts actually looked surprised, as if it hadn't even crossed her mind that her own role in the upcoming nuptials would be of interest to anyone.

Dana got the picture then, sharp and clear. Cameron Roberts had one single focus, and that was the woman standing across the room, looking out the windows at the rain with her back to them. Roberts didn't like the idea of Dana covering the proceedings much more than Blair Powell did, but she'd supported Washburn's idea as the lesser of many evils. One reporter versus twenty, control versus chaos. Nevertheless, Roberts was obviously worried about the cost to Blair Powell's peace of mind.

"I'm not going to make her uncomfortable," Dana said quietly, not wanting the first daughter to overhear. "I think she's incredibly brave and I think she's doing something important for the country, not just in acknowledging her relationship with you, but standing up publicly now, when almost everyone else is wondering if they should be finding a place to hide."

Roberts relaxed infinitesimally and some of the tension eased from her face. Dana hadn't realized how tightly she was wound until just that moment.

"I agree with you." Roberts stood. "I have a plane to catch. If you would give us a moment, please."

"Absolutely. I'll wait outside." Dana held out her hand. "I'm good at my job, Deputy Director. She'll be in good hands."

Roberts smiled as she returned the handshake. "Call me Cam."

"Thanks. Cam."

❖

"Hey," Cam murmured, smoothing her hands over Blair's shoulders. She kissed the back of her neck. "You okay?"

Blair turned from the window, scanning the room. "You got rid of her?"

Cam kissed her. "Don't rejoice yet. She still wants to talk to you. I think she's waiting out in the hall."

"Of course she is." Blair sighed and draped her arms around Cam's neck. "You have to go, don't you?"

"Yes."

"Who are you taking with you?"

"Renée."

Blair frowned. "That's all?"

"I don't need a bodyguard, baby," Cam said gently. "And it really is just a routine interrogation."

"You needed a bodyguard a month ago when someone tried to run you down. Oh, and don't forget that little attempt to blow you up too." Blair forced back the memory of just how close Cam had come to dying that night in the cold, black ocean. She wanted to chain her to a desk, even though she knew Cam would hate it. She almost didn't mind how unhappy being stuck in an office would make Cam, as long as she was safe. And if she thought about *that* for very long, she would be forced to appreciate why Cam wanted to keep her hidden away somewhere, out of harm's way. And she did not want to go there. Oh, this two-way street thing definitely took some getting used to. "What about Valerie? Can't you take Valerie?"

"Renée is an excellent agent."

"I know that. I just thought two would be better—"

"I can't take Valerie where we're going." Cam brushed the backs of her fingers over Blair's cheek. "There's no danger. I swear."

"Call me, okay? Whenever."

"I will." Cam kissed her, then let her go. "Are you ready for Dana Barnett?"

Blair sighed. "Why not."

Cam laughed. "I love you. See you soon."

"See you soon," Blair whispered, watching Cam gather her topcoat and briefcase. She might have been any executive on her way to a midday meeting, except for the .357 pistol holstered against her left side. "Hey, Cam?"

Cam turned with the door half open.

"I love you."

Cam smiled and stepped aside to let Dana Barnett enter. Then the door closed and she was gone. Blair remained where she was, waiting for the familiar surge of anxiety to pass. Cam would be fine, and she would be back soon. No one would come to the door with the message there had been a bomb on a plane, or an escaped fugitive with a gun, or a biological warfare attack. Cam would come home. Blair felt Dana watching her from across the room and shrugged off the melancholy. "Coffee?"

"Yes, thanks," Dana replied.

"Make yourself comfortable, I'll just be a second." Blair filled mugs from the pot in the kitchen and sliced a couple of bagels while she was at it. She put everything on a tray along with cream and butter, and carried them into the living area. "Help yourself."

"Thanks." Dana leaned forward and grabbed a bagel and poured cream into a mug of coffee. "Where's the deputy director going?"

"I don't know."

Dana looked up. "Is that normal?"

Blair grimaced. "Is anything?"

"You've got a point." Dana tried the coffee. It was good. "Does it bother you? The secrecy between you?"

Blair set her coffee aside. "I guess it's time for ground rules."

"Why not. Everyone else has given them to me."

"Mine are pretty simple, really. You can ask me anything you want, but there are certain things I won't answer. I won't talk about my relationship with Cam. I love her and we're going to be married. That's all you really need to know about that."

"I'm not very good at pretending."

"What do you mean?" Blair asked.

"Maybe you believe your own press—that other than the fact that you happen to be two women, your relationship with Cameron Roberts is just like any other relationship—but I'm sure not buying it." Dana leaned back and rested one ankle on her knee. "You know that's complete and total bullshit."

"You really don't want this assignment, do you?"

"No, I decided that I do."

"And you think antagonizing me is a good idea?"

"Maybe," Dana offered, "if it gets you to talk to me."

"I don't talk to people about my personal life."

"How about the deputy director? Do you talk to her about how much her job scares you?"

Blair stood up. "Okay. We're done."

Dana stood. "I'm sorry. I don't have any talent for interviewing. I'm usually trying to get information in the middle of a gun battle or a typhoon, and social niceties are just too damn inconvenient. Thank you for your time."

When Dana started toward the door, Blair called after her. "Why did you ask me that?"

Dana stopped, but didn't turn around. "I saw it in your face a few minutes ago."

"Assuming it's true, why would I want anyone around who's that intuitive?"

"The story here isn't two women getting married, Ms. Powell." Dana pivoted to face Blair. "It's *who* the two women are, and every reporter worth her column space in this country—hell, in the world—knows it. They'll be on you like piranhas."

Blair's temper flared. "And how do you think I feel about that?"

"I imagine you hate it. But if I don't write the story, someone else will—whether they actually know anything or not." Dana slid her hands into her pockets and shrugged her shoulders. "I'll tell the truth. I'll respect the special nature of her job, and yours."

"Better the devil you know?"

Dana grinned. "That's about it."

"I'll have Stark get you the keys to one of the apartments in the building. It will be more convenient."

"I appreciate that."

"I'm going shopping this afternoon. Around two."

"That sounds like fun," Dana said, sounding as if each word were painful.

Blair smiled. "Oh, it will be."

CHAPTER NINE

W ho do we have?" Cam settled onto the rear seat of the SUV across from Savard. The regional office in Virginia had sent two FBI field agents to transport them to the Federal Bureau of Prisons Detention Center where detainees from Matheson's mountain camp were being held.

"Martin Early," Savard replied, passing a folder across the space between them. "Arrested at Matheson's compound. In addition to firing on federal officers, he had recruitment documents in a cardboard box behind the seat of his truck. It looks like he was trying to clear out some of Matheson's paperwork before we showed up."

Cam checked to be sure the mics to the front compartment were off. She didn't know the agents who had met them at the airfield, but that wasn't unusual. The fledgling OHS had yet to recruit a full complement of agents and for the time being was forced to commandeer bodies from other security divisions. She suspected the rumors that the OHS would soon become a cabinet department were true, and once that happened, they'd have more funds and more permanent agents. But for now, the occasional inconvenience of being shorthanded was far preferable to the bureaucratic entanglements that were sure to result as the politicians and directors of various agencies struggled for supremacy in the new security structure. "Early is what—Matheson's third or fourth in command?"

"From what we've been able to put together from duty rosters and memos confiscated during the raid, we can at least put him in the upper echelons. He's a graduate of Matheson's military academy, although he wasn't much of a scholar." Savard spoke quietly, but her tone suggested she was frustrated. Or angry. "We haven't exactly had free access to information. We've been looking for this guy for a month, and finally tracked him down at the BOP in Virginia. Somehow, no one was quite sure where they'd put him."

"That seems to be happening with persons of interest a lot these days," Cam said grimly. She suspected that the DOD or the CIA, or both, were sequestering potential terrorists away from the other security agencies. The failure to predict 9/11 had not yet been laid at anyone's door, and it was doubtful there was any single agency to blame. Nevertheless, no one wanted detainees giving up information that would point to their own agency as culpable. It was politics, and politics always derailed justice. "Does the prison director know why we're coming?"

Savard gave a predatory smile. "No. We just informed him to expect the deputy director late this afternoon."

"No reason for us to share if no one else does." Cam studied the 4x4 color photograph reproduced on the first page of the file. The man was younger than she had anticipated, perhaps mid twenties, and she wasn't certain why she was surprised. Most of her team members weren't a lot older. He looked like a typical all-American boy grown up—blond, blue-eyed, fair complexion. But his mouth was thin and hard and his eyes held nothing but fury and contempt. "What does he do when he's not playing soldier?"

"He's a trucker."

"Interstate?"

"Up and down the East Coast."

"That's convenient," Cam said. "Is there any evidence that puts him in contact with the hijackers?"

Savard looked pained. "I wish I could answer that, Commander. But no one is giving us anything and all our requests for files have been ignored. It's taken us weeks just to pinpoint this guy's location. It's like a shell game—find the detainee."

"Felicia can't dig up anything?" If there was information in any computer anywhere, Cam was convinced Felicia could find it, given enough time.

"She says no."

Cam frowned. "Then someone has decided to shut us out."

"It looks that way to us. Just the same, we're working all of Early's known associates and the truck routes he's run for the last year. We might be able to put him with one of the hijackers, and if we do, that ties Matheson in as well."

"Good," Cam said neutrally. Building a case against Matheson that would stand up in a court of law was going to be difficult given the lack of access to intelligence, although her team would keep working to do just that. She knew what Matheson had done, and she knew that he would keep coming until he was stopped. Men like Matheson didn't consider themselves bound by the law, which gave him the kind of freedom his victims didn't enjoy. Cam valued and respected the need for order and the ascendancy of the common good, but in Matheson's case those finer points of law were long past.

Her goal was simple, to find Matheson and stop him. Apprehending a lone fugitive, especially one with an extensive network of supporters and undoubtedly sizable funds, was a difficult undertaking. Matheson could move around the country easily with very little risk of detection unless he attempted to access bank accounts or return to his known previous locations. So far, he hadn't done that. He'd had no reason to—his friends and colleagues in the patriot movement were sheltering him. She'd already talked with her FBI counterpart, and the surveillance of known patriot organizations had been stepped up. They might get lucky and catch Matheson meeting with one of the ringleaders. Fugitives had been apprehended more than once by some fluke—a traffic stop, being recognized by someone who'd seen their picture on *America's Most Wanted*, an accident that forced them to seek medical care. Somehow, she didn't think Matheson was going to be careless. Even though she doubted they would find him before he made another move, they would continue the hunt. In the meantime, she wasn't going to take anything for granted, not even her own intuition.

Once Dana was alone in the apartment two floors below Blair Powell where she'd be staying for the next few days, she unpacked, which took all of five minutes, and then wandered through the impersonally furnished rooms thinking about the woman sequestered upstairs. Out of the spotlight, when Blair wasn't performing some official function— and Dana had the sense that performing was exactly what Blair did under those circumstances—she was a fascinating woman. Reviews of the first daughter's paintings by several well-known art critics indicated that art was not a hobby for her. Blair had real talent. Most artists shunned the spotlight, preferring to pour their energies into their creations. It must be a burden for Blair to be constantly thrust into the public eye. Add to that the fact that she was a lesbian and involved in a controversial relationship with a woman who was once responsible for her protection, and the tapestry became even more intriguing.

And she's beautiful, Dana admitted to herself as she stood in front of the windows looking down on Gramercy Park. More than beautiful, really. Blair had that sensual spark that set everyone in the vicinity a little bit on fire. Dana grinned ruefully. She'd felt that pull of attraction the first time they'd met, and Cameron Roberts had picked up on it immediately. Nice, getting caught lusting after the first daughter in front of her lover. Great way to start an assignment.

Dana wasn't really worried. She had lots of practice keeping her fly zipped. Spending half the year on the road, or most likely in places where there *were* no roads, wasn't exactly conducive to having a love life. She'd discovered pretty quickly that the stress and uncertainty of danger tended to make people do things they wouldn't ordinarily do. When you weren't sure you'd wake up in the morning, you hated to waste a night, especially if you could spend it with someone else who was just as eager as you to feel alive. The good thing was, most of the time you *did* wake up the next day. Unfortunately, the night before would often come back to haunt you. After a few embarrassing and one painful experience, she'd decided love on the run didn't have much to recommend it. She'd gotten used to going without, but occasionally she got blindsided. Happily, she was in the clear now. She only had to see Blair Powell and Cameron Roberts together for a few minutes to realize nothing and no one would come between them, not that she wanted to. But just witnessing the power of what they shared was enough to banish any lingering fantasies.

She turned from the window and surveyed the nicely appointed but completely sterile apartment and contemplated powering up her computer to investigate the players further. But now that she'd met Blair Powell and Cameron Roberts, she realized that nothing that had been written about them, or speculated about them, was going to tell her anything of real value. Since she was still at least forty-six hours behind in sleep, she stretched out on top of the bed in one of the bedrooms and closed her eyes.

When the knock came on her door, Dana woke instantly and checked her watch. Showtime.

"Be right there." Briskly, she rubbed her face, made a quick stop in the bathroom to douse her face with cold water and chase the cobwebs from her head, and grabbed her leather flight jacket on her way to the door. A small, slim woman with straight jet-black hair and almond-shaped deep brown eyes wearing a well-cut navy suit greeted her when she stepped out into the hall.

"I'm Special Agent Hara," the woman said.

"Dana Barnett," Dana said, feeling foolish since she knew the agent knew her name. And likely everything else there was to know about her.

"If you'll come with me, please."

They rode down the elevator in silence and exited the lobby where an SUV stood idling at the curb. Stark stood by the open rear door, her body partially obscuring the interior as she scanned the street in both directions. A half dozen reporters and a couple of cameramen jostled to get a look into the car around the big blond whom Dana had last seen standing outside Blair's apartment. He was effectively blocking the sidewalk between the crowd and the Suburban.

"Dana!" A woman's voice rose above the general onslaught of shouts. "What are you doing with the first daughter's detail? Are you dating her or is it business?"

Caught off guard, Dana half turned toward the gaggle of reporters and saw cameras raised in her direction. Other people shouted questions, most of which she didn't catch in the general tumult of noise, but she did hear the phrases *sleeping with*, *new lover*, and *where is Roberts?* She also saw a society reporter for the *Baltimore Herald* with whom she'd once had a brief fling. They had been great in bed, but their professional ideologies had been so different they couldn't carry on a conversation for more than five minutes. Looking quickly away, Dana ducked into the back seat behind Hara.

"Jesus," Dana muttered. "Nice reception."

"Welcome to my world." Blair Powell, dressed in dark slacks, black boots, and a burgundy blouse beneath a long black leather duster, occupied the opposite seat. She'd pulled her hair back somehow, taming the thick curls, and Dana realized how different she looked with it worn this way. The wild earthy look had been replaced by cool sophisticate. Both looks were sexy.

Dana met Blair's eyes. "Is that normal?"

"It didn't used to be, but…" Blair glanced out the window at the reporters straggling back to the news vans. "For the last few months it has been."

"What about the man on the street? Are you bothered by people wanting to talk to you?"

"Not really. Unless they notice my entourage," Blair grinned at Hara, "they don't even recognize me."

"I find that hard to believe."

Blair's eyebrows rose. There wasn't anything flirtatious in Dana Barnett's tone, although Blair had caught the barest flicker of interest from her a time or two. The reporter's compliment seemed to be genuine. "Thank you."

"You're welcome." Dana removed a small digital recorder from the pocket of her leather jacket and showed it to Blair. "Do you mind? I'll only use it while I'm actually interviewing you."

"Where do the cards go when you're done with them?" Blair asked.

Dana had half expected Blair to refuse outright, and the question took her by surprise. Most of the people she interviewed were eager for exposure. "I keep them locked in a safe. No one ever hears them except me."

Blair was silent for a moment. "It's all right with me, but I have a feeling there's a protocol for this sort of thing." She glanced at Hara, who appeared relaxed but alert sitting next to Dana. "Do you know, Patrice?"

"No ma'am, but I would suggest clearing it with the chief and the commander."

"Why don't we assume it's all right for now." Blair saw the small red light come on at the end of the device. "By the way, Dana, are you a lesbian?"

Dana laughed and looked at the tape recorder in her hand. "For the record? Yes."

"Not that it matters, of course," Blair added.

"Considering that your marriage won't be legal, why are you doing it?" Dana asked.

"Because it *should* be legal, and because I don't need anyone's permission to promise my life to Cam."

"How does your father feel about it?"

"You should probably ask him about that."

"I'd love to," Dana said, "but I'm not sure I could get past Ms. Washburn to ask him."

"He'll be coming to the wedding. You can ask him then."

Dana sat up straight. "The president is coming?"

"That's not official," Blair said, "so you'll need to wait until the White House officially announces it. Unless you want Lucinda on your tail."

"Are you kidding?" Dana said. "As soon as that word goes out, the number of reporters in Colorado will triple. You're damn right I'll keep it quiet."

The SUV pulled over to the curb and slowed to a stop. Hara shifted toward the door, again blocking the interior as someone on the outside opened it. Dana craned her neck to see around Hara and saw Stark guarding the door again. Then a drop-dead gorgeous blonde in a Fifth Avenue wardrobe climbed in and settled next to Blair Powell. She kissed Blair on the cheek, then set her gaze on Dana.

"Blair, honey, whatever have you picked up?"

"Diane, this is Dana Barnett, the reporter I told you about," Blair said dryly.

"Hello, Dana," Diane said, savoring the name as if it were a fine wine.

Dana felt a pleasant anticipatory rush. The blonde's smoky voice was like liquid heat pouring over her. She leaned across the space between them with her hand outstretched. "I think I'm going to like shopping after all."

"Oh, my dear, you have no idea," Diane purred as she took Dana's hand.

Blair shook her head. "Diane."

"I'm just being sociable." Diane leisurely crossed her legs. "I told you, I don't intend to touch."

Dana laughed. "Do I get a vote?"

"I'm afraid not," Diane replied.

"This assignment gets more difficult all the time," Dana said, and sat back to enjoy the ride.

❖

"I'm sorry, Deputy Director, but I think we've got a problem." The balding, barrel-chested man with the military bearing didn't sound particularly apologetic, although he'd been nothing but distantly polite since Cam and Savard had arrived at the high-security federal detention center. They'd been shown into his office after minimal delay and he had appeared genuinely surprised when she gave him Early's name. Now he withdrew a folder from a pile on his desk, opened it, and studied a list. Then, his expression grave, he said, "Martin Early is in the process of being transferred to another facility. I'm afraid you won't be able to interview him here."

"Where's he going?" Cam asked calmly, although she already knew the answer.

The prison director shrugged. "Your guess is as good as mine. With some of these guys, we're just providing holding services. Bed and board."

Meaning, Cam thought, some other agency was in charge. Since the Patriot Act—designed to broaden the ability to investigate foreign terrorism—had been enacted the month before, the jurisdiction over and civil liberties of suspected *domestic* terrorists had become a bit cloudy. Could be coincidence that the detainee she wanted to interrogate was suddenly bound for destinations unknown, but she doubted it. And now was not the time to discover where in the tangled lines of intelligence the message had gotten out that she was interested. "I'd like to speak to whoever is in charge of his transfer."

The prison director glanced at his watch. "I imagine they're about ready to leave."

Cam stood. "Please relay the message that they should wait. And have one of your people take us to them."

"All right," he said dubiously. "I'll send the message, but these boys don't necessarily listen."

"I think they will this time," Cam said pleasantly. Federal agents recognized chain of command even if they didn't always play nice with other divisions. She motioned to Renée and they followed the guard who came in to escort them. He led them to the ground floor and through a myriad of hallways to the rear of the prison. Outside, a small parking lot was enclosed by twelve-foot-high concrete walls topped with razor wire, infrared cameras, and motion detectors. Two black SUVs and an unmarked black transport van idled in the lot. A young, clean-cut man in a well-fitting blue suit, white shirt, tie, and shiny black dress shoes stood outside the lead vehicle, his arms folded across his chest. He didn't look happy. Cam walked over to him.

"I'm Deputy Director Cameron Roberts from the OHS," she said, extending her credentials. She did not offer her hand. She tilted her head toward the windowless van. "Do you have Martin Early in there?"

"I'm not at liberty to disclose that, ma'am."

"Can I see your ID, please." Cam took his badge holder. It said Federal Bureau of Corrections, but she suspected he was DOD. "Agent Tomlinson, I need to interview Mr. Early on a matter of urgency. I'd like you to delay the transfer until I'm done."

"I can't do that, ma'am, without a direct order from my superiors. I'm sure you understand."

He was stonewalling, as any good agent would. It might take hours to unravel the jurisdictional issues, and even that might not gain her access to the detainee. She was going to have to pull rank, and a parking lot was not the place to do it. "Where's your destination?"

"I'm sorry, ma'am, I'm not at liberty to disclose that information."

"I understand," Cam said evenly. She could feel Renée tense beside her. Her number one was short on patience; they all were these days. But a brawl between agencies, especially with a midlevel agent like this, wasn't going to get them anywhere. "We'll be coming with you." She turned to Renée. "Radio our driver and tell them to come around and pick us up."

Agent Tomlinson's eyebrows climbed above his expensive sunglasses. "I don't have clearance for that, ma'am."

Cam smiled. "That's quite all right. I do."

CHAPTER TEN

"W̱ait a minute," Diane said to Blair and Dana as she dug in
her purse. "I've got a call."

The group slowed, and Dana noticed their three shadows take up
position in front and behind them again. Over the last few hours, she'd
almost gotten used to Hara, Wozinski, and Stark hovering just outside
her direct field of vision. When she had first started walking down
Fifth Avenue with Blair and Diane, she'd been acutely aware of being
followed. Spending time in combat zones had made her highly vigilant
and hypersensitive to anyone encroaching on her personal space, and
when that someone was the size of Greg Wozinski, she was doubly
uncomfortable. In fact, after twenty minutes of having him behind
her—*close* behind her—she was irritable and jumpy. She had no idea
how Blair Powell tolerated this kind of violation of her privacy twenty-
four hours a day.

"Hi," Diane said brightly when she answered the phone, "where
are you? Really? You're finally free?...No, stay there—we're right
around the corner. We'll meet you and buy you a drink." Diane dropped
the phone back into her purse. "That was Emory. I told her we'd join
her at her hotel."

"Great," Blair replied. "I think anything else we have to do, we
can do by phone before we leave this weekend."

Dana whispered a prayer of thanks. She'd actually had a pretty
good time watching Blair and Diane shop. Just the same, the art of
shopping was an acquired taste, and one she had yet to develop. When
she had to attend a formal function, she went with basic black and white,
figuring that would always work. Plus, black traveled well and tended

not to show wrinkles even after hours, sometimes days, in a suitcase. She'd used the time between fittings and discussions to informally interview Blair Powell. A good reporter didn't need to ask questions to learn about her subject. Mostly, she just had to listen. And watch. She'd discovered quite a bit in the last few hours, almost none of which would ever make it into her article.

Diane Bleeker, she soon ascertained, was a lot more than Blair's close friend. Diane was a little bit in love with Blair Powell, and a whole lot protective, and the feelings seemed mutual in a completely appropriate manner. Both women were effortlessly affectionate with one another in a way that Dana had never experienced with any woman. She was envious and intrigued by their relationship and more than a little turned on. Maybe her arousal stemmed from the sheer force of being surrounded by such powerful pheromones. Or maybe she had just gone too long without the singular pleasure of losing herself in a woman. Whatever the cause, her nerves were pleasantly on edge.

They set off walking again and within a few minutes had reached the Plaza. Dana noticed a few heads turn as they made their way through the lobby toward the hotel lounge and bar. Perhaps, as Blair had said, if Blair were by herself on the street, she might go unnoticed, but three women flanked by an entourage in suits scanning the surroundings were pretty hard to miss. Blair kept her eyes straight ahead, and Dana could almost feel the shield she had erected around herself. She wondered about the cost of maintaining that kind of barrier, and thought perhaps it explained why Blair seemed so intimate with those few she let close.

"She's over there," Diane remarked, pointing to a seating area in the corner with several sofas and a low table.

Dana glanced idly to where Diane indicated and nearly stumbled as her gaze honed in on the woman seated there. Blair and Diane, both blond, both beautiful, exuded a sense of brilliance and heat, and being around them was much like basking in the noon sun. The woman who awaited them made Dana think of midnight on the deck of a sailboat when the sky was black velvet sprinkled with diamonds and the breeze promised forbidden pleasures. The petite woman's shoulder-length ebony hair framed a face rendered unforgettable not by perfection but by the bold mouth and deep-set dark eyes. Her complexion held hints of the Mediterranean, adding to her undeniable allure.

"Emory," Blair and Diane exclaimed simultaneously. The three hugged, and then Blair indicated Dana, who stood slightly outside the group, unable to take her eyes off the brunette. "Dana Barnett, Emory Constantine."

"Nice to meet you," Dana said, extending her hand. Dr. Emory Constantine's chin barely came to Dana's shoulder, and Dana had the irrational thought that they'd fit very well together in bed. Just as quickly, she banished the image and prayed Emory didn't read minds. After all, she was supposed to be here getting Emory's story too. Now she wouldn't have to wait until they all gathered in Colorado to get started.

"Hello." Emory's voice was warm and mellow. Her gaze lingered on Dana's for a few seconds before she turned to Blair and Diane again.

Wozinski, Hara, and Stark triangulated positions behind the grouping of sofas, and Dana realized that she stood midway between the perimeter formed by the agents and the inner circle of the three friends. She had often found herself caught between conflicting worlds—democracy and dictatorship, order and chaos, life and death. Despite being used to navigating the limbo of shifting landscapes, she had never felt as much an outsider as she did at this moment, nor been as aware of the desire to be connected. Watching Blair and Diane draw Emory into the fold of their affection, she experienced a pang of loneliness that settled in her chest and made it hard for her to breathe.

Everyone sat down, and Dana found herself next to Emory on a love seat across from Blair and Diane. A waitress appeared out of nowhere and took their orders for drinks. Dana didn't drink much, but she ordered a beer while everyone else ordered wine. She rarely thought about her working-class upbringing, but right at this moment, surrounded by elegance and beauty, she felt the difference. Emory's streamlined black skirt, she noticed, glided up her slender thighs when she crossed her legs. The slight whisper of pantyhose sliding over the surface of Emory's skin made Dana's stomach knot. She caught the barest trace of perfume, an aromatic scent that made her think of shadowed glades and sunlight dappling through a thick leafy canopy. She had the nearly irresistible urge to press her face to Emory's neck.

"Thank God," Dana muttered when the waitress brought their

drinks. She took a long swallow of her beer and tried to distract herself from the altogether enthralling presence of Emory Constantine only inches away.

"So you're really going to take time off," Blair said to Emory. "I hope you're planning to come with us when we leave on Monday."

Emory laughed. "I didn't pack enough for next week. I'll have to go back to Boston first."

"What could you possibly need at a ski resort that we can't lend you?" Diane said.

"There's a slight matter of you being five or six inches taller," Emory pointed out.

Diane waved her hand in dismissal. "We'll manage. Now that we've finally pried you out of your lab, we're not letting you go back."

"When's the last time you had a vacation?" Blair asked.

"I travel a lot," Emory said defensively.

Blair shook her head. "I've spent my life with politicians. It's impossible to snow me with a diversionary answer like that. Vacation. Not business trip."

"Uh...sometime last year."

"There, see," Diane said triumphantly. "You're *not* going back to Boston. The second you do, you'll start in on whatever it is you do and forget about coming with us."

"I'm not going to forget that Blair is getting married," Emory protested. She glanced at Dana with a friendly smile. "Are they this relentless with you too?"

"My situation is a little different," Dana said, realizing that Emory didn't know why she was there.

"Dana is a reporter, Emory," Blair said, the slightest note of apology in her voice. "She's covering the wedding for a Washington paper."

"Oh." Emory's smile disappeared and her voice became distinctly cooler. She shifted slightly away and regarded Dana with thinly veiled suspicion. "I see."

"Allergic to the press?" Dana asked sharply, bothered by the wall Emory had thrown up so quickly.

"Let's just say my experiences haven't been exactly positive," Emory said, obviously trying to be polite. She set her wineglass down with exaggerated care, then looked regretfully at Blair. "I think I'll have to pass on your offer to join your group this weekend."

Blair didn't look at Dana. "I'm sorry, Emory. I wasn't thinking."

"That's quite all right. There's no reason you should be." Emory pushed her hair back from her face with a gesture of weariness. "Would you mind if I caught up with you later? I think I need a little time alone to unwind."

"Of course not," Blair said. "Promise you'll call us later. Diane will be at my place for a while, and we were hoping you could come to dinner."

"I'll call." Emory stood and gave Blair and Diane a quick hug. She nodded to Dana. "Good afternoon, Dana."

"Well, hell," Diane muttered as Emory hurried away. "That puts a crimp in our plans."

Dana put her beer bottle down and stood. "I think I can take care of this for you."

Without waiting for a reply, Dana sprinted after Emory Constantine.

❖

"We're turning off the interstate," Savard reported, checking the highway signs as the SUV slowed at the bottom of the exit ramp and turned west. "Looks like a pretty small road."

Cam stretched her legs and shook some of the tension out of her shoulders. "I imagine this caravan was attracting a bit of attention on the highway. Easier to track by air out there too."

"Air like helicopter or air like satellite?" Savard asked.

"Satellite for sure, possibly both." Cam checked her watch. It got dark early in the mountains, but it was still later than she had hoped. "We're not going to make it home tonight. We'll be lucky if we make it home tomorrow."

"You think we're going to Illinois?"

Cam nodded. "My guess is they're transferring Early and whoever else is in that van to the supermax facility at Marion. The Navy base at Guantánamo isn't ready to hold detainees yet."

"Hell," Savard muttered, "if we don't talk to this guy before he goes down there, we'll never talk to him."

"That's why we're on this road trip."

"You want me to put in a call to base about our change in plans?"

Cam did, because she wanted to get a message to Blair that she wouldn't be home when she had planned to be. On the other hand, even though she *thought* Early's transfer just when she wanted to interrogate him might be a coincidence, she wasn't convinced of it. She also believed their communications with base were as secure as they could make them, but that didn't mean they weren't being monitored. For the moment, she preferred not to broadcast her plans. "Let's wait on that for a bit."

A few minutes later Savard looked out the window again. "Foggy out there."

"We're climbing through the mountains. I don't think I've ever crossed them when it wasn't."

A beep sounded from the console built into the side panel announcing that an occupant in the front compartment wished to speak to them. Cam pushed a button. "Yes?"

"The vehicle just ahead of us is signaling they're going to pull over."

Cam frowned. "Can you see any sign of mechanical problem? A flat tire or engine overheating?"

"No ma'am."

"There's not much of a shoulder on these twisty roads. Be careful we don't hit them."

"Do you want us to stop, Deputy Director?"

Cam considered her options. The prisoner transport van was sandwiched between the two other SUVs. Her vehicle was fourth in line. If the agents in the vehicle behind the van were having mechanical problems, they weren't in any danger. They had phones and were undoubtedly in contact with their superiors. On the other hand, if she stopped, she'd lose the prisoner van and the lead SUV along with her opportunity to interrogate Early. "No, go around them and pull in line behind the van."

"Yes ma'am."

"What do you think that's about?" Savard asked edgily.

"I don't know." Cam had a prickly sensation on the back of her neck and the uncomfortable feeling that she had missed something. She pushed the button on the intercom again. "Let me know if they speed up. And be prepared, they may try to lose us."

"Don't worry, they won't."

Cam tightened her seat belt. She could tell Savard felt uneasy too. At Savard's unspoken request, Cam nodded. "Open the floor compartment."

Savard leaned over while Cam punched in the code to unlock the storage bin beneath Savard's feet. At the click of the lock disengaging, Savard opened it and extracted the shotgun from the clamps that held the weapon in place. She dropped the lid back on the compartment and rested the shotgun across her knees.

"If for any reason we need to leave the—" Cam's words were obliterated by an explosion that rocked the vehicle. The SUV swerved abruptly and Cam catapulted forward. Her seat belt abruptly stopped her motion, and she vaguely registered a bruising pain across her chest. Then she was thrown violently back against the seat as the world dissolved in a dizzying, bone-jarring revolution of screeching metal.

❖

"Emory, wait," Dana called. For a second, she thought Emory would ignore her, but finally Emory stopped in front of the elevators.

Dana couldn't read her expression so she went by instinct. Emory hadn't seemed angry a few minutes earlier, more…sad. "It usually takes longer than five minutes for someone to decide they don't like me."

"It's nothing personal." Emory shrugged and pushed the up button. "It's occupational."

"I figured that out."

"I'm sorry if I appear rude," Emory said, her attention fixed on the elevator doors. "But I'm too tired to watch what I say, especially when I'm relaxing with my friends."

The resentment in her voice was hard to miss. "How about if I tell you everything is off the record unless we agree otherwise."

Emory gave Dana a curious look. "I'm afraid I'll have to insult you again, but I don't believe you."

"Let me guess," Dana said, taking a chance. "You told someone something in an intimate situation and it ended up in print."

"Close enough."

"Then she didn't have any scruples. I do." Dana touched Emory lightly on the shoulder to be sure Emery was listening. "Off the record means off the record."

Emory smiled sadly. "That's what he said too."

He. The disappointment hit Dana like a fist in the solar plexus, but she managed to hide her shock. "Sorry, I just assumed—"

"There's no need to apologize."

"Well, since we don't have to worry about pillow talk, you should feel even safer."

"For some reason, I don't," Emory said, although her expression softened. "You're a lot smoother than he was."

"Glad to hear it." Dana grinned and cupped Emory's elbow, tugging gently. "Come back and finish your wine."

"I'm not usually this easy to persuade," Emory said with a small frown, falling into step beside Dana.

"It's my natural charm," Dana joked, wondering if she imagined the slight tremor beneath her fingertips. Emory's arm brushed hers and she knew she wasn't imagining the pulse of arousal that settled in the pit of her stomach. A news story, even one her boss had sent her out to get, was the furthest thing from her mind. All she wanted was to get to know Emory Constantine better. A lot better.

Cam registered two things at once. Heat and the smell of something burning. The vehicle had come to rest on its side, and she was dangling in her seat belt, her weight supported by the straps across her hips and chest. Breathing in that position was difficult. "Renée! Renée, are you all right?"

"Banged up," Savard gasped. "Nothing serious."

"Stay there until I can check you out." Cam fumbled with the latch on her seat belt and finally opened it. She tumbled the few feet onto the door, which was now really the floor, and landed on her left shoulder. She grunted at the pain, then pushed herself to her knees just as Savard dropped next to her with a bone-crunching thud. The interior lights were out, and as she tried to see Savard, she realized that the air was a hazy red. Panic hit her hard, and for an instant, she saw her father's limo explode in a fountain of fire. Mentally pushing the image away, she grasped Savard's shoulder. "We have to get out of here. How's your leg?"

"Leg's fine." Renée's voice was clear and calm. "I'm okay, Commander. You think anyone's out there?"

"We'll have to climb out to see." Cam pushed upright and fumbled with the door handle on what was now the roof. The first person out would be a sitting duck. "Still have the shotgun?"

In response, Renée chambered a cartridge.

"Once I'm out I'll cover you," Cam said. "Wait here."

"Commander, let me go out first!"

"No." Cam pushed up on the door with all her strength and it banged open. Cautiously she peered out, but all she could see were fingers of fire leaping into the air. A sniper could have her in his crosshairs and she'd never know. Her vehicle wasn't on fire—at least not yet. Something else was burning close by. Although her arms were shaking, she braced herself on the open hatch, pulled herself up, and rolled over the side onto the ground. As soon as she hit, ignoring the rocks digging into her body, she pulled her pistol and put her back to the vehicle. From that position she could see a hundred and eighty degrees. All she saw was smoke. If there was anyone out there, they were well hidden. "Savard. Now. Quickly."

A few seconds later, Savard plummeted next to Cam. "What about the guys up front?"

"Still inside." Cam's eyes finally adjusted to the eerie light. "Our vehicle went over the side. We're down about fifty yards." On her knees, she worked her way slowly toward the front of the vehicle. Another fifty yards down the slope, the van, or what she assumed had been the van, was completely engulfed in flames. "You check our escort. I'll check the van."

"Commander," Savard protested, "let me go down."

"Just watch my back, Savard." Cam edged into the roiling clouds of black smoke. She doubted anyone was still alive in that inferno, but she had to find out. She couldn't just stand by and watch them burn.

CHAPTER ELEVEN

S o are you going to take us up on the dinner offer?" Blair asked Emory. After Emory had returned with Dana, they'd all shared another drink, and as far as Blair could tell, Dana and Emory had made some kind of peace. Emory seemed more relaxed, and Dana couldn't seem to look anywhere but at Emory.

"Before I say yes," Emory said, "who's cooking?"

"We are," Diane said, sliding her arm around Blair's waist. "One of our many talents."

"Then I accept." Emory glanced at Dana. "Are you coming?"

"Well," Dana said hesitantly, "I'm not really sure—"

"Join us," Blair said. Even though she wasn't crazy about Dana's assignment, she liked her. And Emory's question had sounded a lot like an invitation. If Emory wanted Dana to be there, Blair wasn't going to object. She'd felt an immediate affinity for Emory the night they'd shared the stage together at a fund-raiser that turned deadly. Even though she, Diane, and Emory had gotten close, she didn't know a lot about her, except that she was brilliant, kind, and single. There was an ex-husband in her past, but from the way Emory had been studying Dana all night, Blair wondered what had led to the ex part.

Dana smiled at Emory. "Looks like I'll be there."

Emory smiled back. "Good."

Blair stood. "Then I vote we move the party to my place."

The SUV was waiting in front of the hotel entrance, and just as Blair and the others reached the vehicle, the world took a jump into fast-forward. Wozinski grabbed the rear door and yanked it open at the same time that Hara and Stark closed in on Blair and propelled her into the vehicle.

"The rest of you, get in, *now*," Stark shouted as Wozinski threw himself into the front seat and Stark started to swing the rear door closed. Diane had already followed Blair inside, and Dana grabbed Emory and pulled her in just as the door swung shut.

"What is it?" Blair exclaimed as the SUV roared away from the curb. "Paula? What is it?"

Paula shook her head, her fingers against her earpiece as if urging a message to come through. At the same time, she lifted her communicator. "Delta one, priority red. Delta one, priority red."

The second Stark stopped speaking, Blair demanded, "What's happening?"

"I don't know." Stark's body was rigid, her expression stony.

Blair willed herself to think clearly. This wasn't the first time she'd been in this situation. A rapid evacuation could mean almost anything—another terrorist attack anywhere in the country, a biohazard threat in the subway system, an assassination attempt on her father. Someone in a security division somewhere might simply have overreacted to an intercepted radio transmission and called for extreme protective measures without true justification. She wouldn't know until Stark had more information, or until she could speak to Cam. Suddenly, she felt icy cold. She gripped the edges of the seat to keep her hands from shaking. "Get in touch with Cam. I want to talk to her."

"As soon as I can," Stark replied, still apparently screening transmissions.

Within moments, they careened into the serviceway behind Blair's building. Stark unholstered her weapon. So did Hara, and both agents positioned themselves to shield the occupants when the rear door opened.

Blair glanced at her friends. Diane and Emory both appeared stunned but calm. Dana looked fiercely focused and, Blair noticed, she had angled her body so she was between Emory and Hara. If there were armed assailants waiting for them on the street, the gunmen would have to go through two people to get to Emory. Blair took in all of this almost unconsciously, the foremost thought in her mind being Cam.

Where was she? Did she know this was happening? And beneath it all, the one fear she could not allow to surface. The one impossible, unacceptable possibility that all of this was because something had happened to Cam.

"Clear," Stark said to Hara, and opened the door. Both agents immediately jumped out, and Blair could see other members of the team fanning out around the SUV. Stark leaned in. "Ms. Powell, you first, please."

"Come with me," Blair said, taking Diane's hand.

As soon as they stepped out, half a dozen agents surrounded them and in the next second, Dana and Emory followed with several more agents falling in behind. Blair didn't bother with conversation, but half ran as the mass of bodies encircling her surged toward the building. Inside, the elevator to the penthouse was standing open and Stark directed Blair, Diane, Emory, and Dana inside. Hara and Wozinski squeezed in last. Once they were moving up, Blair let go of Diane's hand.

"Do you know anything more?"

Grimly, Stark shook her head. "Not yet."

The elevator doors slid open, and Blair's heart sank. Valerie waited in the foyer, her expression grave.

"Is it Cam?" Blair asked woodenly.

"There's been an incident. I don't have the details." Valerie's gaze never wavered from Blair's face. "Cameron signaled to secure you. You need to move inside your apartment. Now."

Cameron signaled. Blair swayed slightly. *Alive, then. She's alive.*

"How are they?" Savard croaked, choking as smoke engulfed the vehicles and completely obscured the road above them.

Cam shook her head, wiping sweat and ashes from her face. "Anyone in that van is gone. How about our people?"

"I deflated the airbags to get a look at them. The driver is unconscious, the other has at least an open fracture of his femur, maybe his pelvis." Savard struggled to open the rear compartment of the SUV, the lower edge of which was partially buried in rocks and earth. "I need to get to the medical equipment."

Every transport vehicle had at least rudimentary first aid supplies, although not the full complement carried when the first daughter was on board. "Leave it. We need to get these guys out of this thing before it burns."

"All this smoke has got to be attracting attention," Savard shouted as they made their way back to the front of the overturned SUV. "Some kind of rescue team should be here soon."

Cam climbed up on the side of the vehicle, which was now pointing upward, and peered down into the driver's compartment. "Assuming Agent Tomlinson doesn't turn them away." She gripped Savard's arm. "I'm going inside. I'll lift them up and you pull them out. Drag them as far away from here as you can."

Savard frowned and started to protest, but Cam cut her off.

"I'm taller, Renée. It makes sense for me to do it."

"Promise if it starts to burn you'll get out."

"We'll have them both out by then."

Cam dropped down into the driver's compartment, squeezing her body between the men still strapped into their seats and the dashboard. She checked the driver's neck for a pulse and found a thin racy thread beneath her fingertips. He was alive, but shocky. She eased her hand behind his head and checked for obvious fractures in his posterior skull and neck. She didn't feel any open wounds or major malalignment, but as a precaution, she worked her arms out of her jacket, folded it lengthwise several times, and wrapped it around his neck. The makeshift cervical collar might not help much if he had a serious neck fracture, but letting him burn to death wasn't an option. With his neck as protected as she could get it, she braced her shoulder against his chest and unsnapped his seat belt. With both arms underneath his, she straightened to her full height and dragged him up with her. "Can you reach inside and grab him under the arms?"

Savard leaned into the cab and gripped him. "I've got him if you can lift a little more."

"Hold him." Cam re-grabbed him around his hips and shoved upward. Between the two of them, they got him outside. Then she went back for the other one, this time carrying Savard's jacket. She wrapped it around his thigh and pulled the arms tight to act as a splint. He moaned while she worked, but fortunately he was only semiconscious.

He mumbled something about his wife, and for a second, Cam thought about Blair. Jesus, she was going to be so scared. "Sorry, I know it hurts. Hang on. We're going to get you out of here, and then I'll call her for you."

When Cam tried to lift him, she couldn't. Her legs felt like lead and her arms were so tired, she could barely move them. She leaned her head against the windshield behind her and closed her eyes, trying to gather her strength.

"Commander! We've got flames under the vehicle. Get out, Commander."

"Go," the man in her arms mumbled. "Get out."

Cam wrapped her arms around his chest and hugged him against her body. "Forget it. I don't want to face your wife. If she's anything like mine, she's going to be pissed enough as it is."

The man in her arms laughed, a broken sound that ended with a groan. When he spoke again, though, his voice was stronger. "I can pull myself up. Get my hands on something."

Cam ignored the screaming pain in her shoulders and the trembling protesting muscles in her legs, and pushed up with all her strength. "Reach." She felt him raise his arms, heard him slap his hands on metal as he gripped the edge of the opening above them. Then Savard was reaching down for him.

"Hurry," Savard yelled as she pulled the agent out of the truck.

Winded, struggling to stay upright, Cam felt her head spinning. Tears ran from her irritated eyes, and her chest burned with each smoke-laden breath. Visibility had dropped to zero, and for a second, she wasn't certain which way was up. Then hands dug into her shoulders.

"Commander, climb out. Now."

Savard yanked on Cam's shirt, and Cam grabbed the metal above her head. It was hot. Her father had been dead the instant the bomb exploded under his vehicle. She knew that, but she'd had nightmares of him burning for years after. She stepped up on the edge of the steering wheel and launched herself up and through the opening. She tumbled headfirst over the side and onto the ground, landing hard on her back. She wanted nothing more than to stay exactly where she was, except the air was barely breathable and so hot. If she stayed where she was, she wasn't going to make it home. If she didn't make it home, Blair would hurt. She rolled onto her stomach and started to inch away from the burning vehicle.

❖

Blair grabbed Valerie's arm. "What did Cam say? Valerie, what did she say?"

"Stark, secure the residence, please," Valerie ordered.

Wordlessly, Stark unlocked Blair's apartment door and she and Hara disappeared inside. Dana watched the apparent transfer of power, wondering who the icy blonde was. Her expression was remote, her green eyes glacially calm. And yet the air around her vibrated as if her body emitted an energy frequency no human could hear. A single word resounded in Dana's mind. Deadly. Deadly calm. Deadly control. Deadly.

"Who is that?" Dana murmured to Emory. They stood at the outer circle of activity, although Dana didn't for a second think they were unnoticed. She'd felt the sweep of the blonde's eyes as they'd exited the elevator and noted the flicker of recognition when she had seen Emory. When Emory didn't answer, Dana shot her a look. "Off the record, remember?"

"It's not for me to say," Emory said quietly.

"But you know her?"

Emory nodded.

"Are you okay?" Dana asked, realizing that Emory was pale. Her eyes were huge dark wells of worry.

"I never get used to it. Being pushed into a car, dragged away. I don't know how Blair stands it."

Dana rested her hand on Emory's back, hoping to reassure her. "Neither do I. But she's here with friends. That's good."

"Yes."

"You're shaking."

Emory smiled tremulously. "It's adrenaline. I'm all right."

"Adrenaline. Must be why my knees are knocking." Dana rubbed Emory's back in a slow circle. "Looks like we can go inside."

Stark held the door open. "Clear."

Dana noticed that Diane Bleeker stayed near Blair, but her attention never left the woman Blair had called Valerie. Everyone moved inside.

Valerie picked up the nearest phone and spoke quietly, her back to the group. Someone turned on the room lights and drew the blinds over the windows on the far side of the room.

"I feel useless." Dana watched Blair, who stood with her attention riveted on Valerie. Blair reminded Dana of ice statues that looked as if they might shatter if struck by a shaft of sunlight. "Jesus, isn't there any way to find out what's going on? It's driving me crazy, and it's not my lover out there."

"Isn't this what you wanted for your story?" Emory asked, a hint of bitterness in her voice. "The inside scoop with all the drama and pain as a bonus?"

"Is that what you think?" Dana was angry, but the pain in Emory's eyes was so raw, her own annoyance fled. "He really hurt you. I'm sorry."

"No, I apologize." Emory touched Dana's hand for an instant, then quickly pulled back as if surprised by her own actions. "You have a job to do. A great many people believe that what you do is necessary."

"But you don't."

Emory shrugged. "I don't believe the public has a right to know what it cannot process or place into context. Not when ill-informed and misguided public opinion can create wars or halt critical scientific progress."

"And I believe it's the responsibility of people like me to see that the public understands what's important. Don't you think that's the true power of the press?"

"Perhaps, in the best of all possible worlds." Emory shook her head. "I don't think Blair Powell would agree that we live in the best of all possible worlds right now."

"Give me a chance," Dana said, not knowing why it was so important but certain that it was. "Give me a chance to prove that I won't hurt her. Or you."

"Don't you mean trust you?"

"Yes," Dana said fiercely. "Yes. Trust me."

"I don't know that I can do that."

❖

The instant Valerie was off the phone, Blair pulled her out of earshot of the others. "Tell me what you know. Whatever it is."

"Cameron sent a coded digital signal from her cell phone to our base twenty-two minutes ago. The message directs us to secure you here, and lock down the building."

"That's it? You didn't speak to her?"

"No." Valerie paused, then added, "And I don't think you should expect to hear anything from her anytime soon."

Blair fought the surge of nausea. She'd been in this position before. She knew the drill. Communications were a two-way street. Almost any transmission could be diverted, tapped into, decoded. Cam would not risk a security leak in the midst of a crisis. The fact that she had contacted them at all indicated just how serious the situation was. "You can't call her?"

"You know that I can't."

"Do you know where they are?" Blair glanced over at Stark, who stood just inside the door, her hands behind her back, her jaw clenched. Savard was with Cam. Just this morning, Blair had wanted Valerie to go with her. Then it would have been Diane wondering, worrying, fighting back the fear.

"No. We can't triangulate the signal. It's intentionally designed not to be traceable." Valerie lowered her voice. "My feeling is that Cameron believes there's a major security breach—either here or in Washington. She has access to her phone, which suggests she's not being detained, and she was able to send us a message, which indicates she's not badly injured. Both of those facts are very much in her favor."

"But you think she's hurt?" Blair asked.

"I don't know that," Valerie said firmly. "And speculation will do none of us any good. You need to trust Cameron. She's very good."

Blair had the urge to laugh, but it wasn't because she found anything humorous She was struck by the absolute absurdity of discussing whether her lover might be injured or in grave danger with a woman whom she'd alternately envied and resented. "What if it were Diane out there?"

Valerie's expression never changed. "Then if I weren't with her, I would wish that Cameron was."

"You believe in Cam that much?"

"Don't you?"

Blair was taken aback by the mildly challenging tone and then answered firmly, "Yes, I do." She knew it as the absolute truth, and in the knowing, felt her panic subside and calm take its place in the center of her being.

"Well, then," Valerie said, "I have some calls to make. The moment I know something, I'll tell you."

"Thank you." As Valerie started to turn away, Blair caught her wrist. At the question in Valerie's eyes, she said, "I'm glad that Cam has you to rely on."

"I'm not the only one Cameron can count on." Valerie smiled for the first time. "She has you."

Chapter Twelve

How's your leg holding up?" Cam suspected the accident and the rough terrain they'd been scrambling over were taking a toll on Savard's barely recuperated knee. Her own body felt as if it had been run over by a truck with very large wheels, but other than being winded from breathing the hot, polluted air, she couldn't register any serious damage. Savard had only been back to full duty a few weeks, and she probably wouldn't admit to being injured unless she couldn't move at all. "We need to secure the road before we call for extraction. I don't want another team walking into this if there's a sniper up there."

"I'll go," Savard said.

"That's not what I asked."

"I can make it, Commander. And it ought to be me."

Cam didn't agree with Savard's belief that safeguarding Cam was her duty. She also didn't believe that going up the hill was more dangerous than staying where they were. Anyone still in the area who wanted to be sure they were all dead was probably in the process of working their way down the hillside right now. They would likely approach from their flanks, not from directly ahead. The road above was probably clear, but she needed to be sure. "Go. And don't trust anyone, no matter who they say they are. Keep your weapon at the ready and signal me."

"Yes ma'am."

Savard disappeared into the murky gloom. The burning cars were smoldering now, generating more black greasy smoke than flame. The night was closing in around her, and Cam was suddenly aware of being in the mountains in November. It was damn cold. She was in shirtsleeves, and her trousers were soaked from crawling through snow-covered brush. She checked on the two injured agents. Both were either unconscious or asleep. They had been wearing trench coats that they'd removed in the SUV, and now both were dangerously exposed. She needed to get these men to a hospital, but she didn't want to get them killed in her haste to save them. Savard had been gone a few minutes, long enough to have reached the road. Cam was about to start after her when a shower of rocks cascaded down the slope followed by Savard tumbling out of the darkness to land by her side.

"The road is empty, Commander. There's no guardrail where we went over and nothing to really show that we did, except some debris on the side of the road. It's so foggy, I don't think the smoke is all that noticeable to any cars passing by. That's probably why no one has shown up yet."

"People have gone off these highways and been trapped in their vehicles for days before rescue teams ever found them," Cam said. "Tonight, that works in our favor." She removed her cell phone from her pocket and dialed a Washington extension. The phone was answered on the second ring. "This is Cameron Roberts. I need an alpha-level extraction team, including a med-evac helicopter. Engaging the GPS now."

"That signal is going to light up for anyone looking for us," Savard said when Cam disconnected.

"Let's hope our team wins the race," Cam said.

"How long, do you figure?"

"She'll probably send a chopper from Langley. Maybe thirty minutes." Cam settled down on her stomach to wait, facing upward where she could see anyone who approached from above. "Keep an eye on those guys and make sure they stay close together to conserve body warmth."

"What about you?"

"I've been colder." Cam remembered the frigid waters of the Atlantic and how very much she never wanted to be *that* cold again. She needed to stay alert now, because she had to be sure that the next people coming down the slope were there to take care of her injured escorts and get her and Savard out of there. She couldn't afford to let herself get too comfortable, so maybe the bone-chilling weather wasn't necessarily a bad thing. "You watch sectors twelve o'clock through six, I'll take the other half."

"I'm on it." A minute later, Savard added, "And, Commander? You know that request I made about more fieldwork? I'd like to reconsider."

Cam laughed, knowing that Savard wouldn't want to be anywhere other than where she was right now. In some ways, she felt the same. This was what she was trained for. This was what it meant to live her beliefs. And if there had only been herself to consider, she wouldn't even be particularly worried. She did not fear death, although she had no desire to die. She wanted to live a long time and share every moment she possibly could with Blair. And above all else, she wanted to spare Blair the agony she knew Blair would feel if she did not return from a mission. She couldn't imagine losing Blair—in fact, even contemplating it was more than she could tolerate. Without taking her eyes off the murky shadows around her, she said, "Forget changing your duty request, Savard. I'm afraid you just proved you're combat ready."

Savard's quiet laughter pushed back the cold and made the dark just a bit less impenetrable.

❖

"How are you doing?" Valerie asked, joining Diane where she stood before the fireplace. Although the room hadn't been cold, she'd asked Diane to start a fire to chase away some of the gloom. Earlier, she'd ordered the blinds closed against the possibility of outside surveillance, which had added to the claustrophobic atmosphere in Blair's loft. Although she trusted the bulletproof glass to stop most small weapons fire, she didn't trust it to stop a surface-to-surface missile. And it was well past time to anticipate an attack from unexpected sources.

Diane took Valerie's hand and leaned closer to her. "I feel guilty for being glad you're here and not out there with Cam and Renée. Isn't that horrible?"

"No," Valerie whispered. She wanted to hold her. She wanted to kiss her. She also wanted to tell her that everything would be all right, but she didn't. Lies came easily to her, because altering others' perception of reality was what she was good at. So good that few people even knew who she was. That skill had suited her very well up until now—more than once the ability to make others believe a lie had saved her life. Now, what mattered most was that Diane never doubt she was telling the truth. "When I got the emergency evac signal, I ordered Stark's team to secure not just Blair but everyone with her because I knew the team would keep you safe too. Not strictly protocol." She brushed a quick kiss over Diane's hand. "But I didn't care. I need you to be safe."

"Do you think they're all right?" Diane asked.

"Everything I know tells me they're in trouble, but able to maneuver. If Cameron has any opportunity at all to gain the upper hand, she will."

"I know it's going to be hours, maybe days before this is resolved, and you need to be here." Diane caressed Valerie's face fleetingly. "But after that, I need you to come to me. Promise me that you will."

Valerie didn't hesitate, because this was a truth she embraced without question. "I will. I love you."

❖

Dana sat beside Emory on the sofa where she'd started the day twelve hours earlier and watched Diane and Valerie talking across the room. Everything about their body language said they were lovers. Interesting, that Blair's best friend was involved with someone who was obviously high up in the chain of command.

"Is she Homeland Security?" Dana asked Emory.

Emory sipped the coffee that someone had the brilliant insight to make in large quantities. She had a feeling they were all going to need it tonight. "Do you think if you ask the question that I refused to answer previously in a slightly different way, that I'll answer?"

"It's not the same question. Before it was open ended—*Do you know who she is?*" Dana crossed her legs, balancing her ankle on her opposite knee. "*Is she homeland security?* is a factual question. Background. Reference. It doesn't call for disclosure of personal information."

"Is that line of thinking supposed to make me more comfortable around you?" Emory shook her head. "Because it doesn't. It just sounds sneaky."

Dana listened for censure in Emory's tone and relaxed a little when she didn't hear it. Emory seemed to be searching for the ground rules, something that Dana ordinarily tried to keep as vague as possible. With Emory, she didn't want to make a mistake. She had a feeling there would be no second chances, and considering that she hadn't even had a first chance yet, she chose her words carefully. "Usually I have to get information from people who most often don't want to give it. The leader of a terrorist cell living in a cave in the mountains in Afghanistan wants his message to be heard, but he doesn't want me to know the truth. He wants me to broadcast his jihad, but he doesn't want me to know how many men he has, or who funds him, or what he intends to blow up next." For a second, she was back in a jeep in a barren wasteland in a world so brutal that morality was sacrificed on the altar of survival. She shivered, then smiled wryly. "I'm sorry. None of that has anything to do with you."

"You're wrong there." Emory shifted so her knees were touching Dana's leg. "If we're going to be friends, I need to understand what's important to you. And what isn't."

"Are we going to be friends?"

"I don't know." Emory shrugged, her expression almost sad. "My aversion to reporters isn't entirely due to…personal…experiences. I'm not exactly as popular a target as someone like Blair, but my work is controversial enough that I tend to draw a crowd."

"You're hassled by the press a fair amount."

"Yes. Relentlessly, sometimes. And unfortunately, not all the reporters take an open mind to what I'm doing."

"Tissue regeneration, right?" Dana had reviewed some but certainly not all of the voluminous articles on Emory Constantine and her controversial work on stem cell research. It was a hot-button topic with every right-to-life group, extremist religious group, and anti– genetic engineering organization.

"Considering that it's public knowledge, yes, that's the general term for what I do."

Dana leaned closer. Unfortunately, as soon as she did she caught Emory's unique scent, which totally derailed her train of thought. Now was the time to take advantage of the high emotions everyone was experiencing. Barriers were down, control shaky. People said things, did things, admitted things they wouldn't ordinarily if they weren't so distracted and upset. Like blood in the water, a crisis signaled the time for a reporter to strike, and strike hard. Instead, she felt herself holding back. "I'd like to talk to you about your work sometime. What you think people should know about it. What you want others to understand."

"I don't think so."

"Just consider it," Dana said. "You know the only way you'll get public support is by making them understand how research like yours will benefit them."

"You make it sound as if people are only interested in their own welfare."

"Usually," Dana said flatly, "that's the case."

"You're a cynic."

"I prefer to call it realism." As much as she hated to do it, especially considering what she and Emory had been discussing, Dana couldn't ignore her instincts completely. Blair Powell was alone for the first time all afternoon, and Dana had a job to do. She stood up. "Excuse me."

Emory followed her gaze. "Doesn't it bother you, taking advantage of other people's pain?"

"I'm sorry that's the way you see it," Dana said before she walked away. All the way across the room, she could feel Emory's eyes on her, and it hurt to know she had disappointed her. Still, she kept going until she reached Blair, who sat with her back to the room at the counter dividing the living area from the kitchen. "Excuse me, Ms. Powell, may I sit down?"

"Go ahead," Blair said, staring at an untouched cup of coffee on the counter in front of her.

"Can I warm that up for you?"

"No thanks," Blair said, finally angling her head to look at Dana.

Blair's eyes were darker than Dana remembered, and she thought that was probably from the pain she felt coming off her in waves. Dana was no stranger to other people's tragedies, and she was used to interviewing people in the midst of the agony of loss. Tonight, though, it affected her more than usual, because she already felt an affinity for the first daughter. Despite her sympathy, she still needed to know. "What's it like? Being here, waiting, not being able to do anything?"

"You know," Blair said contemplatively, "I don't think anyone has ever asked me that before." She glanced across the room at Diane and Valerie with a fond, sad smile. "Diane wants to protect me. The others do too, even when they hurt so badly themselves they're almost dying." She looked into Dana's eyes. "Do you have any idea how that makes me feel?"

"I imagine when you're not grateful for them caring, you hate it."

Blair laughed bitterly. "That's about right. And it doesn't make me very happy to admit it. Especially to you."

"I'm not writing this down." Dana displayed her empty hands. "No tape recorder. But, *for* the record, tell me why you support your lover doing what she does."

"That's easy," Blair said quietly. "The job she does is essential, and as my father says, only the best should do it."

Dana's heart surged, because the simple truth was always the most powerful. "Have you ever asked her to stop?"

"Yes." Blair's expression became distant, and Dana had a feeling she was recalling a conversation. Her smile flickered, and then settled into one of tender resignation. "I tried to make her choose between me and her duty, but she wouldn't."

"And you gave up trying to change her mind?"

"I love her. I think I mentioned that."

"Yes."

"I wouldn't change anything about her."

"But..."

"But I'll never stop asking her to be careful. I'll never stop telling her I want her to be safe. And I won't give her up, no matter what it might cost."

"May I quote you?" Dana asked gently.

"Ask me again when she's home safe."

❖

"Commander!"

"I hear it." Cam strained to home in on the distant but unmistakable rumble that seemed to be getting closer. With each passing second, the repetitive *thump thump thump* became louder. Rotors. "I think that's our ride."

"I sure as hell hope so, and not Tomlinson deciding to come back and check that van."

"I doubt it. If he was part of that scene up on the highway, he's long gone."

A shaft of light pierced the greasy smoke overhead and swept back and forth over the ground around them. Cam shielded her eyes and tried to make out the markings on the side of the helicopter. Nothing. It least it wasn't a TV news chopper or a local medical helicopter responding to some driver's 911. As she suspected, cars passing along the road above probably had no idea there had even been an accident. That was just as well, because she wanted to avoid publicity. Now all she could hope was that the helicopter had been sent by Lucinda Washburn and not by whoever had decided to eliminate a potentially dangerous witness who knew way too much.

"I think they're landing up on the road," Savard yelled above the noise.

"Keep your weapon trained up the hill until I tell you otherwise," Cam said, getting stiffly to her knees. Finally she pushed herself upright and started up the slope.

Within seconds, she was gone.

CHAPTER THIRTEEN

Around ten p.m., Dana finally saw her chance to talk to the enigmatic, decidedly aloof agent named Valerie. Blair, Diane, and Emory had closed ranks and were giving off *we don't want company* vibes in the sitting area. Stark remained at the door, although she had moved to a chair someone had dragged over for her. Wozinski had delivered food and drinks an hour or so before, and an untouched half sandwich sat on a paper plate on the floor next to Stark. Valerie stood looking out the window through a narrow opening in the blinds. She didn't acknowledge Dana's presence when Dana stepped up beside her.

"We haven't been introduced, but I imagine you know who I am," Dana said.

"Yes," Valerie said.

"Do you have an update on the incident that has detained the deputy director?"

"No comment."

"How long do you think it will be before this country reorganizes its security structure enough to effectively combat terrorism?"

"No comment."

"Creating the Office of Homeland Security looks a lot like a political maneuver to assuage public fears while justifying the surveillance of U.S. citizens on domestic territory."

Valerie continued to watch the street as if Dana weren't even there.

"How long have you been intimately involved with Blair Powell's best friend?" Dana tried another tack.

Valerie turned her icy gaze on Dana. "I can have you removed from this room and permanently denied access to Blair Powell in less than a second. How much do you want to complete your assignment?"

"All right," Dana said slowly, holding Valerie's gaze. "I've been saying this a lot tonight, but off the record, how long do you think it will be before we hear anything?"

"I don't know." Valerie turned her attention back to the street. "The White House has a press department that handles the kinds of questions you're asking."

Dana laughed. "And I believe in the tooth fairy too."

A smile flickered at the corner of Valerie's mouth. "I've only allowed you to stay this long because this morning the deputy director cleared you to have unrestricted access. If it were up to me, you wouldn't be here."

"So you're in charge when she's unavailable?"

"No comment."

"Can you give me your official title?"

Silence.

"How about a last name."

Silence.

"All right, no questions. *I'll* talk." Dana rubbed the back of her neck, calculating how many shots she might have in getting anything out of the Sphinx. "This is how I see things. There's two teams working out of a base somewhere in this building—one is the first daughter's Secret Service detail and the other is some kind of special OHS detachment. The deputy director heads the team of OHS people here— you're one of them, probably second in command. There's some kind of crossover between the two teams, because Stark is following your lead now, which is really unusual for someone in her position." Dana thought about that for a minute. The Secret Service was notorious for not sharing responsibility for their protectees. They usually liaised with the White House press staff during advance planning for public events, but the Secret Service made all the calls on security. And yet Stark readily deferred to Valerie. Why? "Stark knows you. She trusts you. If she didn't, she'd be fighting you every step of the way. How am I doing so far?"

"No comment."

"I'm going to print what I see if I don't have anything else."

Valerie ignored her, still looking unfazed.

Dana worked her hands into her pockets and rocked back and forth, figuring the angles. "There's only one reason for the OHS and Blair's security team to be so entwined. I'm betting some of the OHS detachment here used to be Secret Service." Her heart rate shot up as the pieces fell together in her mind. When that happened, it was always a rush, nearly as invigorating as the adrenaline high of danger or the orgasmic satisfaction of great sex. "Jesus Christ. Blair Powell is the focus of both teams because someone thinks the terrorists are after *her.*"

Valerie sighed as if in disappointment. "Writers have such active imaginations."

"Or maybe they've already tried. When? When was the attempt on her?" Dana couldn't believe the White House had kept this quiet. And now she understood why Cameron Roberts supported her being this close to Blair. Roberts was trying to limit Blair's visibility because she was a goddamned *target.* Oh yeah, there was a story here all right. A hot story. Dana started away, knowing she wasn't going to get anything out of this agent, if that's what she was.

Valerie stopped her with a viselike grip on her arm. "If I were to think you were going to write about any of your theories, I might have to sequester you and restrict all your communications."

Dana wasn't all that surprised by the threat, but she hadn't expected the complete absence of anger. Valerie No Last Name appeared to be completely unprovokeable. Even Cameron Roberts had shown some fire when Dana had pushed about Blair. This woman Valerie fascinated her. And she knew one thing for certain now. There was nowhere she wanted to be for the foreseeable future, except with Blair Powell. "I suppose it's been a long time since you've read the Bill of Rights. You know, the part about freedom of the press?"

"I'm not playing games," Valerie said easily. "Your press pass doesn't protect you when matters of national security are at stake."

"And who decides that?"

"I do."

"Who's going to decide exactly what will be *on* the record, other than the menu for the wedding?"

"I believe that will be up to the deputy director." For an instant, Valerie's cool façade shifted and Dana caught a glimpse of something dark and dangerous in her eyes before Valerie added, "When she returns."

❖

"Can I talk to you for a second?" Emory tugged Dana's sleeve and pulled her away from Valerie, who immediately turned back to the window.

"Sure." Dana followed Emory to the breakfast bar, surprised that Emory had sought her out since she was pretty certain that her talking to Blair had confirmed for Emory just how self-serving and callous she was. She slid onto one of the stools. Someone had turned the lights down so that the area was dim, giving the false impression of privacy. "Something wrong?"

"I thought I should rescue you before you got yourself into trouble."

"Worried about me?" Dana said lightly. Ordinarily, she would be irritated by anyone trying to interfere with her work, but the little frown lines between Emory's dark brows indicated real concern. After witnessing the passionate interconnections between Blair Powell, her friends, and those who guarded her, Dana realized just how much she wanted someone to care about her. To wonder about where she was and to worry if she didn't come home. Maybe that was a pipe dream, but the breathless pleasure she got from the troubled look in Emory's eyes was not a dream. The feeling was real and sweet and she wanted more of it. "It's been a long time since I've had a champion."

Emory's lips parted in pleasant surprise, and as she leaned closer she rested her hand on Dana's thigh. "I can see what you're doing, and you don't know what you're doing."

Dana grinned. "For a scientist, you're remarkably subtle. And at the moment, imprecise too."

"Don't joke. You don't know what's going on here, and if you push these people…" Emory shook her head. "Just do the job you came to do. Write about what a warm, wonderful woman Blair Powell is and how much she cares about her country and how much she loves her father. Write about what it costs her to be open and honest about her life with the whole world watching, and a good part of it criticizing. Write about the beautiful love between Blair Powell and Cameron Roberts."

"I can't just write about the things that are pretty," Dana said. "Or easy. Or what people want to hear."

"Blair's life is not easy." Emory snorted. "Believe me, there are a lot of people who don't want to hear about Blair and Cam."

"I know that. And I will write about her marriage. But what about what else is going on? What about the danger? Who's after her, Emory?"

"Don't. Please don't go there."

Emory's voice was low and almost tortured and Dana had this sudden need to erase her pain. She covered Emory's hand where it lay on her leg. "You know, don't you? You know what's really going on here." Dana began mentally sorting what she knew about Emory and the things she had read about the first daughter. Blair and Diane Bleeker had been friends since they were teenagers. There had never been any mention of an acquaintance with Emory until some brief news clip about the two of them at a fund-raiser early the previous month. But from what Dana could see now, something had bonded Emory, Blair, and Diane in a powerful way. What's more, Emory knew a lot of the inside players in the room. Valerie had recognized Emory the instant she'd stepped off the elevator. "Something happened last month, and you were there, weren't you? When was it? In Boston? Was there an attempt on Blair's life?" Dana had another thought and her stomach clenched. "On yours?"

"I've always been a private person," Emory said as if she were talking to herself. "But I've never had so many secrets in my life." She pulled her hand from beneath Dana's and got up. "I wish you weren't so good at what you do."

"Emory," Dana said urgently as Emory turned away, but Emory did not look back. Her abrupt departure left Dana feeling hollow and unspeakably lonely. For the first time ever in her life, she wished the story didn't always come first.

❖

"Hey," Blair said, squatting down next to Paula's chair. "You ought to try eating some of that sandwich. You've been on duty all day and it might be a long night."

"That's okay. I'm not hungry."

Paula had never learned Cam's infuriating ability to hide her pain, but Blair didn't think Paula was any less good at her job because of it. Paula would do whatever she needed to do, even while she bled to death inside. She was bleeding now, and Blair ached for her. She understood firsthand just how hard it was to silence all the little voices that kept screaming she was going to lose what mattered most to her. But fight to silence the nightmare demons she did, and she would keep on fighting no matter what. "As soon as this is over, I want to get out of here. Tomorrow, let's go to Colorado."

"Tomorrow?"

"Or Sunday. That's only moving things up a couple of days. We were going on Monday, anyhow."

"I'll have to clear it with the commander."

Blair's heart warmed to Paula's automatic certainty that Cam would be back. "Why? You're my security chief. Everything is set out there, right? Mac and Ellen have done all the advance work."

"They probably have a few more simulations to run with local law enforcement and the medical evac teams, but we've been at full readiness since midweek."

"There, see?" Blair grasped Paula's arm. "We've been planning this for over a month. Now more than ever, Cam, and Renée too, will need to rest. I don't care what they say. I don't care who needs to be chased, who has to be caught, who must be punished. For a few days, they need to recover." She leaned closer. "Or, Paula, next time someone's going to get hurt."

"Next time?" Paula whispered. Her gaze swept the room as she checked to make sure that no one could hear them. "Renée barely finished rehab before going on this mission. It was supposed to be an easy trip. If there's been trouble..." Her voice broke and she clenched her fist, the muscles in her arm tightening under Blair's hand.

"Renée will be all right. Cam would never have taken her if she didn't think Renée could do whatever needed to be done, under any circumstances." She gave Paula's arm a shake. "Besides, Renée might be stubborn but she's a professional. She wouldn't have put herself back on active duty if she didn't think she was ready."

Paula smiled. "Renée's idea of being fit for duty is a little bit different than mine."

"Oh, bull," Blair exclaimed. Individually, they each felt they were indestructible, but they lived with the fear that the ones they loved were not. "As I recall, you were the one who didn't want to give up a shift even when you had a bullet hole in your shoulder."

Stark frowned. "That's different."

"Right. It's always different when it's you." Blair was glad to see some of the pain lift from Paula's eyes. "So what do you say? Colorado? We'll hit the slopes and leave all this behind?"

"As soon as I get clearance, and you know where that has to come from. Until the commander gets a handle on..." Paula paused and glanced across the room at Dana Barnett, who was studying them intently. "Your security is a joint operation for the time being, but I'll push for us to go. You're right, they'll need it." She took a deep breath and let it out slowly. "We'll all need it."

Cam and Savard waited until the injured men were removed from the helicopter and transferred to an ambulance, then they climbed out, keeping their heads down as the rotors whipped overhead. They'd landed in a small lot behind a mostly darkened building at Langley Air Force Base. Outside the wavering circle of light cast by the chopper's beams, Cam saw two figures but she couldn't make out their faces.

"By my side," Cam said to Savard. They approached their reception committee with shoulders touching. Cam kept a grip on her holstered pistol as did Savard until she recognized Lucinda Washburn and Averill Jensen, the president's security adviser. "Clear."

"Who were you expecting?" Lucinda asked.

"Right about now, I'm not real sure," Cam said.

"Do you two need medics?"

"Savard does," Cam said.

"No, I don't," Savard snapped. She glanced at Cam. "Ma'am."

Lucinda, dressed in low heels, a dark skirt and jacket, and a silk blouse, looked as if she'd just stepped out of her office rather than out of the helicopter she had probably taken to get from Washington to Langley after Cam signaled her. "You're sure? Because it's going to take most of the night to debrief you."

Cam looked at Savard. "Is there anything wrong with you that a gallon of coffee won't cure?"

"I'm fine, Commander."

"We're good to go," Cam said to Lucinda. "After I make a phone call. And we both need showers. We're covered with ash and smoke."

"The showers we can provide," the president's security adviser said, "but I don't think a call is advisable until we have a better handle on exactly what happened."

"I wasn't making a request." As Cam started toward the building with Savard by her side, she pulled out her cell phone.

❖

Matheson put his book aside and picked up his cell phone, surprised at the unexpected call. Only a very few people had this number, and he changed phones every few days. His surprise turned to concern when he didn't recognize the caller's number. He contemplated not answering for a few seconds, and then decided a brief response would be safe. If he sensed trouble he could hang up before anyone had a chance to trace his location.

"Hello?"

"Hello, my good friend. I believe we have some business to discuss, do we not?" a man said in heavily accented but perfect English.

"I'm always happy to assist a friend, although I don't remember any further bus—"

"Recent events have altered our thinking about the value of certain items. Perhaps we can choose a convenient time and place to confer."

Matheson checked his watch. Still a little more time. "Of course, of course. I'll have my second contact you with details."

"Thank you, my friend." There was a pause. "Do not delay."

The caller disconnected and Matheson considered his alliance with the men whom under other circumstances he would consider enemies. The enemies of his enemy had become his friends. God did work in mysterious ways.

CHAPTER FOURTEEN

Blair's and Paula's cell phones rang simultaneously in stereo, and Blair saw the same mixture of hope and uncertainty flash across Paula's face that rushed through her. She yanked her phone off her waist. "Cam?"

"Everything's okay," Cam said quickly. "I'm sorry I'm so late."

Late? She's worried about being late? Blair would have laughed— or cried—at the absurdity, but she knew Cam meant it with her whole heart. Turning her back to the room, Blair lowered her voice and cradled the phone in her palm as if it were Cam's face. She wanted to touch her so badly and refused to think about how long it might be before she could. Only one thing really mattered at this moment. "Are you hurt?"

"No," Cam said firmly. "No, we're both all right."

"How long can you talk?" Blair heard her own voice and was amazed at how calm she sounded. Inside, she shook with the release of hours of tension and fear. She wanted to say, *Come home, now. I need you.* She knew that wasn't possible. She *knew*, but that didn't ease the ache in her chest.

"I've just got a minute." Cam sounded apologetic. "Are you okay?"

"Better now." Blair took a breath, the first unhindered pain-free breath she'd taken in hours. "When will you be home?"

"I don't know yet. Are you sure you're all right?"

"Lonely."

"Me too," Cam said softly. "I'm sorry for worrying you."

"I know. Are you sure you're safe?"

"Yes. Are you with friends?"

"Everyone's here. Everything's under control." Blair knew better than to ask where Cam was, or about what had happened, or who she was with. All those questions would have to wait. She had what she needed most. Cam was unhurt and out of danger and coming home. "You sound hoarse."

Cam coughed, clearing her throat. "Maybe a little scratchy. No problem."

"You're not hurt?" The last time Cam had sounded this way someone had tried to kill her. The idea of someone physically assaulting her lover made her ill. The reality haunted her dreams and stalked her waking moments. "Darling?"

"No. There was…some smoke."

Blair sighed. Cam would try to keep the details from her, not because Cam didn't trust her, but because she didn't want to worry her. And Blair would force it out of her, not just because she needed to know what monsters lurked, waiting to destroy her world, but because Cam needed to talk so the monsters wouldn't slowly destroy *her*. "Later about that, then, Roberts."

Cam laughed. "Okay, baby."

"Can you tell everyone to get out of our apartment now?"

"Soon. Not tonight, though. Not until I have a better handle on the incident."

The incident. The event. The operation. The mission. Code words for danger. Euphemisms for death. "I'm not going anywhere until you get home, but I've about had it. Which means you need to get your ass back here."

"I will. Just as soon as I can. I promise."

"And no side trips." Cam would know she meant that whatever retaliation might be necessary, she didn't want Cam to be part of it. There were agents trained to do what needed to be done—Cam did not have to be the first on the scene any longer. When the silence stretched longer than a few seconds, Blair said, "Do you hear me?"

"I'll do my best, baby."

And Blair knew that was all she could ask. "Come home soon. I miss you."

❖

A silent female lieutenant waited inside the locker room while Cam and Savard showered. She provided them with black military-issue BDUs and T-shirts and then escorted them to a small, drab conference room with a table that seated twelve, an outdated pull-down projection screen at one end of the room, and a coffee cart with a huge urn that Cam hoped was filled with hot coffee at the other end. Lucinda sat at one end of the conference table with Averill Jensen.

"You two are looking a little better," Lucinda said.

"We're good to go," Cam said.

The lieutenant stepped out into the hall and closed the door, leaving the four of them alone. Cam tested the urn with her hand, grunted in pleasure when she felt the heat, and searched the metal cabinet beneath the cart for cups. She filled a Styrofoam cup with coffee and handed it to Savard, then got her own. Savard followed her when she sat down at the conference table.

"What happened?" Lucinda asked.

Cam gave a recap of the events. "I don't suppose you two have anything to add?"

Jensen look surprised. "Like what?"

"Like whether or not this was a sanctioned neutralization?"

Lucinda glanced at Jensen, eyes narrowed. "Averill?"

"No," he said, sounding defensive. "Why would you ask? Isn't it obvious that Matheson or one of the other patriot organizers was trying to eliminate Early before he could identify them or disclose other vital information about their operations?"

"It's never wise to accept the obvious," Cam said quietly, watching Jensen carefully. Lucinda Washburn and Andrew Powell she trusted unequivocally, but they were the only two she could say that about other than Blair and the members of her team. Jensen she didn't know that well. "How many people knew we were planning to interrogate Early today?"

Now Jensen turned in his seat and looked to Lucinda for help. Lucinda shook her head and said, "Nothing happens in a vacuum, and there is no such thing as airtight security. You know that better than anyone. The minute you get in a cab, someone knows about it. Flights had to be arranged, the local office in Virginia was contacted for an escort, the prison commander was advised that you were coming. No one knew you were going to see Early, at least not that I'm aware of."

"How many other detainees from Matheson's compound are being held there?" Cam asked.

Lucinda grimaced. "I don't know, and for some reason, I can't find out. No one seems to know. Everyone who *should* know claims not to."

"Bureaucratic snafu or intentional lockdown on information?"

"I wish I knew that too," Lucinda said, obviously frustrated. She leaned forward, her eyes gleaming. "Listen, Cameron. I don't know who blew that van off the highway. Right now, we don't even know how they did it. Have any thoughts on that?"

"It might have been a car bomb triggered by a radio signal," Cam said, "but judging by what happened out in the Atlantic last month, it could just as easily be a surface-to-surface missile again. You've got a team looking at the wreckage out there now, don't you?"

"Yes."

"Unfortunately," Savard put in, "I don't think discovering the how is going to tell us anything about the who. Almost anyone can get military ordnance these days—foreign terrorists, domestic militants, your average Joe Survivalist down the street."

"Agreed," Cam said. "What we need to concentrate on is who wanted Early dead."

"I would think Matheson would be at the head of that list," Lucinda said grimly.

"Possibly," Cam said, far from certain. Matheson had eyes and ears in high places, that was clear. She didn't believe for a second that Valerie's handler was the only person in the Company with ties to Matheson. Operations like Matheson's didn't go undetected without more than a few people helping to keep it quiet. Every security branch had its share of hawks and superpatriots who believed that the end justified any means, if the end was preserving national supremacy. Such people were not above aiding militants, funding false flag operations designed to incite public support for armed retaliation, even orchestrating the assassination of political figures. "If Early had close ties to Matheson and was privy to things certain people didn't want him talking about, it might not have been Matheson who wanted him out of the way."

Lucinda's face hardened. "You're talking about someone on the inside, one of us."

"On the inside, maybe," Cam said grimly. "But not one of us."

"But those were federal agents driving that prison van," Savard protested. "No one inside would…"

"Collateral damage." Cam leaned back, suddenly more tired than she'd realized.

"The SUV ahead of us pulled over right before the prison van was hit," Savard said, her disbelief turning to fury. "If we hadn't been there, there would have been a clear shot at the van and both the lead car and the follow car would have been out of the blast zone. But then we pulled in behind the van and drove right into the field of fire!"

"That's my read too," Cam said, rubbing at the tension between her eyes.

Averill Jensen squared the empty pad of paper in front of him. He had uncapped his pen earlier as if he were going to take notes, but had written nothing down. "We'll do everything we can from our end to trace the leak, if there was one. There won't be a paper trail, but calls were made."

Cam shrugged. "It has to be done, but it could take weeks. I think we simply have to assume that none of our communications are secure." She looked pointedly at Lucinda. "Not even in and out of your office."

"Where does this put us in terms of tracking down Matheson?" Lucinda asked.

"About where we were before," Cam said. "My people are combing personal histories, electronic data, reports from FBI and ATF agents inside the patriot organizations, looking for connections." The dull throb between her eyes accelerated to a full-blown headache. "We're monitoring known cells, tracking targets on watch lists."

"He's running circles around us," Averill said bitterly.

Cam eyed him coldly. "Almost twenty men, none of them nationals, entered this country over a period of several years, established identities, trained on flight simulators, and managed to pull off an orchestrated terrorist attack without the combined power of all the security agencies in this country being able to detect them. Finding one U.S. citizen who has spent his entire life preparing to go into hiding is going to take plain old grunt work and a hell of a lot of luck."

"You don't think we'll get him," Lucinda said wearily.

"Oh, we'll get him," Cam said, "because we won't quit until we do." What she didn't say, what she refused to think about, was what he might do first.

❖

Blair felt all the eyes in the room on her as she walked over to Paula. "Let's compare notes."

Stark smiled, but she looked worried. "Everything's fine, nobody's hurt, and it was just a little unexpected detour. Does that fit with your version?"

"Pretty much. Did Renée sound okay?"

"She sounded pumped." Stark laughed briefly. "There's a reason she went into the FBI and I went into the Secret Service. She wants to chase bad guys, clean up the streets, strike a blow for justice. Me, I want to see that those responsible for justice stay safe. I don't need the rush like she does."

Blair squeezed Paula's shoulder. "She's no cowboy. Neither is Cam. But I know what you mean. I got the same story you did, pretty much. Cam did tell me that Renée was okay."

"Renée told me the commander was okay too."

"Then I guess we can assume they're both walking and talking." Blair closed her eyes for a second. "You should take a break now. You've been on duty all day."

Paula glanced across the room at Valerie, who stood apart from Blair's friends talking on her cell phone. "I'm too keyed up to sleep right now."

Blair knew she should sleep, but the bed would be too cold and empty and her mind too filled with unwelcome images of what life might have been like had things turned out differently. She announced to the room at large, "I'm going to work. Diane, Emory, you're welcome to stay here tonight. The guest room is empty and—"

"Actually," Valerie interrupted, "for the time being, *everyone* is staying here. The deputy director feels that the situation is still too unstable to decentralize our personnel, and she doesn't want anyone left unguarded. So I suggest you all get comfortable for the night."

Blair joined her friends while Valerie walked over to converse with Stark. "There's food in the refrigerator and wine in the cooler under the counter. Diane, you know where all my clothes are. You and Emory can grab whatever you need."

"I've got an empty guest room in my quarters," Dana offered.

"Now that's a lovely invitation," Diane said playfully, "but I'm going to have to turn it down." She raised an eyebrow in Emory's direction. "Why don't you take her up on it?"

"I think it's a good idea," Blair said, when Emory didn't answer. "We're all here until at least tomorrow, so everyone might as well be comfortable."

Emory shrugged, avoiding Dana's gaze. "Sure, makes sense." She hugged Blair and whispered, "I'm so glad she's okay."

Blair returned the embrace. "So am I. Thanks for being here. And you are definitely not going back to Boston now."

"I surrender." Emory laughed. "One of the many advantages of living with my mother is when I'm traveling and forget something, she can send it to me. I'll have her ship what I need out to the resort. That way, when everyone's ready to leave, I can go with you."

"Excellent," Blair and Diane said simultaneously. Dana, Blair noticed, had a particularly pleased glint in her eye.

❖

"The bedroom is down that way," Dana said, pointing as she closed the door to the apartment. "Bathroom also. I didn't have time to stock the kitchen, but there's coffee, soda, and some snacks in the cabinet."

"I'm not hungry, thanks," Emory said, holding the bundle of clothes she'd borrowed from Blair in her arms.

Dana leaned back against the door, giving Emory as much space as she could. Emory looked tired and a little anxious. "Do I make you nervous?"

"No," Emory said in surprise. "Why would you?"

"Well, there's the reporter thing."

"That's doesn't make me nervous. It just annoys me."

"What about me being a lesbian?"

Emory stared, then burst out laughing. For a second, she was afraid she wouldn't be able to stop. The entire day had had an atmosphere of unreality. She'd started out in a meeting with four uptight potential foundation donors who had the scientific knowledge of a colony of ants. It had taken her two hours just to explain what her research was all about and another two to convince them that it was worthy of their exalted contributions. Then she'd discovered that her friends had brought the enemy into their midst in the person of Dana Barnett, and try as she might, she couldn't really bring herself to dislike her. In fact, she felt an unexpected attraction to her—or at least to her dogged determination and her absolute, unshakable sense of purpose. Then she'd been whisked out of the hotel and thrown into the midst of Blair and Paula's nightmare, where she'd spent hours feeling alternately enraged and helpless. Now Dana was suggesting she might be worried about something as harmless as her making a pass? "In case you haven't noticed, some of my best friends are lesbians."

Dana grinned. "This is probably the only time I've ever heard that cliché when it is so not a cliché. But your best friends are, like, girlfriends." Her eyes grew smoky. "I'm not."

"Do you intend to seduce me?"

Dana's heart nearly stuttered to a stop, then raced so fast she was breathless. She hoped she still looked cool and collected, because her temperature had just shot up over the boiling point. "Do you want me to?"

Emory hesitated, suddenly wanting to be very very clear. Dana watched her as if her next words were the most important words Dana would ever hear. Did she *want* Dana to seduce her? Was she inviting her to? The idea of being with a woman wasn't foreign to her—how could it be, when Blair and Diane had become her friends so quickly and so deeply. She'd felt attraction to women now and then throughout her life, but the pull had never been overwhelming. She had written the fleeting feelings off as being perfectly natural and had always assumed she was heterosexual, until she married a man for whom she soon discovered she had no particular passion. What had surprised her most about her marriage was that she yearned for more. Their eventual divorce had been mutually agreeable and completely amicable, even though what underlay her discontent eluded her. "I'm sorry. I don't know."

"Why are you apologizing?" Dana tried to appear relaxed while every muscle in her body was vibrating. She wanted to cross the few feet between them and take Emory's face in her hands. She wanted to kiss her, very gently and very thoroughly. She wanted Emory to say yes.

"I feel like I've given you the wrong impression."

"You haven't." Dana smiled wryly. "You've been crystal clear about your opinion of me."

"We're not talking about you being a reporter," Emory said.

"Sure we are." With another woman, Dana might not have pressed the point, but Emory wasn't just any woman. "I'm a reporter, and you might forget it for a few hours, but it will be there in the morning. It will be there between us the next time I ask Blair Powell a question you think will hurt her. It will be there when you confide in me and then wonder if you can trust me."

"You're right. I must be more tired than I thought to have forgotten that." Emory ignored the pang of disappointment, and secretly thanked Dana for being honest and more realistic than she was apparently capable of being at the moment. "I'm going to go take a shower and then go to bed."

"Good night, then," Dana said.

"Good night." Emory started down the hall and then slowed to look back over her shoulder. Her smile was a little sad. "You don't have to stay out there, you know. I trust you not to seduce me."

Dana pushed away from the door and followed her, wondering why she had not taken advantage of what she had seen in Emory's eyes. For a moment, there had been both vulnerability and desire.

CHAPTER FIFTEEN

Before dawn, Saturday

Dana awoke to the soft sound of footsteps in the hall outside her bedroom. She wondered if Emory had had as much difficulty falling asleep the night before as she had. Knowing that only a thin wall and her own reluctance separated them had kept her in a hot sweat for hours while her conscience warred with her body. Rationally, she knew that one wrong step would destroy any chance she had of any kind of relationship, even friendship, with Emory. But her libido taunted her for being a coward and not taking advantage of the hesitation she'd seen in Emory's eyes. For a long time she had stared into the dark, her skin as hot as it had ever been under the desert sun, her nerves jangling with the anticipation of incoming mortar fire, while she debated knocking on the bedroom door next to hers. She'd never been as aware of a woman she hadn't even kissed.

Finally she had fallen asleep and dreamed of shells bursting in a moonless sky, raining fire down on an earth that shuddered under the onslaught of exploding mortar rounds until the sound of Emory's movement outside her closed door had pulled her from the midst of battle. Dana swung her legs over the side of the bed and scrubbed her hands over her face. She'd gone to sleep as usual in a T-shirt and boxers, both of which were damp now. She cocked an ear but heard nothing, the apartment as quiet as if she were alone. Maybe she was. Maybe Emory had gone upstairs to see her friends. Maybe she'd decided not to stay after all and was on her way uptown to her hotel.

Dana bounded from bed and was ridiculously relieved when she opened her door to see light coming from the other end of the apartment. She walked down the hall and discovered Emory sitting at the kitchen table staring at Dana's computer.

"You're up early," Dana said.

Emory regarded Dana as she stood at the end of the hallway. Her dark hair was disheveled and her face pale beneath her tan. Her nondescript gray T-shirt clung to her torso, damp in places with sweat. Her arms and legs, her whole body, was lean and tight. She wasn't beautiful, not in an ordinary way, but she was nevertheless breathtaking.

"I woke you. I'm sorry," Emory said.

"No." Dana's voice was brittle with fatigue. "I got thirsty." She made her way to the refrigerator and pulled out a can of soda. She held it up. "Want one?"

"No, thanks."

Dana leaned against the counter and sipped the soda. Barefoot, Emory wore a white ribbed tank top and loose navy sweatpants. She wasn't wearing a bra, and it was obvious. Although petite, her breasts were full with a hint of dark nipples beneath the white cotton. In the desert, Dana had gotten used to seeing women and men in various states of undress, and although she might notice a woman's attractive body, it hadn't made her throb the way looking at Emory did. She had to concentrate not to reach down and pull her boxers away from her suddenly very sensitive flesh. Aware that Emory was watching her, she asked, "Are you okay?"

Emory drew one foot up onto the chair and wrapped her arms around her knee. "Restless. I didn't think I was going to fall asleep, I was so keyed up, and when I did…" She shrugged.

"Bad dreams?"

"Anxious ones." Emory contemplated what terrors had visited Dana in the night, because she gave every sign of having awakened from a nightmare. "How about you?"

Dana was so used to avoiding any kind of personal conversation, she almost gave one of her noncommittal answers. Then she thought about the fact that she was alone with a woman at four thirty in the morning, and she didn't want to pretend it didn't matter. "I'm still getting the last skirmish out of my system. It'll be another few weeks before I adjust to sleeping in a bed and not listening for incoming fire."

Emory frowned. "Are all your assignment so dangerous?"

"No, usually they're really cushy ones like this." Dana smiled and Emory laughed.

"Oh yes, tonight was nothing but fun and games." Emory glanced toward the digital clock on the stove. "I wonder if Cam is back yet."

Dana noticed the familiarity with which Emory referred to the deputy director. Whatever had happened to bond that group together, it had been significant. "When did you meet all of them?"

"Last month in…" Emory shook her head. "I don't even know how to have a conversation with you because I'm afraid anything I say will end up in print."

Dana pulled out a chair and sat down facing Emory. She nodded toward her computer. "Were you looking for something? My notes on Blair Powell, maybe?"

"What? No! I saw it and wanted to check my e-mail for messages from the lab, but then I realized I couldn't just use your computer." Emory couldn't believe Dana was insinuating she might be going through her personal documents. "Why would you even think I was reading your notes?"

"I don't."

Emory narrowed her eyes, astonished that Dana could anger her so easily. She was used to dealing with confrontational, argumentative, even obnoxiously rude people without losing her temper. Dana made a mildly insulting insinuation and she completely lost her composure. "Then why did you ask? You don't know me well enough to make that kind of accusation."

Dana rested her elbows on her knees and supported her chin on her interlaced fingers, grinning slightly. She tilted her head from side to side. "Well, you don't know me, either, but you suspect the worst."

"With good reason," Emory snapped. "I watched you questioning everyone you could tonight, including me. That's what you do. It's all a means to an end for you, isn't it?"

"I was working part of the time tonight, you're right," Dana said, struggling not to let her temper take over. "Does it make any difference to you that the White House specifically requested that I do this job? And the deputy director—Blair Powell's lover—*insisted* that I do it? Do you think I like following the first daughter around, imposing on her privacy?" Angry at the situation and angrier still that Emory blamed her for it, Dana shot to her feet. "I'd rather be back in Afghanistan being bombed."

Emory jumped up as Dana stalked away and grabbed her wrist. "Don't say that."

Dana spun around. "Why?"

They were so close, Emory could see the tiny flecks of silver in Dana's eyes. Heat poured off Dana in waves, and Emory didn't know if it was from anger or the simple force of her personality. Whatever the cause, it ignited her inside and she felt her nipples tighten in response. Completely unbidden, she brushed Dana's cheek with her fingertips. "I don't know. It scares me to think of you in danger."

Dana sucked in a breath and closed her eyes. "You shouldn't do that."

"What?" Emory asked, her voice so low and husky she didn't recognize it. She didn't recognize her body either. Her limbs felt liquid, and her breasts ached. She looked down and realized she still held Dana's arm. She wanted to guide Dana's hand to her breast, knowing somehow those strong, tanned fingers would turn the ache to pleasure.

"Don't touch me like that." Dana opened her eyes to find Emory staring at her, her lips parted in faint surprise, the expression in her eyes absolutely unmistakable. "Unless you want me to touch you back."

"I don't know what I want," Emory said. "I don't know why I feel this way."

"What way?" Dana whispered.

"Like I want your hands on me. Like I've always wanted that."

Dana groaned and took a step back. "The last twelve hours have been crazy. You'll feel different when the sun comes up."

Emory laughed a little unsteadily. "I said I wasn't worried about you seducing me. I didn't think I'd be the one doing the seducing."

"You haven't seduced me yet." Dana gently disengaged her arm from Emory's grasp. Emory's fingers were soft, so soft, and she knew she'd be dreaming about those fingers gliding over her body for a very long time. "But I'm weakening really fast."

"I'm sorry." Emory flushed with embarrassment. "I don't want you to think I'm one of those women who wants to bed her lesbian friends just to see what she's missing."

"Don't apologize. I'm not that easy to offend." Dana grinned.

"Besides, I've had some pretty good times with married women who wanted a little no-strings fun for an afternoon."

"I'm not one of those women," Emory said sharply. She instantly pictured Dana with some sexy, curvaceous model type tumbling around on a motel room bed in the middle of the afternoon and felt a surge of jealousy that was completely foreign to her. When she and her husband had stopped having sex, she thought he might have gone outside the relationship to satisfy his needs, and the possibility never bothered her. She wasn't even involved with Dana, and she hated the thought of her pleasing another woman. Or being pleased by one. "God, I think I'm losing my mind."

"Hey, Dr. Constantine," Dana said, leaning forward to tuck an errant strand of midnight hair behind Emory's ear, "I think you should remember that stress does funny things to our systems. Give yourself a break."

Emory couldn't help herself. She caught Dana's hand and held it against her cheek for just a second. She was right, Dana's hand felt strong, and even though her fingers were chafed from the sun and the sand, they were also gentle. She imagined them rubbing over her nipples and shuddered, releasing Dana's hand. "I don't think it's wise for you to touch me, either. My nervous system seems to be short-circuiting."

Dana wished she had pockets to jam her hands into, because she wanted them back on Emory's body. She wanted to see that flash of surprise and need in Emory's eyes again. Christ, she wanted to take her to bed. "Okay. The no-touch rule is now in effect for both of us. Deal?"

"Deal." Emory experienced that confusing mix of disappointment and relief again and pointed to Dana's computer. She needed to do something normal, to ground herself somehow, because she didn't recognize who she was right now. "Do you mind if I check my mail? I need to let my chief tech know I won't be back until the end of next week."

"No, go ahead." Dana was acutely aware that she was not only standing in the kitchen in her underwear, she was totally turned on, completely hard, and thoroughly soaked. "I'm going to grab a shower."

"Are you sure you don't want to stay while I use your computer?"

"Jesus, Emory." Dana wanted to tear her hair out or grab the woman and…do what? Have her on the kitchen table? Drag her into the bedroom for a quick romp? Yes! No, no, she didn't. What she wanted was for Emory to look at her again with hunger in her eyes and know that it was for her, and her alone. No uncertainty, no confusion, no doubt. And that was not going to happen. "Maybe we should try trusting each other too. I'll go first. You can use the computer whenever you want to."

"Dana," Emory called just before Dana disappeared down the hall.

Dana turned. "What?"

"I know you have a job to do, and I don't understand all the reasons that it's important, but I believe you that it is. I'll try to remember that."

"Thanks."

Then Dana disappeared and Emory sat motionless, listening until she heard a door close and the shower come on. Burying her face in her hands, she willed her out-of-control body to quiet. Her seething arousal wasn't helped by the image of herself sliding open the shower door, slipping under the hot spray, and pressing her breasts against Dana's slick back. She moaned and forced her hands to move to the keyboard, when what she really wanted was to roam them over Dana's body or at the very least, to quench the burning in her own.

Instead, she typed in the password to her Webmail and focused on the messages. Whatever strange and incomprehensible addiction she had developed for Dana Barnett, it would pass if ignored. All she had to do was concentrate on what really mattered. Her work.

CHAPTER SIXTEEN

B lair put her paintbrush aside when she heard Ramsey murmur into his radio. Despite her objections, Valerie had insisted that an agent remain inside her loft for the remainder of the night. Once she had started painting, she could almost ignore his presence, but as the hours ticked away, part of her mind waited for some sign of Cam's return.

Now she tried to read his expression from across the room. The blinds were closed but she knew it had to be after dawn. She wasn't tired. While she'd worked, she hadn't been aware of her body at all. Usually she would paint until her forearm cramped, but tonight she hadn't even been aware of that. She opened and closed her hand. Her fingers were stiff.

She started forward as Ramsey moved toward the door. "Is it Cam?"

"If you'll wait right there, Ms. Powell," he said as he dropped his right hand to the holster on his hip and opened the door with his left, completely blocking her view of the hallway outside.

She kept her eyes fixed on the door as Ramsey sidestepped, opening it wider. Cam walked in, scanned the room until she found Blair, and smiled.

"Hi, baby," Cam said.

"Hello, darling." Blair hadn't realized how cold she'd been, or how deeply the hollow ache had penetrated, until the sound of Cam's voice warmed her and the sight of her face filled her empty places. Even as her world slipped back into place, she searched for any signs of trouble. Cam looked exhausted, which she had expected, and was wearing military-issue clothes instead of her own, which wasn't good. Something had contaminated Cam's suit, possibly the smoke she hadn't wanted to go into detail about. But it might have been blood, and Blair raked her gaze over Cam looking for any sign of injury. There was a scrape on her cheek but it didn't look deep. She'd washed her hair— there might be an injury there. A quick visual survey wasn't going to be enough. She wouldn't be satisfied until she checked every inch of her. But first, she had to touch her.

"Thank you, Agent," Cam said to Ramsey without taking her eyes off Blair. "You can finish your shift outside in the hall now that I'm home."

"Yes ma'am," Ramsey said, and disappeared, closing the door behind him.

Blair slid her arms around Cam's neck, pressed close, and kissed her. "Interesting outfit. I always knew you wanted to be a soldier."

Cam rested her cheek against Blair's head and chuckled. "And here I thought you'd find it sexy."

"What I find sexy is you naked in bed. Although the BDU's *are* a nice touch." Blair ran her fingers through Cam's hair and stroked the back of her neck. "How are you?"

"Glad to be home." Cam searched Blair's eyes, looking for traces of pain, and skimmed her thumb over Blair's chin. "You haven't been to bed."

"I've been working. Lost track of time."

"Uh-huh."

"You're one to talk," Blair griped, backing up and capturing Cam's hand. She tugged her arm, then stopped abruptly when Cam winced. "What?"

"Too much time on airplanes in the last—"

"Don't even try." Eyes flashing, Blair pulled Cam's shirt out of her BDUs and lifted it with both hands as high as her breasts. Then she saw the swath of bluish-purple running from Cam's left shoulder to her right hip. "God *damn* it."

"Seat belt. It's nothing."

Blair held up her hand to stop the words that she didn't want to hear. "What else?"

"Nothing more. We had an accident on the road." Cam sucked in a breath when Blair growled. "Okay. Someone took out a prison van with the man I wanted to interrogate inside. We drove right into the blast and it flipped our SUV. I got banged up. Bumps and bruises." Cam cradled Blair's face and forced Blair to meet her eyes. "Nothing more, I swear."

"You can swear all you want. Get your ass into the bedroom." Blair pulled away and went to retrieve the phone.

Cam frowned as Blair punched in numbers. "What—"

"Emory?" Blair said, ignoring Cam. "I'm sorry to get you up so early. What? Oh, good. Could you please come up here and take a look at Cam...Thanks."

❖

Blair wasn't surprised to see Dana with Emory when she opened the door. As she let them in, she said, "Hi, Emory, Cam's in the bedroom. Down the hall past the kitchen. I'll be right there."

"Morning," Dana said, waiting just inside the door to gauge her reception. She half expected Blair to tell her to leave, but she had come here to get the real story behind the woman, and this was the story. She'd been on her way back to the bedroom after her shower when she ran into Emory on her way out. Emory hadn't been happy about her tagging along, but she could hardly say no.

"Everyone's up early, I see," Blair said, taking in Dana's wet hair.

"Long days make for short nights, sometimes. How's the deputy director?"

Blair gave her a long look. "She's tired. Long day."

"I've wondered sometimes," Dana said, hooking her thumb over the edge of her jeans pocket, "who protects the protectors. Last night, watching you wait for hours for some word, I could only guess how frustrating, how agonizing, it had to be. But you were just waiting your turn to act, weren't you. Now it's your turn to stand guard."

"She's my lover. I'm not doing anything special."

"I don't mean to disagree, Ms. Powell," Dana said, "but you taking care of her goes beyond the private and personal. She's a deputy director in the OHS. What she does is important to a great many people on a great many levels. Like you, she's important because of who she is and what she does."

"I know that." Blair glanced in the direction that Emory had gone. "I don't want Cam's position profiled in this article. I don't want her made into a target."

"I think everyone in the country, probably in a good part of the world, knows who she is. You don't seriously think your relationship is a secret?"

"Of course not. We've made public statements, but that doesn't mean I want to call attention to what she does. Just keep the news focused on the issue of gay marriage."

"While it's true what you're doing is important in terms of raising social consciousness," Dana said, "the public is much more interested in people, rather than issues—especially people who appear to lead charmed lives."

"Charmed." Blair laughed shortly. "That's not a word I would've chosen."

"What would you have chosen?" Dana asked.

"Indentured." When Dana's eyebrows rose, Blair added hastily, "And no, you can't quote that."

"You don't give me a lot to print."

"Print this. Cameron Roberts is a devoted public servant and a loving partner, and she has never neglected one for the other, sometimes at great cost to herself." Blair sighed and shook her head. "And now, I need to go and check on her."

"Thank you," Dana called after her, wondering how it would feel to have a woman love her that intensely. She'd never quite imagined it, never thought she wanted it. Now, she wasn't so sure.

"Hey," Blair said as she slipped into the bedroom. Shirtless, Cam sat on the side of the bed in just her sweatpants. Emory stood by her side.

"Hi." Cam stood, reaching for a T-shirt draped over a nearby chair. Her movements, Blair noticed, were slow and careful.

"How is she?" Blair asked Emory.

"I'm working at a disadvantage here. Without even a stethoscope," Emory said with a shake of her head, "I can't exactly say anything definitive. But I haven't seen or heard anything that makes me too worried."

Cam slipped her arm around Blair's waist and kissed her temple. "Like I said. Bumps and bruises."

"Shut up. I wasn't asking you." Blair kept her attention on Emory. "You don't think she needs x-rays or anything?"

"I'm not exactly a country doctor who can divine illnesses from the laying on of hands, you know. I'm a researcher, and I haven't treated patients in almost ten years." Emory glanced at Cam. "But unless you're underplaying your symptoms, I think some rest and anti-inflammatories are all you need."

"I'm not minimizing anything," Cam said. "I'm not going to be moving at my normal pace for a couple of days, but I don't feel like there's anything serious going on."

"Can she fly?" Blair asked.

"Tomorrow," Emory said. "Not today. I just want to be sure that those sore ribs aren't going to lead to any kind of problem."

Blair rubbed Cam's back, afraid to hug her. "Today you sleep. Tomorrow we're going to Colorado. For vacation."

Cam said nothing for a few seconds, then nodded. "Okay. As long as—"

"Uh-uh," Blair said with a vigorous shake of her head. "No buts, no contingencies. We're going. We're getting married in a week, and I want everyone to relax and enjoy themselves for a few days first."

"All right," Cam said. "I'll talk to Stark and make sure the advance team is prepared."

"I already did that," Blair said.

"Did you?" Cam grinned. "Then I guess it's all decided."

Blair kissed her. "Guess so."

❖

"Why is it that no one around here can keep normal hours?"

Dana spun around at the sound of Diane's voice and, catching sight of Diane coming from the room opposite where Blair had disappeared, swallowed hard. Diane wore a pale blue silk robe closed with a sash looped carelessly at her waist. Her hair framed her face in careless disarray, the gold tips brushing her neck as she glided forward on bare feet. She was so very obviously naked beneath the thin silk, and so effortlessly seductive, that Dana responded out of pure instinct. She pictured her tongue following the trail of those silky strands as they wafted back and forth over the soft skin of Diane's neck. She felt the weight of Diane's breast in her hand and the plump firmness of her nipple under her thumb. As soon as the images registered in her conscious mind, she jerked her gaze away. And discovered Emory and Blair, who had returned while she was lost in the Siren's call, watching her. Emory immediately looked away, but not before Dana saw what looked like anger eclipse her features. Perfect. Caught literally drooling over another woman, and one who was clearly involved on top of it. Hell.

"Well," Diane said, breezing by on her way toward the kitchen. "Is someone going to enlighten me as to the cause of this outrageously early gathering?"

Blair leaned against the breakfast counter. "Cam is back. Emory was just taking a look at her."

"Oh, good," Diane said with a sigh, sliding onto one of the stools next to Blair. She grasped Blair's hand. "And how is she?"

"She's good," Blair said, her voice softening. "She's good."

"And what about Renée?"

"Cam said she sent her home to bed and gave Stark orders to see that she stays there."

"Somehow, I don't think *that* will be a problem." Diane smiled. "Maybe now things can get back to normal."

Blair snorted. "Is Valerie with you?"

"No. She's…wherever…doing whatever."

While Blair and Diane talked, Dana followed Emory into the sitting area. She pointed to the empty spot next to Emory on the sofa. "Do you mind?"

"No," Emory said quietly, "go ahead."

Emory was still wearing the sweatpants Blair had loaned her and had thrown the blouse she'd had on the day before over the tank top, leaving it unbuttoned. Dana couldn't help but notice the curve of her breasts and the slight swell of her nipples beneath the thin layers. Diane Bleeker was a beautiful woman and any lesbian would have to be dead not to notice. But looking at Diane had not stirred her blood the way the sight of Emory, dark circles under her eyes, in baggy sweatpants and a rumpled blouse, did. Dana not only wasn't dead, she had been struggling with simmering, unfocused arousal for hours. That restless need had crystallized when Emory had innocently caressed her face, and now she couldn't stop thinking about touching her. "Is everything okay?"

"More or less. Things are finally calming down around here."

"I'm sorry if I upset you earlier," Dana said.

Emory regarded her curiously. "Which time?"

Dana smiled ruefully. "I don't know. Every time?"

"You haven't done anything you need to apologize for. You certainly don't have to explain what you do or why you do it to me." She started to rise. "I'm going to try and get a little sleep."

"Do you want me to stay up here?"

Emory glanced across the room at Diane, and then quickly away. "That's entirely up to you."

Dana stood up quickly, blocking Emory's path to the door. "I'm not interested in Diane Bleeker."

"I think that's really good," Emory said, avoiding Dana's eyes. "Because I think Valerie would shoot you."

"I was just caught off guard there for a second when she...when I saw—"

"Don't. For God's sake, do you think I need to know why the sight of a beautiful woman arouses you?"

"It doesn't," Dana snapped. "Well, it does. Sometimes. Jesus." She lowered her voice. "It certainly did an hour ago. Downstairs with you."

"We had a deal, remember?" Emory sidled around her.

"That was a no-touch deal. Not a no-talk-about-it deal."

Emory looked into Dana's eyes. "I'm expanding the parameters of our agreement."

"Why?"

"Because. I don't know what I'm talking about half the time."

Dana smiled. "That's okay, I do."

"Just concentrate on writing your article without jeopardizing Blair or Cam, okay?"

"I'm not going to jeopardize them." Dana gripped her hand. "You said you were going to trust me. Did you forget about that too?"

Emory looked down at their joined hands and brushed her thumb over the top of Dana's fingers. "I remember."

A soon as Emory pulled her hand away, Dana wanted it back again. The tiny bit of contact made her almost dizzy. "Emory."

A knock on the door prevented Emory from answering as everyone turned in that direction. Blair crossed the room and asked who was there.

"It's Valerie."

A look that Dana interpreted as worry, followed by resignation, crossed Blair's face just before she opened the door.

Valerie stepped inside, her eyes going first to Diane, then settling on Blair. "I'm very sorry to disturb you. I need to speak with the deputy director."

"She's resting," Blair said. "Can't it wait?"

"I'm afraid not. I'm sorry."

"Valerie," Blair said so quietly Dana almost didn't hear her. "She needs a few hours—"

Cam appeared from around the corner of the partition separating the kitchen from the bedroom beyond. "I'm awake."

"Well, you shouldn't be," Blair said, rounding on her sharply.

"I'm still a little too wound up to sleep anyhow." She slipped her arm around Blair's shoulder and squeezed briefly. Then she turned to Valerie, her entire body instantly on alert. "Do you need me downstairs?"

Valerie scanned the room. "Here is fine, if we could talk alone for a few minutes."

"Let's go in the other room." Cam led Valerie down the hall and they disappeared.

Silence fell and no one moved. Blair looked like she wanted to follow Cam, but didn't. Dana definitely wasn't leaving unless someone ordered her to. Then Emory sat back down on the sofa.

"Well," Diane said with a sigh, "I guess I might as well get dressed."

Blair braced both arms on the granite countertop and lowered her head. After a pause, she looked up, her face composed. "I'll make coffee."

CHAPTER SEVENTEEN

"What have you got?" Cam didn't want to give in to the pain in her chest and right side. Compromising, she sat on the side of the bed because standing upright hurt enough to be distracting, and she needed to focus on what Valerie was about to tell her. Although Valerie's ivory blouse and black slacks were barely wrinkled, Cam doubted she'd been to bed at all in thirty-six hours. "Sit down. You look beat."

"Are you hurt badly?" Valerie asked, shaking her head when Cam indicated a nearby chair.

Cam relayed the details of the event. "Early and the van driver are dead. Renée and I are still walking around, but the two local agents with us both ended up in surgery."

"Matheson? Or friendly fire?"

Cam smiled bitterly. "What's your guess?"

Valerie folded her arms under her breasts and leaned back against the wall. "Considering the time frame—less than twelve hours from the time you made arrangements to interview him and your arrival there? I'd put my money on the Company."

"If you're right, that means our communications are completely transparent. Probably someone in DC is monitoring our reports and requests."

"Unless of course you've got a Company mole inside your team."

Cam regarded Valerie steadily. "We don't."

"You trust me?"

"I do. And so do the others." Cam suspected from the strain in Valerie's eyes that she'd been driving herself hard searching for some clue as to who might have been behind the most recent attack.

"What do you suggest we do about locking down our security?" Valerie asked.

"We don't go outside our team for anything. We fly private. We drive rental cars. We use our own people or Tanner's people if we need backup."

Valerie rubbed her arms as if she were cold. "I think…"

"What?"

"You might consider sending disinformation to Washington."

"You're suggesting that I mislead the White House chief of staff and the president's security adviser?"

"That's what I would do, but I'm not sure that my advice is good for your career." Valerie smiled thinly. "I'm not exactly trained to work inside the system."

Cam laughed. "My career path has been a bit uncertain since the moment I saw Blair Powell. And since September, it's the last thing I'm worried about. Right now, I agree with you—we don't know who we can trust, so the best course is to trust no one except each other." She rotated her shoulder and tried to rub some of the stiffness out of her left arm. "You came down here with news, I take it."

"The FBI has been watching a suspected cell in the Buffalo area for the last six months. Reports show an increase in activity since September," Valerie said.

"What kind of activity?"

"New faces turning up, more phone calls, and a rash of Internet communications in the last few weeks."

"How'd we get this?"

"You wanted us pulling intelligence from all sectors on suspected domestic activity, and when reports from this area went hot, Felicia started monitoring everything coming out of the local field office up there. When several cell members made calls to the same number, the FBI started monitoring *that* number on the theory it belonged to the ringleader. Last night whoever is using the target phone called someone in Virginia."

"Virginia. *After* the prison van was hit."

"That's right. Possibly unrelated."

Cam knew there had to be more. "Did we get a fix on who was called?"

Valerie shook her head, obviously frustrated. "No. Cell phones. We got as far as the local tower, but no trace after that."

"But we know where the tower's located?"

"Felicia's got that. It's not much of a lead, but we know Matheson has connections in that area."

"It's more than we've had. Let's see if we can narrow down the location." Cam stood. "Pull addresses and property records on Matheson's family, his academy graduates, any and all known associates, the detainees from the raid on his compound, and known patriot members. Look for anything within a hundred-mile radius of that tower."

When Cam started toward the hall, Valerie stopped her with a hand on her arm. "You should get some sleep."

"I'm good for a couple more hours."

"Maybe, but you look like hell." Valerie laughed quietly when Cam frowned. "And Blair's been up all night. Waiting to hear about your status was rough on her. Chances are we won't come up with anything, and if we do, it's going to take more than a couple of hours. Felicia knows what to do until you get there, but I'll go over your directives with her."

Cam closed her eyes and took a deep breath. "Blair wants to leave for Colorado tomorrow. If we're closing in on Matheson, I need to be here."

"All the more reason to spend some time with her now. Take a few hours."

Cam glanced at the bedside clock. "I'll be down by noon."

"I'll clear everyone out of here so you two can get some rest."

"You should take a break yourself," Cam said.

"As soon as I go over things with Felicia."

"That wasn't a suggestion, you know."

"I know."

"Thanks for handling everything here last night," Cam said, relenting and sitting back down on the bed. "And thank you for looking after Blair."

"You don't need to thank me." Valerie smiled wryly. "And Blair doesn't want anyone except you to look after her."

"All the same, thank you for keeping her safe."

"You can always count on us to do that." Valerie paused. "But you can't keep doing this to her, Cameron."

Valerie left and Cam slowly removed her clothes. She lay back and closed her eyes, but she couldn't obliterate the memory of Blair's torment and the knowledge that she had been the cause of it.

❖

Dana sat on the arm of the sofa in her temporary apartment watching Emory gather her things. "You could always stay here, you know, until we leave tomorrow. You wouldn't have to pay for another night at the hotel."

Emory folded the sweats and T-shirt that she'd borrowed from Blair and stacked them on a nearby chair. She wore another outfit of Blair's, jeans and a dark green sweater, for the trip back to her hotel. She'd had to roll the cuffs of the jeans several times to make up for the difference in their height. "That's probably not a great idea. Would you mind returning these to Blair later today?"

"Sure. Why is it not a good idea?"

"Are you intentionally being dense?"

Dana grinned. "I try not to make assumptions."

Emory cut her a look. "There's something very strange going on between us, and I think it's better if we get a little distance."

"It's called attraction," Dana said completely seriously, "and I don't think distance is the answer."

"What is the answer?"

"Ordinarily, I'd suggest a date," Dana said, "but I'm here on assignment and my schedule, as you might have noticed, is constantly changing. I can't very well take you out to dinner when Blair might decide she wants to hop a plane to Colorado."

Emory shrugged. "You're right. Bad timing." She collected her purse and grabbed her coat out of the closet by the door. "Besides, I don't date women."

"Yet."

"You are remarkably sure of yourself." Emory thought she should probably be annoyed, but she wasn't really. Part of her wanted to stay exactly where she was. Actually, part of her very much wanted Dana to kiss her. And that was why she knew she should leave.

"I'm not sure of anything where you're concerned," Dana said, moving closer. She took Emory's coat and held it for her. When Emory turned to slip her arms into it, Dana pressed against her back, rubbing her hands over Emory's shoulders and down her arms. She put her mouth close to Emory's ear. "But I know the last thing I want is distance between us." She skimmed Emory's hair back with the tips of her fingers, exposing her neck, and kissed her softly behind the ear. "If you stay here, we can get to know each other better."

Emory shivered and closed her eyes, glad that Dana couldn't see her face because she wouldn't be able to hide what that kiss had done to her. She leaned her back into the front of Dana's body and felt Dana's hands tighten on her arms. Dana's breath blew hot and fast against her skin. "You're breaking the no-touch rule."

"I know," Dana whispered, her voice husky. "I'm sorry. I stood it as long as I could. God, you smell good."

"It's Ivory soap." Emory laughed shakily.

"Don't ever wear anything else." Dana slid her arms around Emory's waist and slipped her hands inside Emory's coat, pulling Emory more tightly against her.

Dana's hands rested on the sweater covering Emory's abdomen, and Emory could easily imagine those bold and possessive hands on her skin. She couldn't remember ever wanting to be kissed more than she did at that moment, and she worried that she was allowing herself to be attracted to Dana's attraction to her. Dana was, after all, infuriatingly charming and relentlessly sexy. "I don't do one-night stands."

"Thank you for telling me that," Dana said quietly, turning Emory to face her. She put her hands back inside Emory's coat, resting them on her waist just above her hips. She ran her thumbs up and down Emory's abdomen. "But I don't want to go to bed with you."

"You don't?" Emory had a hard time focusing on anything except the fiercely intent expression in Dana's eyes and the pleasure that spiraled from beneath Dana's hands into her depths. She was horribly, terribly aroused and frighteningly close to letting something happen she would regret. And she couldn't seem to stop.

"No," Dana murmured. "This is what I want."

As Dana leaned closer, Emory knew she was about to be kissed, but the reality was nothing like she had expected. True, Dana's mouth was soft and hot and certain, but Dana was surprisingly patient. She took her time, teasing Emory with the tip of her tongue, waiting for Emory to kiss her back. Caught off guard by the gentle invitation, Emory responded, stroking over the surface of Dana's lips and tongue because it just felt so damn good. She clasped a hand behind Dana's neck and sank into her, moving against her in a way completely foreign to her and so completely right. She pulled away from the kiss and struggled to control her out-of-control body. "I don't...I can't..."

"Shh," Dana said as she caressed Emory's cheek. Her hand trembled. "We're not. It's okay." She kissed her again, slowly, and drew back. Her chest heaved and she fought to steady her breathing. "I was thinking we could start simple. You know, with a kiss or two."

Emory nodded dumbly, trying to envision kissing her—just kissing—without bursting into flames. Well, she'd never been afraid of a challenge. "Okay. Yes. That sounds reasonable."

Dana grinned. "Reasonable."

"You suggested it," Emory said hotly. "So don't look so damn supercilious."

"Hey," Dana said, raising both hands in surrender. There was no reason Emory had to know she wanted her so badly she ached all over. She needed to get a grip on her runaway libido just as much as Emory needed time to get comfortable with hers. Then they could have a nice, adult interaction with no one getting disappointed or hurt. "I agree. Reasonable is good."

"You agree?" Emory asked suspiciously.

"I do. Absolutely. How about I walk you back to your hotel. You can tell me all about tissue engineering on the way."

"All right, but that doesn't mean I'm coming back here later."

"I promise. No expectations." Dana just had to figure out how to convince her body of that.

❖

Blair pulled the shades and stripped by the side of the bed. Slipping under the sheets, she turned on her side to face Cam. She stroked Cam's hair and kissed her cheek. "Valerie ordered everyone out, and me to bed."

"And you listened?" Cam teased.

"I could hardly disagree." Blair snuggled closer, drawing one leg over Cam's thigh. "How are you feeling?"

"Better. The Motrin kicked in." Cam urged Blair down into the position they normally slept in, with Blair's cheek on Cam's shoulder, and kissed her forehead. "Both of us could stand to get some sleep."

Blair smoothed her hand over Cam's chest and down the center of her abdomen. "What did Valerie need to see you about?"

Cam hesitated, her natural instinct not to worry Blair surfacing even as she knew what she had to do. What Blair needed her to do. "We got a little bit of a break. We might have a lead as to Matheson's whereabouts."

"What will you do if you find him?"

Blair's tone was casual, but Cam felt her tense and the hand that had been playing over her abdomen grew still. "We'll go after him."

"We?"

"The last time I shared our intelligence, someone warned him and he slipped through our net." Cam couldn't keep the fury from her voice. "That's not going to happen again."

"But I thought that was because Valerie's handler was working with Matheson and tipped him off. There's no way that can happen again."

Cam sighed. "No, that particular leak has been taken care of. But I can't trust that he was the only one who wanted Matheson to succeed, and what happened yesterday afternoon makes me suspect Matheson has more friends on the inside than we realize."

Blair sat up so she could look directly into Cam's face. And so that Cam could see hers. "I understand, I really do. I know he has to be stopped. I know how badly you want to stop him." What she had to ask next—opening herself, revealing herself—went against every instinct and everything she was, but she did it without hesitation. Cam meant that much to her. "I need it not to be you who goes after him. Please, Cam. Send someone else."

"Ah, baby," Cam murmured. She wanted him dead, but she could live with him behind bars. What she couldn't live with was him free to come after Blair again or help orchestrate another savage attack that could cost hundreds, possibly thousands of lives. Matheson and everything he represented was the reason she did what she did. In many ways, fighting men like him made her who she was. Valerie's voice played in her mind. *You can't keep doing this to her, Cameron.*

For as long as she could remember, Cam had relied on her duty to give her a sense of purpose and meaning, even in the darkest moments. After Janet had been killed and she'd been tormented by guilt, when she'd felt dead inside and disconnected from everything in her life, her duty and Valerie's humanity had been her only salvation. She was not that person any longer, and she had other duties, perhaps even a greater duty, beyond that to her country. "We have no evidence that he has a large force with him. Hopefully I'll only need a small team to apprehend him." She took a deep breath and let it out slowly. "I'll put Savard in charge."

"And you won't go?"

Cam took Blair's hand. "I won't go."

Blair bowed her head and kissed Cam's fingers. "Thank you."

Cam shook her head. "Don't thank me. I love you. You let Stark and her team protect you, and I know how much you hate it. You do that because I need it."

"It doesn't feel like the same thing."

"It is." Cam threaded her fingers through Blair's hair and drew her back down beside her. She kissed her. "It's exactly the same thing."

"This love thing is really hard, isn't it?" Blair murmured.

Cam laughed. "It is. But I wouldn't change a thing." She guided Blair on top of her and shifted her legs so their bodies melded. "And it definitely has its advantages."

Blair skimmed her mouth over Cam's breast. "Let me show you just how many."

CHAPTER EIGHTEEN

Renée found Paula working at the desk that used to be Cameron Roberts's in the far corner of the command center. Other than the agent watching the monitors at the opposite end of the room, the place was empty. It was five p.m. on Saturday, after all, and the agents who were off-shift were probably either with their families or out enjoying themselves. She couldn't remember a time when Saturday night had seemed any different than a weeknight. She and Paula hadn't had an evening alone together since before 9/11. And they weren't going to tonight, either.

"We got a hit," Renée said. "I'll be leaving soon. Probably won't be back until late morning."

Stark put her pen down and pushed the work aside without looking up. After a pause, she shifted slowly in her chair and looked up at Renée. "You're heading the mission?"

Renée nodded. The OHS team routinely shared intelligence with Blair's protection detail, especially when the information impacted the first daughter's security. This mission didn't, not yet, but they all had a stake in tracking Matheson down. Especially Paula. Renée didn't want to worry her lover any more than necessary, but she'd already changed into her black camos and T-shirt. She wasn't wearing her weapons yet, but Paula had to know what kind of operation was planned.

"Where?" Paula asked.

"Where we suspected. Virginia."

"How many people are going with you?" Paula asked.

"Enough. All good people." Renée checked that the other agent's attention was occupied, then squatted down beside Paula's chair and put her hand on her knee. "I won't be able to call until it's over, but I will as soon as I can."

Paula held Renée's hand in both of hers, her head bowed as if she were studying the surface of Renée's fingers. She rubbed her thumb over Renée's knuckles. "You're okay? You didn't get much sleep."

Renée leaned closer. "I'm fine, sweetie. I hate for you to worry."

"Make sure someone has your back, okay?" Paula raised her head, her eyes dark with thinly disguised anxiety. "Don't be a hero."

"I don't plan to be." Renée kissed her. "We've got more than enough of them around here already."

"Okay then," Paula said, forcing a smile. "So I'll see you tomorrow sometime. We may be on our way to Colorado by the time you get back."

Renée brushed her thumb over Paula's cheek, then straightened. "Then I'll see you on the slopes. Love you."

"I love you too," Paula murmured.

Renée turned and walked swiftly away, knowing that the best way for her to ease the worry in her lover's eyes was to get the job done, get it done right, and come home. That was exactly what she intended to do.

❖

Blair closed her book and dropped it onto the floor beside the couch. She could feel Cam's tension from across the room. "Why don't you go downstairs."

"In a few minutes." Cam leaned over and kissed Blair's forehead. "Trying to get rid of me?"

"Actually, yes. You're driving me crazy with your pacing."

"I'm not pacing."

"We're going to have to have the floors resurfaced in front of the windows, darling. You've walked off the varnish."

"Sorry," Cam muttered.

"Sit for a second." Blair patted the space next to her. They'd slept all morning, then Cam had showered and gone to the command center. She'd come back a little over an hour before so they could eat dinner together. Cam tried to hide it, but Blair could tell she was distracted. "You're sending a team out, aren't you?"

Cam settled next to her and leaned her head back. "Yes."

"Is it big?"

"We might have Matheson's safe house."

Blair tensed. "How?"

"Felicia tracked a suspect cell phone call to the Norfolk area. We found a property in the tower radius owned by a man named Jeremy Barton. He's the son of an Army buddy of Matheson's. We're hoping Matheson is there."

"Did Lucinda call in the special ops?"

"Not this time," Cam hedged, since Lucinda didn't know about the operation. No one did. "We're going in fast and light. Just our people and some of Tanner's."

"Is Tanner here?" Blair knew her childhood friend employed a security force that was made up of ex-military people, and after seeing them in action she began to suspect that Whitley Industries had more involvement in what was happening in the Middle East than she had ever realized.

"Not Tanner. She flew Steph down with a couple of men."

"What if Matheson *is* there and he's got a force with him?"

Cam shook her head. "We've got satellite images—no cars, no real signs of activity for the last five hours. He knows we know who he is, and I expect he's doing everything he can to stay under the radar. I doubt he's going to have direct contact with any of his people, because he's got to know we're looking at everyone he's ever been associated with. A lone man is the hardest to track."

"When will you know?"

"Our team will arrive around midnight."

"God, another sleepless night."

Cam pulled Blair closer, settling her in the curve of her body. "If this operation is still ongoing in the morning, you'll have to leave without me."

"That's not happening." Blair ran her finger down Cam's arm. Usually Cam dressed for work in a dress shirt and tailored pants, even when she spent the day in the OHS offices downstairs. Today she'd worn jeans and a faded blue cotton shirt. She looked sexy in either outfit, but Blair realized how rarely Cam was off duty these days. She wasn't leaving for Colorado without her because she wasn't entirely certain that Cam wouldn't become wrapped up in something else that absolutely needed her attention and forget to come. "I'll wait."

"I know it's a bad time—"

"It is what it is, Cam," Blair said, surprised to find that she wasn't angry. Oh, she was outraged at the uncertainty and vulnerability they all lived with every day, but she certainly wasn't upset with her lover for doing what had to be done. "I'm sorry this is so hard for you. The waiting."

Cam grimaced. "I'm not sure I'm cut out for this deputy director job. It doesn't feel right sending my people out on a mission while I stay here."

Blair laced her fingers through Cam's. "I know you're doing this for me, and I appreciate it. But—"

"I don't want you to thank me. We've already been over that."

"I wasn't going to thank you." Blair gave Cam's hand a shake. "I was going to point out that my father thinks you're the right person for this job, and Lucinda agrees, and so do I. And not just because I don't want you in the field." She rested her chin against the tip of Cam's shoulder and circled Cam's waist with both arms. "One person can't fix this, darling, you know that. But you have a team that might be able to."

"That's right. *My* team. *My* people." Cam sighed. "I should be there to have their backs."

"You do have their backs, by sending the best to do the job. You're the team leader. You hold them all together."

Cam rested her forehead against Blair's. "It's a lot easier to *do* than to stay behind and worry."

Blair laughed and shook her head. "That's something you don't have to tell me, my love."

"I'm sorry for that." Cam buried her face in Blair's hair. "I just hate *watching*."

Blair felt Cam tremble and was instantly alert. This wasn't fear— Cam never gave in to fear. This was something deeper. "Hey, hey." She tightened her grip. "What is it?"

After a pause, Cam said so quietly Blair could barely hear her,

"I keep thinking of that night when Janet was undercover and the operation went to hell. All I could do was watch while the trap closed around her. By the time I got to her..."

"Oh, baby." Blair stroked Cam's hair. Cam rarely talked about the night Janet, a narcotics detective and Cam's on-again, off-again lover, was killed, but she knew the story. At least the details Cam had been able to share. Janet had been undercover, and somehow, the federal agents and the local detectives had failed to coordinate a raid on a warehouse where drugs were being exchanged for counterfeit money. Janet had been caught in the crossfire and killed. Cam had been shot trying to get her out. "Is that why you're always the first to stand in front of the bullets?"

"Believe me, I don't have a death wish," Cam said. "I'm just doing my job."

Cam's voice was muffled against her neck, but Blair could hear the pain. "I know. But no one wants you to protect them at the cost of your life." She rubbed Cam's back and tried not to think about Cam taking the bullet that was meant for her. "Especially not me or any of the members of your team."

"No one's going to be doing any dying," Cam said, straightening up. "I'm sending them in with a satellite link to the command center. I'll have audio and video, and at the first sign of trouble, I'll pull them out. If Matheson so much as points a squirt gun in their direction, he's a dead man."

Blair smiled as cold, hard fury settled in the pit of her stomach. "That sounds like a perfect plan. Especially the last part."

"I need to go." Cam kissed Blair. "Thanks. Thanks for letting me get that out."

"Anytime. I love you." Blair squeezed Cam's shoulder, then gave her a little shove. "So go take care of your people."

❖

"Explain to me again the part about the...extracellular matrix stuff," Dana said. Without raising her head, she scribbled in a tattered brown leather notebook with one hand and reached out with her right for her coffee cup.

Emory slid the glass mug closer to Dana's fingers, noticing again the faint roughness to her fingertips. Several of her knuckles were marked with small healing lacerations. "What happened to your hands?"

"Hmm?" Dana looked up, surprised to see that the Starbucks had filled up sometime during the last hour. She'd been too busy getting down everything Emory explained about tissue engineering and stem cell diferentiation to even notice. She hadn't expected the impromptu interview, and she didn't want to miss a single sentence. Her research had indicated Emory was considered one of the world's authorities in tissue engineering, but she was just now beginning to understand how significant that really was. Emory's work could lead to a means of growing organs in the laboratory for tissue transplantation. "So you could grow a kidney, and someone wouldn't have to wait for a donor, right?" Dana pushed a thick lock of hair off her forehead and absently sipped her cold coffee. "Or, Jesus, a heart. Right?"

"Theoretically, yes." Emory smiled at Dana's intensity. She'd never before experienced the kind of pleasure she had gotten over the last hour describing her work to Dana. She hadn't thought she'd had an ego, but every time Dana complimented her, she felt a rush of heat.

"That could be big, right?" Dana said. "I mean really big. Like Nobel Prize big, right? It could change the entire face of transplant surgery."

Emory covered Dana's hand, which was clenched around her now forgotten coffee cup. "We're a long ways away from that kind of territory yet."

Dana frowned. "I don't get why anyone would object to your research."

"I understand some of the objections, theoretically at least," Emory said. "Any scientific tool—any kind of tool at all, really—has a potential for misuse. Look at nuclear power. If appropriately harnessed, the power of the atom could free us from dependency on natural oil and gas. But what's the first thing we make? Bombs so huge, so devastating, they can destroy entire cities and hundreds of thousands of lives." Emory shrugged. "There are those who think *today a kidney, tomorrow an infant*. And then...." She quickly grew serious. "There are some who feel that what we're doing is an affront against God, or an abomination of nature, or just plain egomaniacal. There are lots of arguments. I'm sure you know them."

"People can get pretty wound up about those issues," Dana said casually.

"That's putting it mildly."

"Did you know the person who attacked you in Boston?"

"No, he wasn't…" Emory stopped suddenly and pulled her hand out from under Dana's. "Why are you doing this? Why are you using what's happening between us to take advantage of me?"

"How am I doing that?"

"By treating me like a story."

"You *are* a story. You, Emory. You." Dana's expression darkened and when she leaned forward, her eyes sparked with anger. "Don't you get it, Emory? If you're in danger, publicizing it makes you safer. Letting the world know you're a target for hatemongers and zealots will force the foundation to give you more security. It will make local law enforcement agents more alert the next time you step onto a stage. You're an important person. Maybe one of the most important people in the world. What part of that don't you get?"

"I don't need you to worry about my safety."

"Well, that's just fine, but I already do." Dana reached across the table and grabbed Emory's hand. "And I happen to like holding your hand. I happen to like *you* a lot."

"I don't like you *using* the fact that I like you." Emory kept her voice down even though she wanted to yell. "Is that why you kissed me earlier? Because you know it makes me stupid and senseless?"

"How can a simple little kiss make you stupid?"

"I don't know," Emory hissed, "but it does. I can't think. All I can do is feel how hot your mouth is and how soft your lips are and how much I want you to keep kissing me. The tips of your fingers are rough, did you know that? I think about you rubbing them—" She closed her eyes. "Oh my God. Now I don't even have to kiss you and I lose my mind."

All the air left Dana's chest as her stomach did a slow somersault. She knew Emory wasn't trying to seduce her. In fact, it sounded like the last thing in the world Emory wanted was for something to happen between them. But just thinking about Emory wanting to be kissed—wanting to be kissed by her—was the sexiest thing she'd ever experienced. "It's a damn good thing we're sitting in a coffee shop right now."

Emory opened her eyes. "Why?"

"Because I want to kiss you like you've never been kissed, and I don't want to stop until we're both naked and I'm inside you and I can watch you come."

"I really haven't thought beyond kisses," Emory whispered. "So you might want to back up a step or two."

Dana grinned, but her legs were shaking. If she'd been standing up, she might've fallen down. "I'm not using you, Emory. Yes, I want to write about you and what you do. But it's more than that. I want to know you. I want to know why you do it." She pulled her chair around the side of the small, round pedestal table until they were side by side. She kissed the side of Emory's neck. "I want to know what pleases you. What frightens you. What makes you happy." She turned Emory's face to hers and kissed her on the lips. "I want to make love to you."

Emory traced her fingers over Dana's mouth. "You have such beautiful lips. But I'm not ready to have an orgasm in a coffee shop."

"I was thinking we would probably wait until we were in bed."

Emory laughed. She wished they were alone so she could curl up in Dana's lap and kiss her and be kissed, and touch her and be touched. Her body had never felt so alive. "I'm glad we're not alone right now."

"Why?"

"Because I think I would let you take me to bed, and I'm not ready for that." She laughed again, her voice shaking as much as her insides. "Well, at least not all of me is ready."

"Okay." Dana eased away but kept Emory's hand in hers. "No orgasms tonight. But will you come back with me? Just stay in the apartment with me. I promise I won't ask you any questions."

Emory looked down at Dana's hand and ran her thumb over the scratches. Then she looked into Dana's eyes. "What if I want to ask you questions?"

Dana wanted to say no, but how could she ask for what she wasn't willing to give? She nodded. "All right. But I have one stipulation."

Emory quirked an eyebrow.

"You did agree earlier that a kiss or two would be a reasonable expectation on my part."

"One or two." Emory appeared to be considering it. "As long you promise not to get greedy."

"I'm not usually greedy by nature," Dana said. But where Emory was concerned, all bets were off.

❖

Cam stared at the monitor, which provided a still image of the country house and the surrounding grounds where they believed Matheson had gone to ground. No lights, no vehicle in the drive. She clenched her jaw as Savard's voice came over her radio feed.

Place looks deserted, Commander.

"Deploy your teams," Cam told her. The satellite image wasn't precise enough, especially at night, for her to track the movement of individual team members, and as the minutes dragged on the muscles in her neck screamed from tension. She should have been there. What if word of their plans had gotten out somehow? What if there was an ambush? What if she was wrong and Matheson had laid in a force like the cadre that had hit the Aerie?

Nothing, Savard reported. *The bastard's like smoke.*

Cam closed her eyes. Where the hell was he? Matheson on the move was going to be twice as hard to locate and three times as dangerous.

❖

Matheson passed through Cumberland, Virginia, and headed north on Route 220 into Pennsylvania at 4:10 a.m. Right on schedule, he noted with satisfaction. The rental car that had been delivered to his safe house a little before midnight was appropriately nondescript, the kind of midsize low-budget sedan any businessman might drive. When he pulled into the parking lot of the Denny's restaurant, there were a dozen others like it parked nearby. He got out and stretched, then made his way beneath the still-dark sky to his hastily arranged meeting.

He stopped just inside the door, pretending to survey the newspapers in the coin-operated boxes while scanning the area. Considering the hour, the restaurant was more crowded than he had expected with truckers and travelers heading north to the turnpike. All the better. In his bland khaki jacket, dark trousers, and tab-collar blue shirt, all purchased in the men's department of a low-end chain store, he doubted any of the busy waitresses would remember him in an hour. That might not be the case for the man he was meeting, which was why he detested doing business in public places. However, the alternative—a clandestine rendezvous—was unacceptable when he couldn't bring backup. Here, at least, he was unlikely to be targeted if his *friends* decided he was no longer useful. Of course, he was under the same constraints himself, but he had no doubt that when the time came to eliminate any unwanted associates, his men would rise to the occasion.

"Breakfast for one?" a careworn blonde asked him as she automatically handed him a shiny laminated menu.

He took the menu and smiled. "Thanks, I'll just grab a booth if that's okay. My business partner just ducked into the john."

"Sure, go ahead," she said, already turning away.

Matheson settled into the bench seat of one of the smaller booths facing the door and ordered two coffees, giving the waitress who barely looked at him the same story. A minute later, another traveler entered, took a quick look around the room, and walked directly to Matheson's table. Dressed in casual business clothes, he too would have gone unnoticed as easily as Matheson if he hadn't been so obviously foreign. Matheson resented the necessity of working with nonwhite men, finding them inherently untrustworthy and lacking in true moral character. But war demanded that men sacrifice, and the cause sometimes necessitated unusual alliances. This one had so far proven valuable.

"Good morning, my friend," the dark-skinned man said as he sat down across from Matheson. His English was even less noticeably accented than it had been on the phone.

"Morning," Matheson said, taking a sip of his coffee. Weak, just like all diner coffee. "While I'm always happy to be of service, I'm afraid my schedule is very tight today."

"Yes, I imagine you have a plane to catch, do you not?"

Matheson's gut tightened, but he knew the man was fishing. No one except his most trusted man knew his destination was the Pittsburgh airport. "I didn't expect we would meet again."

"While our previous venture was successful beyond our greatest expectations, circumstances have changed since last we talked."

Matheson managed not to smirk. Yes, things had certainly changed. The country had gone on red alert and the military was kicking terrorist ass in Afghanistan. Soon, the U.S. would make its presence felt in other parts of the Middle East, he was certain. The show of force wasn't enough, but it was a beginning. He contained his smile and waited.

"The item of mutual interest," the man said smoothly, pushing his coffee cup aside untouched. "We no longer wish to divest ourselves of it." He spread his hands as if he were discussing motor parts and not the first daughter of the United States. "We believe it has value in our forthcoming negotiations."

Matheson leaned back casually, thinking furiously. Eliminating Blair Powell had always been his main agenda, but only a side note for these men. Why, suddenly, had they taken an interest in her? And what negotiations? He resented being played, especially by men who weren't fit to polish his boots. He met the dark eyes across from his. "Valuable how?"

The foreigner shrugged. "Consider it currency."

Currency. Trade. Exchange. Matheson's lips curled as he considered the advantage to his own long-range goals. If the president's daughter were suddenly the bargaining chip between the U.S. government and foreign terrorists, he wondered how long the president would pay lip service to his policy of not negotiating with terrorists. The president's capitulation would strike another blow to his credibility and further weaken his paper tiger government.

"We're talking about a very expensive commodity," Matheson said.

"Money is of no consequence to us."

"Twenty million."

"A very reasonable sum. You can send information regarding payment through the usual channels. We would prefer a midweek delivery. We have a busy schedule too."

The foreigner smiled with obvious satisfaction and Matheson

wanted to put a bullet between his eyes. Instead, he rose and carefully placed payment for the coffee plus a fifteen percent tip on the table. If he couldn't deliver as promised, he could always fall back on his initial plan and kill her. "Consider it done."

CHAPTER NINETEEN

Sunday

Dana barreled out of her bedroom and nearly ran over Emory in the hall. Emory obviously had just come from the shower, since her hair lay in damp wavy strands on her shoulders and she wore nothing except a large white bath towel rolled over just above the tops of her breasts.

"Sorry," Dana said, grasping Emory's shoulders to steady her as she stumbled backward. She tried really hard not to look down at Emory's breasts, but she failed. And when she looked back up, she knew Emory had noticed. "Sorry."

"For what?" Emory asked, enjoying the off-balance look in Dana's eyes. And enjoying the appreciation in them too. She'd never given much thought to her body. She was happy that she was fit and healthy. But she wasn't so self-deluded as to pretend she didn't know others considered her attractive. That was nice, but didn't rank high on things that were important to her. Except in the last two days. She loved that Dana found her attractive. Knowing that she could somehow make worldly Dana as off-kilter and unsure of herself as she seemed to be gave her a thrill. She wondered how much more excited she would feel if Dana actually put her hands where her gaze had just lingered.

"What?" Dana asked, sounding dazed.

Emory smiled. Dana wore jeans, a navy T-shirt with long sleeves that she pushed up to her elbows, and scuffed brown boots. Her almost-tight T-shirt outlined her small, neat breasts and narrow waist. Sexy, God, she was sexy in a completely unstudied way. "Sorry for what?"

"Uh, for almost running you over." Dana backed up a step. Emory smelled like Ivory soap again, and her skin was flushed. Probably just from the heat of the shower, but Dana just *knew* Emory's skin would be exactly that color when she was aroused. And she wanted nothing more in the world than to open that towel and slide her hands over the full breasts that lay beneath it. She wanted it so much she was choking on desire.

"Did you sleep all right?" Emory asked, trying to decipher Dana's expression. Lean and hungry. She'd never really thought about what that phrase meant until just this moment, but that's exactly how Dana looked at her. As if she were ravenous and wanted to taste her. Emory backed up in the other direction, fearful of broadcasting her arousal because she had no idea how to hide it. She licked her lips and cleared her dry throat when Dana continued to stare. "Were you going somewhere?"

"Coming to find you," Dana said. "Patrice Hara called down. We're on schedule to fly to Colorado today. Blair is looking for you. She said to give you the message to come up."

"I'll get dressed and pack, then." Emory circled around Dana to get to her own room. Just before she went inside, she turned back to where Dana still stood in the hall. "I had a nice time last night. Just talking and watching television. I haven't done anything that simple in a long time." Emory hesitated. "And I liked the good-night kiss too."

"So did I." Dana grinned a little, recalling the exceptionally soft, exceptionally warm, and exceptionally wonderful kiss they had shared just before going to their separate bedrooms. Emory had been the one to lean forward when they stood outside their adjacent doors to say good night. Emory had kissed her first. "It was a great night. Even if we had sworn off orgasms for the evening."

Emory laughed. "I don't know about you, but I didn't swear off orgasms. Just not together."

"Are you saying you…" Dana closed her eyes. "Oh man, that is so so unfair."

"I'll see you in a few minutes."

Dana heard a door shut, and when she opened her eyes she was alone. She'd probably been awake the night before, restless and aroused, while Emory had been lying in the dark in the room next to hers, touching herself, making herself come. If she'd known, she doubted she would have been able to keep from going next door. But Emory had said she wasn't ready, and more than Dana wanted her—and it felt like she wanted her more than she'd ever wanted any woman in her life—she wanted Emory to want it too.

She'd just have to be patient, but God, it was hard, when she couldn't seem to think about anything except tasting her, and touching her, and making her sigh with pleasure.

"Perfect," she grumbled, returning to her bedroom to grab her luggage. "Absolutely perfect time to be obsessed with a woman who might not even end up being interested—right when I'm in the middle of not just one, but two or three big stories."

"Are you talking to yourself?" Emory said from the open doorway.

Dana spun around. Emory was no longer wearing a towel, but the silk T-shirt tucked into casual black slacks had almost the same effect. She was still beautiful and sexy. She was drying the ends of her hair with a hand towel, and after a few seconds she tilted her head quizzically.

"Dana?"

"Yes. I'm talking to myself. Well, apparently if you heard me, I'm talking to both of us."

Emory laughed. "Do you know that you don't make a lot of sense sometimes?"

"We're not even kissing, and I'm stupid and senseless just from looking at you."

Slowly, Emory lowered the towel, and the look on her face changed from amusement to surprise. "If you didn't look so flummoxed, I might not believe you. You don't know what's going on any more than I do, do you?"

"Not exactly." Dana grinned. "I understand some of it. The part where we get naked…"

"That part I get." Emory took a deep breath. "I came to ask what I should do with my luggage."

"Leave it inside the front door. Someone will pick it up and bring it down to the cars."

"I'll be ready in a just a minute."

Dana lifted her battered canvas travel bag. "I'll wait for you in the living room."

"Okay." Emory turned away, then looked back. "I'm trying not to worry about the fact that I don't understand what's going on. And just for the record, I really like the way you look at me."

And then she was gone, leaving Dana feeling totally out of her depth and, strangely, not caring.

❖

"Hey! Look who's here," a small, wiry redhead exclaimed when Emory and Dana walked into Blair's loft.

"Steph!" Emory hurried toward the woman. "I didn't know you were going to be here."

"Tanner decided to give me some time off."

While Dana watched, the redhead—Steph—draped an arm around Emory's waist way too casually, pulled her into a full body hug, and kissed her on the mouth. Dana narrowed her eyes, taking in the black fatigue pants, black T-shirt, and black boots. Jesus Christ, a mercenary. Well, these days they were called contract workers or security personnel or some other equally bland term, but they were mercenaries just the same. Where the hell did she come from? And what the hell was she doing pawing Emory? Dana checked the rest of the room. A power meeting was underway, by the looks of things.

Blair and Diane were in the sitting area, cups of coffee and a tray of bagels and muffins between them on the low table. Greg Wozinski sat on the arm of a chair near the door, drinking coffee and talking to Paula Stark, who was flanked by two burly jarheads dressed like the tough little number still fondling Emory. A gorgeous coffee-skinned woman with shoulder-length coppery gold hair stood next to the breakfast bar in conversation with Cameron Roberts. When the woman, whose body radiated tension, turned to survey Dana with an intense, flat gaze, Dana pegged her as federal. Not part of Blair Powell's personal security detail—probably FBI. Valerie was missing, but then she often was—part of the OHS team, but still a loner. Dana's skin prickled. She was getting the picture, a picture that said Cameron Roberts had put her OHS squad together by pulling from existing agencies, which made sense. Secret Service, FBI, civilian contractors—and Valerie? No Last Name Valerie had come from someplace deep and dark. Another story there.

As much as Dana wanted to stay and drag Steph away from Emory, she was working. She walked over to Blair. "I hear we're heading for the mountains."

Blair smiled. "At last."

"Looks like you've picked up a lot of new people."

"Just some friends who dropped by." Blair pointed to the muffins. "Have something to eat."

"Thanks." Dana sat down, poured a cup of coffee, and balanced a blueberry muffin on a napkin on her knee. "Where did you come by the private guys?"

"They work for a good friend of ours," Blair said. "You'll meet her in Colorado. Tanner Whitley."

"Why do I know the name?" Dana frowned, then checked out Steph, who was still in animated conversation with Emory and the other two guys in black. "Whitley as in the Whitley Corp?"

"That's right."

"I heard they might be helping out with personnel and technical support over in the desert," Dana said casually.

Blair glanced at Diane, who raised her eyebrows as if to say she had no idea and if she did, she wouldn't admit it. "Tanner has a lot of business interests I don't know about."

"Tanner Whitley. She's the daughter, right? The one who inherited the whole Whitley empire?"

"That's the one."

"Really," Dana said, her interest escalating. No wonder the president's daughter appeared to have civilian contractors as part of her security team. Irregular, for sure. But it would explain why they were trusted. The real question was, why weren't regular agents being used if Blair needed more security? Something had happened to cast doubt on the usual channels, and Dana was willing to bet it all went back to Boston, or maybe even before that. Whatever had gone down, Cameron Roberts and Paula Stark were distrustful of agents from inside the system. Jesus. What the hell was going on?

"So you all know each other?" Dana asked.

"Tanner and Diane and I have been friends forever," Blair said.

Diane Bleeker laughed. "Not exactly forever, Blair darling, but close enough."

Diane's blond hair swirled elegantly around her long, graceful neck, and in her casual slacks and black cashmere pullover, she looked younger than Dana had first thought. She realized they'd all probably been in school together. She sipped her coffee. "That must have been fun— the three of you in school together."

"Well, Blair and Tanner were a little on the wild side," Diane said self-righteously. "I was the model of decorum."

Blair snorted. "God, what an awful liar."

"Oh, all right," Diane said, nudging Blair's calf with her toe. "We all had our moments. But just look at us now. Tanner swore she never wanted the business. Never intended to settle down." Diane shook her head "Now she's married, to a career naval officer of all things, and you're about to make a big public splash with a Fed." She took Blair's hand. "What a ride."

Blair gave Diane an affectionate look. "And it's not over by a long shot."

Dana was struck once more by the clear and unself-conscious tenderness between the two women. Throw in Tanner Whitley and there had to be a great sidebar there, but the story was none of her business, and no one else's either. She averted her gaze just in time to see Steph run her hand down the outside of Emory's arm and briefly squeeze Emory's hand.

"Who is *she*, exactly?" Dana asked before she could stop herself.

"Besides yummy, you mean?" Diane replied, her tone teasing.

Dana hoped she wasn't glowering.

"She works for Tanner," Blair repeated. "And she's a friend."

A very good friend, at least of Emory's from the looks of it. Dana couldn't ever really recall being jealous before. Not the way she felt right now. Like she wanted to physically put herself between Steph and Emory and make some macho statement about ownership and beat her chest like an idiot. Emory would probably think she'd lost her mind. She probably had.

"She and Emory look really good together, don't you think?" Diane said, reaching for a bagel.

"Stop it," Blair muttered.

Dana gritted her teeth.

"I'm sorry." Diane laughed. "But since I'm the only one who never gets to see her girlfriend, I'm allowed to act out a little bit."

"Where is Valerie, anyhow?" Dana asked.

"I don't recall mentioning her name," Diane said, suddenly serious.

"You didn't have to."

"You're really good at this reporter thing, aren't you?"

Dana grinned. "Some people think so."

"It's not like you're not going to see us together," Diane went on. "At least, I hope you will. If Cameron decides to let her out of this building sometime in the next few days."

"Diane," Blair said quietly.

"It's okay," Dana said, surprising herself. "We're off the record here. And I already figured out that Valerie is part of the OHS team. Diane's not giving anything away." She put her empty coffee cup and napkin aside and leaned forward, focusing on Blair. "I understand there are certain things that need to be kept confidential—like the identities of your security people and the members of the deputy director's team. Being around everyone like this all the time, it's pretty easy to figure out the players. I want you to understand that I don't have any intention of compromising them."

"I believe you," Blair said. "But you're not the first reporter I've ever met. You have some biologic imperative to poke into things."

Dana grinned. "You're right. I won't deny it."

"And I also know that you have this obsessive need to not only inform, but to use the power of the press in the name of what you consider justice."

"Consider? Isn't justice immutable?"

Cam walked up behind Blair just as Dana asked the question and rested her hands on Blair's shoulders. She leaned over the back of the couch and kissed Blair, murmured hello, then regarded Dana intently. "Not when justice depends upon the human assessment of merit, or of right and wrong."

"Then how do we administer it?" Dana asked.

"We have laws," Cam said. "And sometimes the course is so clear, the laws are redundant."

Blair covered Cam's hand and squeezed gently, but her eyes were on Dana. "You may *not* quote that, Dana."

"I wasn't going to. And for the record, I agree." Dana stood, deciding it was time to meet Steph. "What are the plans when we get to Colorado?"

Blair brightened. "If there's enough snow, I'm going skiing."

"It'll be dark," Cam pointed out.

Blair swiveled around to kneel on the couch, draped her arms around Cam's shoulders, and pulled her down into a serious kiss. "There will be moonlight. You can do anything by moonlight."

Diane sighed. "Should I remind you that some of us are going to be solo for at least another day?"

"I'm sorry," Cam said apologetically. "She should be able to follow us tomorrow."

"If she doesn't," Diane said, poking Cam's shoulder vigorously, "I'm going to hound you until she arrives. You haven't experienced misery until you've been around me when I'm unrequited for too long."

Cam grinned. "I wasn't aware that ever happened."

"Now can I quote you?" Dana asked.

Laughing, Diane looped her arm through Dana's and bent her head close. "I've got a better idea. Why don't you stand in for Valerie until she arrives at the resort. I hate being without an escort."

"You're going to have to define stand in," Dana said playfully.

"That's something I'll think about." Diane frowned. "And *that's* certainly new."

Dana managed to avoid being captured in the hypnotic seductiveness of Diane's sultry gaze, only to realize Emory was standing a few feet away watching them. "Hi."

"Hi," Emory said with just the slightest bit of chill in her voice. "Have I missed out on plans for a party?"

"Not my idea of a party," Diane said wryly. "Blair is going skiing later."

"Good," Emory said. "I hope they've got plenty of extra gear at the lodge, because I'm going to join her."

"I think everyone has lost their minds," Diane said. "I for one intend to sit before the fire with a glass of wine and think about absolutely nothing at all."

"Do you ski, Dana?" Emory asked.

"I do, but I have a feeling I'm going to be outclassed by everyone here."

"Well then you can join me by the fire." Diane smiled mischievously. "Adding logs and whatnot to make sure we stay warm."

"Thanks," Dana said, "but if Emory doesn't mind company, I just might try the slopes."

"Company would be nice," Emory said softly.

"Good, then it's a date," Dana replied, fervently hoping that would be true.

❖

The colonel handed the binoculars to Matheson, who lay beside him in the snow on the side of a mountain in Colorado. A huge timber lodge and smaller cabins lay in a cleared area of forrest a quarter mile below them. "The main lodge, the individual cabins, and the ski lift are in rifle range from here. The SSM is another alternative." He turned and indicated one of several narrow, overgrown trails that ribboned through the snow-laden woods below them. "With snowmobiles we can traverse down the other side of the mountain to our vehicles and onto the interstate in under ten minutes."

"And you've prepared the rendezvous point for emergency evac?" Matheson asked, accepting the binoculars.

"The vehicles are ready and waiting. The weapons too. All well camouflaged."

"You're sure no one noticed your reconnaissance?"

"The nearest village is six miles away, and it's ski season. Lots of tourists. Plus, reporters are beginning to arrive in town. A few have already been up here trying to get an advance story from the innkeeper. No one paid any attention to me." The colonel shrugged. "I've seen Secret Service people at the lodge, but they can't cover the whole mountainside. With all the trails and heavy tree cover, even aerial recon is difficult. I imagine they'll keep her under close protection when she's outside."

"I'm glad she likes to ski." Matheson studied the idyllic, rustic scene below them, imagining Blair Powell stepping out onto the wide front porch of the chalet in the morning sun and directly into his gun sights. So easy. So beautiful.

He sighed. Taking her alive would be so much more difficult, and he wasn't at all certain that the pleasure would be as intense. For now, he would keep his options open. After all, his *friends* were not the ones in charge, and never would be. This was his country.

CHAPTER TWENTY

Late Sunday Night
Colorado

E mory turned at the sound of footsteps on the porch behind
her and smiled as Dana approached. "How did the interview
go?"

"Amazing." Dana joined Emory at the railing of the wide deck that
fronted the ski lodge. At just after nine, the moon was high and partially
shrouded in clouds. The only illumination came from the windows
behind them and the glow of the huge fire burning in the stone hearth
in the common room. Shadows danced across Emory's face. Despite
the near zero temperature, Dana found the crystal-clear mountain air
invigorating. She felt alive in a way she hadn't in years. She wondered
when she had stopped feeling, when she had replaced emotion with
activity. She couldn't pinpoint just when she had abandoned the idea
of a relationship and substituted danger for desire. But she knew the
exact moment when all that had changed. It had happened that day in
the hotel when Emory heard she was a reporter and her expression had
gone from open welcome to closed reserve. Emory's withdrawal had
been like a door slamming shut on her heart, and she'd immediately
wanted to wrench it open again. She'd spent every moment since
trying. "Besides being a world-renowned artist, Marcea Cassels is an
incredible woman."

"You've hit the jackpot in terms of stumbling upon newsworthy
people," Emory commented.

Dana searched her face for signs of criticism, but didn't find any. She realized then that Emory didn't consider herself one of those remarkable people. She hesitated, then said, "My editor sent me here with orders to interview you too."

"I gathered that much from the questions you were asking the other day at the coffee shop."

"How do you feel about it?"

"Uneasy. Uncomfortable."

"Then he'll have to be content with the social events of the next few days," Dana said, "and the interviews I already have."

Emory looked surprised. "Just like that? You'll ditch the story?"

"Yes."

"That doesn't sound like you."

Dana shrugged. "It isn't. But I care about you, and I don't want you to be uncomfortable because of something I've done." She leaned closer, her mouth close to Emory's cheek. "I only want to make you uncomfortable in a good way."

Emory laughed a little shakily. "You're succeeding."

"Glad to hear it." Dana risked stroking Emory's cheek. She wasn't so much concerned that someone would see them as she was at her inability to stop at a simple touch. She'd thought about Emory all day, thought about kissing her, thought about the hot, sultry taste of her mouth and the way her lips slid over hers when they kissed. She imagined how it would feel to hold her breasts in her hands, to squeeze and mold them until Emory whimpered.

Fantasizing about Emory had kept her pleasantly occupied on the slopes when she couldn't keep up with Emory and Blair. She could ski, but with nothing like their speed and skill. She hadn't minded. She'd been more interested in watching Emory than the slopes, anyhow. She'd loved how athletically graceful and exuberantly free Emory had been. She wanted to put that look of unfettered joy on her face. Without thinking, she cupped Emory's cheek.

"Dana," Emory murmured, leaning into Dana's hand. "You can interview me, as long as we're clear that only what I tell you during the course of the interview itself gets into print."

"Okay," Dana said, her voice husky.

Emory searched Dana's face, her eyes questioning. "I thought you'd be more excited."

"I couldn't be more excited." Dana brushed her thumb over the corner of Emory's mouth. "I can't stop thinking about kissing you. I want to kiss you—everywhere."

Emory caught her breath, a spiral of excitement coursing through her. She gripped the wooden railing with one hand and squeezed tightly, hoping Dana couldn't tell she was trembling. She'd been standing in the dark, watching the incredible night sky unfold overhead, and trying to imagine a casual physical encounter with Dana. She was far from a blushing virgin, and the idea of being with a woman didn't seem strange. Diane and Blair weren't her first lesbian friends and even if they had been, she'd thought of being with a woman before. She just hadn't met one she wanted, not the way she wanted Dana. The idea of sex with Dana disconcerted her, not because Dana was a woman, but because Emory wanted her so much. She'd never craved another's touch the way she craved Dana's, as if the need were more than physical. Nothing ever distracted her, especially when she decided to put something from her mind. But she couldn't keep Dana from her thoughts. She was aware of her, no matter where she was in a room. Just looking at her gave her a twinge of pleasure. She could even handle a one-night stand, if that's the way things turned out. What worried her was that one short night might not assuage her hunger. "I don't know what to do about you."

"I know what you mean."

"Do you?" Emory pulled away, gently breaking their contact. "I want to go to bed with you and I have no idea why."

"Do you like me?"

Emory laughed. "I do."

"Good, because I like you too." Dana glanced through the window behind her to the interior of the lodge. Figures moved beyond the glass, but they were alone on the veranda. She unzipped her ski parka and then did the same to Emory's. Turning her back to the railing, she leaned against a post and pulled Emory close. Their coats opened to allow their bodies to touch. Emory settled into the vee between her thighs and Dana wrapped her arms around Emory's waist. "I've been wanting to kiss you all day."

"Then perhaps you should."

When their mouths met, Emory snugged her pelvis tighter into Dana's crotch and gripped the waistband of Dana's jeans with both hands. They fit together as if they had kissed a thousand times.

Dana meant to go slow, but the tease of Emory's tongue between her lips was like fuel to a fire and desire blazed through her, destroying restraint. She deepened the kiss and skimmed one hand under Emory's sweater, sliding up to cup her breast. When Emory moaned and pressed into her palm, her mind emptied of thought and her body surged with uncontrollable want. She sucked on Emory's tongue and found her nipple through the thin silk covering her breast. When she squeezed, Emory shuddered against her.

"God, Dana, I can't do this here."

"I'm sorry," Dana groaned, forcing her hand away from Emory's breast. "I'm so sorry."

Emory pressed trembling fingers to Dana's mouth. "Don't say that. I think I'm the one who told you to kiss me."

"You didn't tell me to start pawing at you," Dana said, disgusted with herself for not treating Emory more carefully. "I just couldn't stop."

"I love knowing you want me." Emory rested her forehead against Dana's. She took a slow breath and let it out. "Would you come to my cabin tonight?"

Dana kissed her very carefully. "Are you sure?"

Emory withdrew a key from her pocket and pressed it into Dana's hand. "I'm very sure."

"When?" Dana said urgently.

Emory laughed, loving the sound of desire in her voice. "I promised Blair I'd partner with her at cards for a while. After that, I'm all yours."

❖

"Blair seems relaxed," Marcea said.

"That's because she's winning." Cam leaned back on the sofa next to her mother, crossing her legs at the ankle. She sipped her wine and enjoyed the sight of Blair laughing, her hair loose, dressed in faded jeans and a navy V-neck sweater that made her eyes seem impossibly blue. At moments like this, Cam was both saddened and joyful. Blair's rare exuberance reminded her of just how much the burden of being a public figure, and lately, a secret target, weighed on her. If Cam could give her anything, it would be peace of mind. But as that was beyond her ability, she would give her as much freedom to be herself, safe and unafraid, as she could. "She loves competition."

Marcea softly tapped Cam's knee. "It seems you're well matched in that regard."

Cam chuckled. "True."

"Are you looking forward to Saturday?"

"I am." Cam shifted her gaze from her lover to her mother. "It means something, to say out loud in front of friends and family what you know to be true in your heart."

"It does. I'm so happy for you, Cameron." She touched Cam's hand. "So if you're not nervous, what is it that's bothering you?"

"Nothing," Cam said quickly.

"I imagine that doesn't work with Blair," Marcea observed easily, "any more than it does with me. I've been hearing the things you don't say for a good many years."

Cam studied her wine. "Nothing specific, but ever since September..." She shrugged. "I can't help feeling something else is coming, and not knowing when or how or from where makes me uneasy."

"This seems like an ideal location," Marcea observed. "Only one main access road, the individual cabins are not too isolated despite being private, and we're halfway up a mountain. I would imagine securing your perimeter is easier here than it would be in the city."

"You learned a lot as an ambassador's wife." Cam smiled, but they both knew caution wasn't enough. It hadn't saved her father from being killed by a car bomb.

"Yes." Marcea took Cam's hand. "You will take care of yourself while you're taking care of her, won't you?"

"I will."

"Good." Marcea released Cam's hand and scanned the people gathered in the common room. "Having a reporter this close must be a challenge."

Cam regarded Dana, who leaned against the fireplace, a beer in her hand, her moody gaze riveted to Emory. "It's working out better than I expected. Barnett's a straight shooter, and she seems to have found a way to get Blair to trust her."

"Blair would value honesty," Marcea said. "And of course, Dana falling for a good friend probably wins points with Blair too."

"Is that what's happening, do you think?"

Marcea laughed. "I don't claim to be an expert, but even I can read what's in Dana's mind right now."

Cam grunted. "Even with Dana on board we still have to allow the media some access. I held them off when we arrived today, but we have a short press conference scheduled tomorrow."

"You don't like it."

"No."

"Blair must find it difficult," Marcea said.

"Having her friends here helps."

"I'm looking forward to meeting the infamous Tanner and her captain."

"You'll like them," Cam said. "When is Giancarlo arriving?"

"Wednesday. He had business he couldn't wrap up until then."

"I rather thought you might be the first one to get married," Cam said.

"Oh, I'm very fond of him, but marriage is not something I'm quite in the market for. I have my work, as does he, and when we do find time together, it makes the pleasure even more enjoyable."

"I can understand that." Cam grinned as Blair whooped and raked in a fistful of cards, obviously having won a big hand. "I don't think I'll ever get tired of being around her."

"No, I can't imagine you will," Marcea said gently. "That's the difference between loving someone and being in love with them."

At that moment, Blair shifted in her seat and glanced in Cam's direction. She grinned and mouthed *I love you.*

Cam smiled back, but she was thinking how dark her world had become after losing her father. She couldn't fathom losing Blair. And she knew, no matter what she had to do, she would never let that happen.

❖

"Can I talk you into the hot tub?" Blair asked, hooking her arm through Cam's as they navigated the snowy path to their cabin. Unlike the last time they'd stayed at the lodge, before she and Cam had become lovers, they weren't staying in the main house. Doris, the owner, had insisted they take the honeymoon cabin, the last one in a line of several surrounded by trees with a large private deck and hot tub. Diane had the cabin next to Blair's, although it was barely visible now with only the moonlight illuminating the mountainside. Emory had another closer to the house, Marcea had one, and another was reserved for Tanner and Adrienne, when they arrived. Other guests and team members had rooms inside the lodge.

"You won't even have to try hard," Cam replied.

Blair slowed as they climbed the steps to their cabin. "How are you feeling? Are your ribs hurting?"

"Nothing a few minutes in the hot tub won't cure." Cam slipped her fingers beneath Blair's hair and cupped the back of her neck, stroking her as Blair unlocked the door. "Emory looked like she was a pretty good partner."

"We killed them." Blair pulled off her coat as she stepped into the cabin. The décor was rustic ski lodge, with comfortable sofas, chairs, and coffee table in the main room by the fireplace. A small kitchen occupied the rear of the cabin and opened onto the back deck. A door on the left led to a separate bedroom with a king-sized bed and adjoining bath. "Do you want wine?"

"I've had enough." Cam glanced over her shoulder, noting Wozinski on the trail. She knew he would walk a perimeter around the cabin before returning to his post farther up the trail. She closed the door. "Give Greg a minute to finish out back."

"I'll grab towels and meet you at the back door, then," Blair said.

A few minutes later, Blair reappeared in the kitchen wrapped in just a towel. Cam quickly stripped and grabbed the other towel. "I already opened the tub."

"Good. Race you." Blair opened the back door and ran outside, Cam close on her heels. The air was sharp, cutting clean, and Blair felt wonderful. Poised on the top step of the hot tub, she turned to take in Cam, breathlessly beautiful beneath the stars. "I've been thinking about this all evening." She slid into the steaming water.

Cam joined her, bracing both hands on the rim of the tub on either side of Blair's shoulders, legs straddling Blair's hips, trapping her. She inclined her head and kissed her. "Have you now."

"I have." Blair gripped Cam's hips. "I've been thinking about how you taste."

"I've been thinking about this too, and my picture was a little different." Cam eased a hand between their bodies until she cupped the hot, silky mound between Blair's legs. Blair spread her arms out along the edge of the tub and let her head fall back, her lids heavy, her breath coming slow and deep.

"Mmm," Blair murmured. "I definitely like your picture."

"Good." Cam squeezed rhythmically, her thumb swiping the base of Blair's clitoris each time she massaged her. She kissed her mouth, her neck, and nipped at the skin beneath her ear. The muscles in Blair's arms stood out as she clutched the side of the tub, her hips rising and falling below the bubbling water.

"Feel good?" Cam muttered, her teeth raking the column of Blair's neck.

"Better than." Blair swirled her hips in invitation. "I want you inside."

"You'll come."

Blair laughed, her throat arched and exposed. "You're right, I will. I want to."

Cam licked the mist from the hollow at the base of Blair's throat and slipped into her. Instantly, Blair closed around her fingers and Cam groaned. She sucked the tight muscle that ran along the pounding pulse, murmuring her approval when Blair covered her hand and pushed her fingers deeper.

"God, Cam, I love you," Blair whispered. "I'm getting close."

"I love you." Cam settled onto the bench and pulled Blair into her lap. Blair's arms came around her neck and Cam cradled her against her body as she moved slowly inside her. Blair's clitoris stirred against her palm and Blair made a small broken sound. "You like that, baby?"

Blair pressed her face to Cam's neck, her hands fitful on Cam's shoulders. "I'm going to come."

Cam kissed her eyes, her mouth, and rocked her gently even as she pushed in short, hard thrusts between her legs. "You're beautiful, so beautiful."

Blair arched in Cam's arms and gave one sharp cry before shuddering uncontrollably for several moments. Cam didn't move as Blair tightened and pulsed around her.

"Ah, God," Blair sighed. "I can't believe I haven't gotten used to you yet. I can't last even when I want to."

"Why try? We can always do it again."

Lazily, Blair lifted her head and combed her fingers through Cam's hair. "Let's go inside. I want you in my mouth."

"Jesus," Cam groaned, her stomach tightening. "I think you could *talk* me into an orgasm right about now."

Laughing, Blair stood, water cascading from her flushed body. She held out her hand. "Let's find out."

❖

From his blind in the forest a hundred yards away, Matheson watched through the night goggles, first as the president's daughter climaxed with a wild cry of triumph, then as she stood naked in the moonlight a few moments later. Had he not just seen her waste her power and her beauty on another woman, he would have thought her perfect. Although his penis was hard, his mind was clear. She was tainted, defiled. If her death served the cause, she might at last be redeemed.

He hunkered down inside the thermal bag, shifting to make room for the sniper rifle cradled like a lover along his side. It would not be long now.

CHAPTER TWENTY-ONE

At the sound of soft knocking on her cabin door, Emory took two steps forward, then faltered to a stop. Her hands were shaking. Her entire body was shaking. She'd never done anything remotely like this in her life.

"Emory," Dana called softly from the other side. "Everything is negotiable."

Smiling, Emory found her legs and made it to the front door. She pulled it open, a blast of frigid air streaking past her as if determined to put the fire out on the opposite side of the room. Dana stood hunched in the doorway, her hands in the pockets of her jacket, her hair windblown.

"Come inside. You look like you're freezing."

"It took me a few minutes to make it onto the porch."

Emory closed the door and leaned back against it. "Really? So I'm not the only one who's nervous?"

"Not by a long shot."

Dana unzipped her jacket. Beneath it she wore a dark T-shirt tucked into her jeans. It was easy for Emory to see the curve of her breasts outlined by the tight material. Dana wasn't wearing a bra, and that simple knowledge made Emory tighten inside. She pressed her hands flat against the door, willing herself to stay in place. Her mind couldn't quite make sense of what she was doing, but her body labored under no such confusion. She wanted to touch Dana, everywhere. She remembered what Dana had said on the porch just a few hours before. *I want to kiss you, everywhere.* Imagining it, Emory grew wet. "I can't believe I invited you to come to my cabin for sex."

Dana smiled crookedly. "You did, didn't you."

Mutely, Emory nodded.

"We don't have to, you know." Dana indicated her jacket. "Do you mind if I take this off?"

"Of course not. There's wine in the refrigerator. Some fruit and cheese too, compliments of the lodge. Would you like some?"

Dana shrugged out of her jacket and hung it on a coat tree just inside the door. Closer now to Emory, she took her hand. Emory's fingers were cold, despite the fact that the room was warm. The look in Emory's eyes had gone from stark confusion to wary interest over the last few minutes. Better, but not anywhere near comfortable enough for them to do anything other than talk. "Let's sit by the fire. I'm not hungry for anything except your company."

"You say the nicest things," Emory whispered.

"All true." Dana drew Emory to the sofa in front of the fire and sat down, coaxing Emory to curl up by her side. She shifted until her back was in the corner and Emory reclined in her embrace. Dana wrapped her arms around her, both hands resting lightly on Emory's midsection, and kissed her. "This is nice."

Emory threaded her arm around Dana's waist and rested her head on Dana's shoulder. She loved the way Dana's body felt, hard and strong, but yielding in just the right way. They fit together effortlessly. She kissed Dana's neck and felt her stiffen. "Don't you like that?"

"No, I do." Dana swallowed and stroked Emory's hair. "I like it a lot." She turned slightly onto her side and stretched so they lay facing each other on the sofa. "Being close to you like this…I can't think of much else except how good it feels."

"It feels good to me too." Emory traced trembling fingers along Dana's jaw. "I appreciate you not rushing me."

"Like I said, everything is negotiable." Dana shifted, easing her leg between Emory's thighs. Her stomach was tight with excitement and her clit ached. She struggled not to move, not to press herself against Emory. "We've done pretty well with the kissing so far. That would probably be safe."

"Oh, you think so?" Emory laughed shakily. "I never got excited lying next to a man this way. Not like I am now." She caressed Dana's back, then her ass. Her breath came faster as the surface of her skin became electric, her vision tunneling until all she saw was Dana's face. "Kiss me, and we'll see how long we last."

Not long, Dana thought, as she covered Emory's mouth with hers. She teased with her tongue, sucked gently, licked the full, soft surface of Emory's lips. Emory moved in her arms, unconsciously seductive, and Dana tightened her hold. Unwilling to break the kiss, even to breathe, she grew dizzy and desperate with need. Finally, she pulled away with a short gasp. "Time. I need a break."

"Why?" Emory's eyes were cloudy, her face soft with arousal. She stroked Dana's cheek before running her hand down the flat of Dana's chest and cupping her breast through her T-shirt. Dana groaned and arched her back.

"God, Emory, I'm so wound up. I can't—"

"I want to make love to you," Emory whispered. "Can I do that? I think if I touch you, I won't be so afraid."

Dana forced back her desire. "What are you afraid of?"

"Of losing myself in this terrible need I have for you."

"Whatever you want, whatever you need," Dana whispered. "We can stop now."

"Could you?" Emory asked urgently. "Because I can't. I don't want to. Will you let me touch you?"

Dana nodded, knowing she was already lost.

"In the bedroom. I want to be able to see you, touch you." Emory pushed Dana away gently. "Let's go in the bedroom."

Dana stood, her legs unsteady. When Emory rose, she circled her shoulders, and Emory grasped the back of her jeans. Together they walked to the bedroom. Emory turned on a lamp on the dresser.

"Should I take off my clothes?" Dana asked.

Emory pulled down the covers, then, with her eyes on Dana, she lifted her sweater over her head and let it fall. She wore nothing beneath it. "Come here."

Dana obeyed, her gaze lifting from Emory's softly swaying breasts to her face. "God."

Smiling, Emory gripped Dana's T-shirt and pulled it from her jeans. When the backs of her fingers brushed Dana's stomach, Dana moaned. Emory looked down, surprised to see Dana's hands clenched at her sides. "What's wrong?"

"Don't you know how beautiful you are? I want to touch you." Dana's voice was hoarse, strained with the effort to contain her surging arousal.

"Then you should." Emory lifted Dana's hands to her breasts. When Dana's fingers closed around her, she tilted her head back and sighed. "I love the way your hands feel on me. I fantasized about your fingers on my nipples, squeezing th—" She groaned when Dana did. The faint roughness of Dana's skin was exactly as she'd imagined. "Yes. Like that." She leaned heavily against Dana as her arousal spilled from her. "But you can't do that to me any longer. I'll get too excited and forget what I'm doing."

With a choked groan, Dana dropped her head to Emory's shoulder, dragging her hands down to Emory's waist. "I'm not sure how long I can take this, Emory. If I touch you again, I won't be able to stop."

"Just a little while. Just be patient a little while." Emory ran her hands up and down Dana's back, tracing the hard muscles along either side of her spine. Then, pulling back just enough to get her hands between them, she unzipped and unbuttoned Dana's jeans and pushed them down. Dana was nude beneath these too, and discovering it, Emory gave a small cry of pleasure. "I love your body."

"I don't usually come easily," Dana confessed, "but right now I feel like—I'm on the edge, Emory."

"Whatever happens, it's all right," Emory soothed, rubbing the back of Dana's neck. She kissed her and felt Dana quiver against her. It was heady, knowing she could do this to her. She probed her mouth, slowly and thoroughly, until they were both shuddering. Then she stepped back, opened her slacks, and swept the remaining barriers away. "Your jeans. Take them off."

Within a minute, they were both naked. Emory climbed under the covers. "Lie down with me."

When Dana stretched out beside her, Emory propped herself up so she could take her all in. Long waist, lean legs, small breasts. Her body was strong, hard, essentially female. She brushed her fingers over Dana's stomach and marveled when her body tightened like a bowstring. "Are you very excited?"

"Oh yes." Dana clutched the sheets with her left hand and gripped Emory's shoulder with the other. "If you touch anywhere near my clit, I'm going to come."

"What do you like?"

Dana gave a strangled laugh. "Right now? Anything."

"I'll rephrase. What would you like me to do right now?"

"Lie on top of me," Dana whispered. When Emory did, Dana wrapped her arms around her and tilted her hips so that Dana's leg rested against her center. "Oh yeah. That's good."

"Mmm."

Emory kissed her, rocking indolently in the curve of her pelvis, their breasts gliding together. Dana skimmed her palms up the outside of Emory's torso, feathering her fingers over the outer curve of her full breasts. Emory moaned and drove her hips harder between Dana's legs. The alternating pressure and relentless friction pushed Dana higher. She wanted to let go, needed to let go, but more than that, she wanted Emory to have whatever she wanted. Dana dragged her mouth away. "You feel so good. You're going to make me come like this."

"I want to see you first." Emory braced herself on her arms, then pushed down on the bed until she was between Dana's legs.

Dana would have objected to the sudden absence of that hot mouth on hers, the sweet torment of Emory's hands, if she hadn't felt the warm rush of Emory's breath between her legs. She'd never had a woman take her this way, so slowly, so simply, so thoroughly. When Emory stroked her finger between her legs, she cried out. "Oh God. Don't touch me. Emory. Don't."

Emory laughed. "I most certainly intend to touch you." Attentive to the desperate tenor of Dana's voice, Emory shifted her fingers away from the one spot she most wanted to caress. Dana was hard and swollen and more beautiful than she had ever imagined. She trailed her fingertips up and down the crease between Dana's thigh and her center, inches from where Dana pulsed and trembled. Emory wanted her in ways she hadn't thought possible. Fiercely, wildly. Pressing her palms to the insides of Dana's thighs, she pushed, spreading her legs, opening her. Dana groaned and lifted her pelvis, beckoning.

Ever so carefully, Emory brushed a kiss over Dana's clitoris.

Dana's body spasmed. "I won't last."

"Can you make it to ten?"

"I don't think so," Dana gasped. "I almost came then."

"It's all right, if you have to." Emory kissed her again, a little more firmly, but still fleetingly. Dana clutched her shoulder, and Emory sensed that Dana wanted to force her mouth down on her. She loved Dana's restraint almost as much as she wanted to break it. She licked her, and Dana tried to twist away. She held her legs more firmly and licked her again.

"God," Dana cried out, her hips rising. "You have to make me come. Emory, please."

"Mmm." Nearly blind, barely breathing, Emory sealed her mouth around Dana's hard length and slowly, tenderly sucked. Dana jerked against her mouth and grew even harder between her lips.

"Oh, *yes.*" Dana's voice broke.

Emory concentrated intently, imprinting every tremor, every cry, every twist and turn as Dana writhed in the throes of her orgasm. Doors long shuttered flew open, barriers fell, defenses shattered. There would never be another first time for her, for them. There would never be another moment as life altering as this. Emory knew victory as surely as she felt her every vulnerability laid bare. When Dana finally arched away, tears streaked Emory's cheeks. She pressed her face to Dana's quivering abdomen. "Thank you."

"Emory," Dana whispered, feeling drugged. She wanted to sit up, she wanted to pull Emory into her arms, she wanted to give her pleasure for pleasure. She could barely lift her hand and just managed to stroke Emory's face. She felt the wetness on her fingertips and her heart clenched. "What is it? Emory, what's wrong?"

Emory shook her head. "Nothing is wrong. Everything is right."

"I want to hold you, but I can't move. Help me."

Laughing softly, Emory moved farther up the bed and stretched out on top of Dana again. Their legs entwined, their breasts cleaved, their mouths fused. Emory burned. Her skin, her muscles, her clitoris. Flame. She needed to be touched. Desperately. "Dana," she gasped, not knowing the words. "I need you."

Dana's strength returned in a rush and she rolled Emory over, following until she was poised above her on her knees and arm. She trailed her fingers between Emory's legs. "Here?"

Emory's eyes opened wide and she clamped her hand over Dana's, pressing her fingers against the places that ached. "Yes. There. There. Oh God. Touch me, Dana, touch me. I want… I need…"

"I know." Dana lowered her head to Emory's breast and took her nipple into her mouth. She sucked, playing her tongue over the smooth, firm tip while she traced one finger around the echoing hardness below. Emory's clitoris strained, ready to burst. She pressed, circled. "Here?"

"Yes," Emory choked. "Yes."

Dana kissed her way up the center of Emory's throat to her mouth, circling her fingers faster between Emory's legs.

"Dana," Emory breathed in wonder. "Oh Dana."

Dana kissed her as she cried out, drinking her pleasure as she poured out her passion. Emory's cries dwindled to soft sighs, but her clitoris remained full and throbbing. Dana slid inside her, felt her muscles tighten, and stroked the still-hard prominence with her thumb. Emory's thighs tensed.

"I...Dana...oh," Emory stuttered as she pushed down against Emory's hand. "I'm going to come again."

Dana rubbed her cheek over Emory's breast, feeling her heart hammer against her ribs. "I know. Let it go. Let it go, baby."

"Oh God," Emory cried.

When Emory quieted, Dana eased onto her side and pulled Emory close, her fingers still inside her. "Okay now?"

Emory snuggled her face in the curve of Dana's neck, her arms draped bonelessly over Dana's body. "I've never felt anything like that in my life."

"Good start, then."

"Oh, very good start. Perfect." Emory kissed Dana's throat. "I'm sorry. I think I'm falling asleep."

"That's okay."

"Don't you need to..." Emory faltered, trying hard to think but her mind was so hazy. "Are you excited? Do you need..."

Dana kissed Emory's forehead. "Yes. I am. But it will keep."

"For how long?"

Dana laughed. "Until the next time."

"'S wonderful," Emory muttered. "Wonderful."

"Go to sleep now." Dana rested her cheek against Emory's head. She didn't want to go to sleep. She didn't want to waste a moment of this night. This night that, no matter what followed, marked the beginning of the rest of her life.

CHAPTER TWENTY-TWO

Monday

Cam rolled over, trying not to wake Blair, and checked the bedside clock. The alarm was due to go off in two minutes. Blair slept with her back to Cam's front, her hips cushioned in the curve of Cam's pelvis. Cam shifted closer and wrapped her arm around Blair's midsection. When she kissed the side of Blair's neck, Blair murmured and drew Cam's hand to her breast. The nipple hardened and Blair sighed.

"Baby," Cam murmured, "we need to get up."

"Can we cheat?"

Cam laughed. "We could, but I don't trust those reporters not to show up early. I'd prefer to have clothes on when they arrive."

Grumbling, Blair rolled onto her back and pulled Cam down for a kiss. "Quickies like last night are nice, but I'm getting that *wanting you to make love to me for an hour* feeling."

"If you hadn't put me to sleep quite so efficiently last night, I would have taken care of that for you."

Blair grinned. "I love knocking you out. It makes me feel virile."

"Virile, huh?" Cam smoothed her hand down Blair's belly and brushed her fingers between her legs. She was wet. "Not the first thought that comes to my mind."

"I meant like potent and powerful." Blair tilted her hips and opened her legs. "Five minutes. Five minutes to take the edge off until we can steal a couple of hours to ourselves."

Cam settled against the pillows. "Come up here."

Blair got to her knees and straddled Cam's chest. When Cam cupped her ass and guided her down, she closed her eyes and took the pleasure only Cam could give her.

❖

Matheson wrapped his thin thermal blanket around his rifle and buried it in the snow at the base of a forked pine. He wouldn't need it for the close-in action he had planned, and the extra few seconds it would buy him *not* to tip off the agents guarding his quarry would be vital. Next he secured the extra ammo clips for his automatic in the pockets of his jacket. Then he chewed a K-ration bar and observed the shift change taking place at the rear of the cabin. Every four hours throughout the night, the agents had changed. Now an agent in winter BDUs made his way around the side path to the back deck, climbed the steps, and stopped next to the hot tub to speak to the woman who had had the last watch. Matheson smiled, thinking about the hot tub scene. Best surveillance duty he'd ever had. He couldn't radio his second with an update yet because the Secret Service would have monitoring devices to pick up any transmissions in the area. He estimated he would have five seconds before the agent outside Blair Powell's back door realized what he had planned.

❖

Emory sat up in bed and ran her hand over the empty place beside her. The space was still warm. She heard water running in the bathroom and relaxed. Dana hadn't left. The bathroom door opened, and when Dana emerged, naked, Emory smiled. "Hi."

Dana slid back in bed and kissed Emory. "Hi. How's your morning going?"

"It's different."

"How so?" Dana's tone was light but she looked worried. "Morning-after regrets?"

"No." Emory ran her fingers through Dana's hair. "But I have never been at such a loss as to what I should say. Or do."

"Anything bothering you?" Dana propped her head on her elbow and caressed Emory's shoulder and arm with the other hand.

"Not that I can think of, although my mind is a little fuzzy still." Emory stroked Dana's hip.

"Sleep okay?"

"In between waking up to have sex with you?" Emory shook her head, not quite believing how many times she'd come and amazed that she wanted to again, already. "I feel great. Should I apologize for not letting you get any sleep?"

"Hardly. Everything about last night was fantastic." Dana dipped her head to kiss Emory's breast, then rolled her tongue lazily around the swiftly hardening nipple. When Emory moaned and held her head more tightly to her breast, Dana ignited, just as she had every time Emory had reached for her in the night. Emory was magic in bed. As wary as Emory was out of bed, she was equally unreserved in it. She asked for what she wanted and seemed to delight in pleasuring Dana, leaving Dana endlessly hungry for her. Dana moved to the other nipple while continuing to toy with the one she had abandoned.

"You make it really really hard for me to think," Emory complained weakly. Needing more contact, aching for Dana in a way she had never before experienced, she pulled Dana on top of her. She kissed her, fusing their centers while massaging the strong muscles in Dana's shoulders and back. "Oh God, that's good."

Dana braced herself on her arms, thrusting harder and faster between Emory's legs. Emory's nails dug into her skin, raked the length of her back, and clutched at her ass. Emory's eyes flew open and the awe and pleasure skating across her face made Dana's clit swell and pulse.

She groaned.

"Oh, you're going to come, aren't you," Emory said, wrapping her legs harder around Dana's hips. "I love it when you...oh. God... I'm..."

"You too." Dana gasped and her eyes slammed shut. "Oh Christ."

They clung to one another, straining, shivering, crying out. Then Dana's arms folded and she collapsed into Emory's embrace. Emory stroked her hair, the back of her neck, her shoulders.

"I love what you do to me," Emory whispered.

"You kill me."

Emory smiled, physically satisfied and supremely content. She thought about what she'd said last night, that if she made love to Dana, kept control, she wouldn't lose herself. How foolish she had been. She hadn't been able to keep Dana out of any part of herself. She hadn't known what true need was until Dana had awakened it in her, and answered it. "God, I don't know what I'm going to do."

Dana raised her head, a frown forming between her brows. "About what?"

Emory traced Dana's mouth with her fingers. "About you. About this hunger I have for you."

"It's new for me too," Dana said. "But last night feels like a beginning. I'm not going anywhere." She glanced at the clock and grinned ruefully. "Well, not permanently. But I have to go now."

"Work?"

"'Fraid so." Dana rolled out of bed.

Emory missed her immediately.

"I have a pre-press interview scheduled with Blair, and if I don't get going, I'll be late." Dana kissed Emory quickly and grabbed her clothes before she gave in and did what she wanted to do, which was taste her and tease her and make her come again. And again. She pulled on her jeans and T-shirt. "Can I see you later? Alone."

"Yes." When Dana leaned down for another kiss, Emory curled an arm around her neck and, unable to stop at just a light kiss, plunged into her mouth, drinking her in. When she let her go, she knew she would ache for her for hours. "But I can't promise I won't attack you the instant I see you."

"I'll hold you to that." Dana ran a hand through her hair and shook her head. "Jesus. I really don't want to go."

Emory yanked the covers up to her chin and clutched them to her body. "Go now. Go, or I'm going to drag you back down here and I'm not going to let you up again today."

Dana backed away, her eyes devouring Emory. "Think about me."

"You have no idea." Emory sighed. "I haven't been able to think about anything else since the moment I saw you."

Dana slipped out the bedroom door and Emory collapsed into the pillows. Her body was in turmoil, but her mind was as clear and calm as it had ever been. For the first time in her life, she didn't have to understand something to know it was right.

❖

Matheson watched Cameron Roberts stride down the path toward the lodge just as another agent he didn't recognize headed toward the cabin. That made three agents stationed somewhere in the vicinity of the cabin. He was neither surprised nor deterred. The president's daughter was never alone, but there were usually fewer people around her while she was in her private quarters than out in public. That's why he had organized the first strike on her loft. This cabin wasn't much different. The main lodge was crawling with agents, and according to the White House press bulletin the previous day, a press conference was scheduled later on in the morning. His window of opportunity to get to her was very small, and would never be perfect. Fortunately, surprise was on his side. And of course, so was God. If he'd wanted to kill her, she'd be dead by now. For the moment, at least, he would attempt to deliver what his foreign friends had requested. He removed the Glock from its holster and set off into the woods. If he approached the cabin from the side farthest from the lodge, he would be invisible most of the way.

He drew in a deep breath of sharp mountain air. It was a great day for a hunt.

❖

"Morning," Dana said to Paula Stark as she climbed the steps to Blair's cabin. She indicated the door. "I'm expected."

"Morning." Stark knew the day's schedule, including the media circus that was planned for noon. Nightmare was more like it. Controlling traffic up and down the mountainside was going to be a challenge, and despite ID checks and required press passes, limiting Blair's exposure to the press and the curious was essentially impossible. Short of keeping Blair inside, absolute security was unattainable. Nevertheless, it was Stark's job to provide just that. "She's waiting."

"Thanks." Dana knocked and Blair answered immediately. "I hope I'm not too early."

Blair smiled. "You're right on time. Come on in. I just put fresh coffee on."

Dana stepped through the door and removed her jacket. She'd barely had time to grab a shower, pull on fresh jeans, a T-shirt, and pullover before rushing back to Blair's. When she had passed Emory's cabin, it took all her willpower not to detour for just a minute. She'd resisted because she knew that a minute was not going to be enough, and she could hardly keep the president's daughter waiting. Nevertheless, she couldn't help wondering if Emory had gone back to sleep, curled around the memory of their night together. Pushing away the images that threatened to stir her up and wreak havoc on her concentration, she indicated the coat tree. "May I?"

"Of course." Blair headed back toward the kitchen. "Hungry? I've got bagels to go with that coffee."

"Sold."

As Dana followed, she heard a thump on the back porch. Snow sliding off the roof, most likely. A new storm had blown in sometime before dawn, and already several new inches had accumulated on the path.

❖

The guard on the rear deck jerked to attention when a figure appeared around the corner of the cabin. Without hesitating, he stepped forward, his hand sliding inside his jacket. "That's far enou…"

Matheson raised the pistol and fired. Blood blossomed on the agent's forehead, and he fell. Before the body landed, Matheson reared back, kicked the back door open, and vaulted into the kitchen.

"Good morning," he said pleasantly as he leveled his gun on the first daughter. "Is that coffee I smell?"

"Who are you?" Blair quickly backed up into the doorway, hoping to shield Dana from the intruder's line of sight. If he didn't see her, Dana might have a chance to get out. She judged the distance to his gun hand. Not enough room for a roundhouse kick, but with luck a well-placed snap kick might work.

Before Blair could try, Matheson rushed her, spun her around toward the living room, and shoved her with a fist to the middle of her back. "Move."

Blair shouted a warning to Dana before crashing into an end table. Matheson clubbed Dana in the temple. As she fell, the front door burst open. Stark raced inside, shouting into her transmitter, her gun sweeping the room.

Matheson opened fire.

❖

As the red-alert signal came over her receiver, Patrice Hara jumped up from the small dining room table, knocking her coffee cup to the floor. "Greg!"

Wozinski crashed through the double doors from the kitchen. "I heard it!"

"Someone advise Commander Roberts!" Patrice raced for the door.

Seconds later, she and Wozinski sprinted down the snow-covered path toward Blair's cabin. Vaughn ran up the trail toward them from the far side of Blair's cabin. Patrice shouted into her radio. "Stark? Julio? Status?"

"Jesus," Wozinski panted when his receiver remained silent. "Where are they?"

Patrice caught movement out of the corner of her eye and pivoted, her gun extended. Cameron Roberts ran toward them over the hard-packed snow in her shirtsleeves, her weapon out, her face a study of eerie calm.

"Report?" Cam barked, never slowing her pace.

"Don't know." Patrice stepped aside as the commander barreled past, then rushed to catch up. "I got an interrupted transmission from... oh Jesus."

Everyone except Cam skidded to a halt. Blair stood framed in the doorway of the cabin. A man in winter BDUs stood behind her, watching them approach. He held an automatic pistol to Blair's temple.

"Hara, Wozinski, stay back," Cam shouted, halting at the foot of the path that led to Blair's cabin. Then she leveled her weapon on the man in the doorway. Matheson. At last. "Let her go."

Matheson smiled. "I don't think so."

Cam's head felt like it might explode. She was going to kill him for touching Blair. Not now. Later. She would kill him later. She forced back the terror at the sight of the gun against Blair's head. Not like Janet—Blair, not Janet. Blair. He would not take Blair. Cam eased slowly forward in the unblemished snow, one step at a time, her weapon steady in a two-handed grip. "What do you want?"

"That's far enough." Matheson pushed the gun barrel into Blair's temple, and Blair winced, coming up on her toes to relieve the pressure.

Cam was close enough to see the expression in Blair's eyes. Fear, yes, but above all, fury. Good, Blair would need that anger to keep her head clear. Cam halted. *Dead man. You're a dead man.*

"What do you want?" Cam repeated calmly. If he'd wanted Blair dead, he would have shot her and been long gone.

"Tell the president to expect a call."

"I can help you get what you want." Cam took another cautious step forward. Twenty yards. She was good at twenty yards, but not good enough. Always trade for something. She would have to break a few rules, but this was Blair. "Let's work together here."

"Why should I do that? I hold all the power." He looped an arm around Blair's neck and jerked her against his chest, shielding his body further. "I have her."

"You know how it works," Cam said, playing to his ego. "Show of good faith. You give me something, I make a call to the right person."

"And what would you want?"

"I need to come inside. Then I'll make some calls."

"No," Blair cried, her voice muffled from the pressure of Matheson's arm on her throat.

Matheson laughed. "We've got enough people inside already."

"Then I'll trade places with her. I'll be a lot more useful to you than her. I know who holds the power in Washington. Do you really think it's her father?" Cam laughed and took another step. Almost close enough. If she could just draw his fire. She was counting on her team to have gotten someone into position with a sniper rifle. "Me for her."

Blair struggled in Matheson's grip and cried out when he fisted his hand in her hair, yanking her head back. His expression hardened. "Maybe everyone will feel more inclined to be helpful if I put a bullet in her."

"All right, all right," Cam shouted. "If you hurt her, you'll have nothing to bargain with."

"I've got a lot to bargain with. One of your agents is bleeding out on the floor just inside," Matheson said conversationally. "And I've got

another one who's going to have quite a headache if she ever comes to."
He smiled. "I've got plenty of currency."

"You know what I'm talking about," Cam said, standing rigid, her gun still trained on him. She didn't raise her voice, but it carried through the clear cold air like steel slicing flesh. "Hurt her, and God Almighty could be in that room and it won't save you."

"What makes you think God isn't in this room?" Matheson dragged Blair backward into the cabin. At the last instant, he turned his gun on Cam.

Blair's scream was lost in the sound of gunfire.

CHAPTER TWENTY-THREE

For the span of a heartbeat, Cam stood her ground with bullets singing around her head, praying for a one split-second glimpse of Matheson's unprotected body. But the bastard was smart, and he held Blair so close that only an inch or two of head and torso was visible. She was a good shot, but not good enough to risk Blair's life. Cam held for another heartbeat, petitioning the universe to bend to the force of her will, but it would not yield. She dove to the ground chest first, barely registering the pain lasering through her bruised ribs. When silence fell, she rolled to her knees, breathing hard, and trained her weapon on the closed cabin door. She wanted to storm the cabin, she wanted to be in that room with her hands around Matheson's neck. She wanted to shout that if he hurt her, if he so much as *touched* her again, she would tear his still-beating heart from his chest with her bare hands.

"Commander," Hara called from somewhere behind Cam. "Commander, take cover, for God's sake."

Cam stood up, her gaze riveted to the cabin, and slowly backed away. Take cover. What kind of cover did Blair have inside that cabin with a maniac? When Cam reached the trail in front of the cabin and saw no activity from inside, she holstered her weapon and sought out her people, who had taken positions in the trees around the clearing. Hara and Wozinski had been joined by the other members of Blair's security detail along with Steph and the rest of Tanner's team. All told, a dozen formidable professionals. Someone, probably Hara, had deployed them to cover the cabin should Matheson try to escape, with or without the hostages.

Cam needed to formulate a counterattack. Matheson was going to move fast, and he had the advantage as long as Blair was alive. That he intended to kill her was a given. At some point, Blair would no longer have value as bargaining currency, and then Matheson would execute her. Cam had only one option—kill him before he ever had that chance.

"Steph," Cam said, "put your best sniper on that door. Put another on the rear. I want only you, me, and Hara to have a channel to them. I give the go."

"Yes, ma'am."

"Make sure we have a tight perimeter on the cabin. Then evacuate the other cabins, get everyone into the lodge, and post someone on all the entrances. No one leaves without my say-so."

"On it." Steph spoke into a throat mic as she ran toward the closest cabin.

"Hara."

"Commander?"

"I need aerial surveillance. Have Wozinski contact the president's advance team in town and tell them we're canceling the press conference because we need extra time to secure the road up here. Do *not* apprise them of the situation here. Then put Greg and one of Steph's long-range shooters into the air in our bird."

"Yes, ma'am." Hara started away.

"Hara," Cam said.

Hara looked back. "Ma'am?"

"If I go down, you have the command." Cam stared at the cabin. "He's going to try to move her. Soon. He's going to come out and she's his ticket to freedom. Do not let him put her in a vehicle. Give the sniper the green light to fire at will."

"Understood." Hara's voice was raspy with tension.

Hara disappeared and Cam signaled for one of Steph's men to take up the position that Hara had vacated. Then she went in search of Mac Phillips. She found him hunkered down behind a boulder, an assault rifle trained on the cabin. "Stark's down."

"Could you tell—"

"Status unknown." Cam fisted her hands. "Dana Barnett's in there too. That's all we know."

"Jesus."

"Do you have people on the back?"

"Two teams."

"Good. Who was on the back door?"

"Julio." Mac shook his head without taking his eyes off the cabin. "There's a body on the porch. Must be him. No way Matheson could have gotten past him unless he took him out."

"I agree." Cam's head was buzzing, her instincts were at war. Her heart and a good part of her mind screamed for her to get Blair out now, get Blair away from him, get Blair to safety. But her training demanded she be calm and dispassionate—assess the situation, plan for contingencies, and ultimately, execute a counterattack. The Secret Service did not *re*act, it acted. She could not allow Matheson to dictate the plays. She knew that. But she wanted to be inside that cabin with Blair more than she had ever wanted anything in her life, and she didn't care if she died trying. Not the way she needed to be thinking. She closed her eyes and directed every bit of willpower she possessed into resurrecting her professional shields. She would do this by the book, until she had no other choice.

"You think he's alone?" Mac asked.

"Looks that way. So far." Cam's nerves settled as she focused on the problem. "No covering fire when any of us took position, and these kind of guys don't pass up a ready target. Besides, I think the only way he could have gotten this close without being detected was to come alone or with one or two others."

"Bold plan but makes sense."

"The lone gunman," Cam said bitterly. "The hardest to defend against. Christ, he could have skied to within a hundred yards of here from almost anywhere on the mountain and we wouldn't have known."

"What does he want?"

"What do any of these fanatics want? Someone to listen to them. The semblance of power." She raked a hand through her hair. She was afraid it was more than mere political fanaticism this time. She feared his true target was Blair and always had been. Her shirt, wet from her dive into the snow, had frozen and chafed her skin. She shivered. "He'll tell us soon enough. In the meantime, I need you back inside the lodge.

Set up a command post and monitor any and all transmissions in or out of this area."

"With respect, Commander, I think I'll be of more use out here. Maybe you should take the inside—"

"No," Cam snapped. "He's got partners somewhere. He wouldn't walk into this if he didn't have someone on the outside waiting to help him disappear. The more we know, the more we limit his options. I don't want him to think he's in charge."

"Right. Okay." Mac looked uncomfortable. "Are you going to call for backup?"

Cam shook her head. "We have all the people we need right here, and I know just how good they are. We bring in hostage rescue or a spec ops team and we'll have chaos. I'm not putting him under that kind of pressure. Not with our people inside that cabin with him." *Not with his gun on Blair.*

When Mac looked like he would say more, Cam cut him off. She knew she'd probably lose her creds over the decision. That didn't matter. Nothing mattered except getting Blair and the others out. "What's Valerie and Renée's ETA?"

"They should be landing right about now."

"Good. Go ahead and brief them, then I want to see them both." Cam scanned the area, checking to be sure she had people in appropriate vantage points. "Double-check that everyone has radios and put them on delta frequency. Then get back to the lodge, Mac." She tore her eyes from the cabin and met his. "That's where I need you. I need to know what he's doing. I'm blind out here."

"Yes ma'am." Mac crouched, ready to move away, but still he hesitated. "I'll send a vest and a dry shirt down for you."

"I'm okay."

"You might be out here for a while."

Wordlessly, Cam nodded. She would be here until Blair was safe. Time was immaterial.

❖

Emory had heard gunfire before. The first shot had brought her upright in bed as she struggled to make sense of the sound. She knew what it was but her conscious mind refused to embrace the idea. The second and third reports had followed closely on the first, and instinctively she'd rolled out of bed onto the floor, no longer able to deny the reality. The eerie silence that followed was more unnerving than the gunfire. Staying low, out of sight of the bedroom window, she quickly grabbed her clothes and jumped into the bathroom. Hastily, hands shaking, she pulled on jeans, a sweater, and boots. When she dared to peek out the window she saw armed figures moving at the edge of the woods, but she couldn't make out who they were. Heart hammering, she dashed into the main room and snatched her jacket and cell phone. She wished she had a gun. After the first attack on her life, she'd gotten a license and learned to shoot but she refused to carry a weapon. Despite the threats made against her, she did not want to answer violence and hatred with more violence. She wondered now if she had been wrong.

She knew she was safer inside the cabin than outside, and she knew that someone would come. Crouched on the floor behind the sofa, she hoped it would provide enough cover from an errant bullet. Waiting was the hardest thing she'd ever done.

When a sharp knock on the door was followed almost immediately by a voice calling, "Emory, it's Steph. Let me in," Emory jumped to her feet.

"What happened?" Emory asked anxiously as she held the door open just wide enough for Steph to slip inside.

"There's been an incident at Blair's. I need to get you and the others up to the lodge."

Emory grabbed Steph's arm. "What do you mean by incident? Is she hurt?"

A muscle in Steph's jaw bunched. "It's a hostage situation, Emory. I don't have much time. Let's go."

"Oh my God. Dana. Dana was supposed to meet with Blair. Is she there?"

"We're not sure who's in there."

Stunned, Emory glanced in the direction of the bedroom. Was it possible that less than an hour ago she and Dana had lain together in that bed, making love, talking about the next time? What if there was no next time? What if Dana never came back? Emory couldn't take it in.

Blood rushed from her head and her vision flickered. The room turned gray at the edges and she swayed. "This can't be. She was just here. We made lo—"

Steph grabbed Emory's arm to steady her. "Jesus, Emory. I didn't know about you two. I'm sorry."

"It's…we're…new." Angry at herself for almost falling apart, Emory shook her head. She clenched her hands until her fingers ached. Better. "What can you tell me?"

"Until we get a head count up at the lodge, we won't know for sure who's with Blair. The perp said someone was unconscious. It might be Dana."

"What's going to happen?" Emory asked urgently as Steph opened the door and guided her outside with an arm around her and her gun at the ready. Now that they were outside, Emory could see agents shielded by boulders and trees ringing Blair's cabin.

"We're going to get this guy," Steph said resolutely. "Trust us."

Emory wasn't used to relying on others to take care of what was important to her. And Dana was very important to her. "I know how to shoot. I practice at the range regularly. I can help."

"You've never shot a person." Steph led Emory quickly up the path toward the lodge. "It's a lot different than a paper target."

"He's hurt my friends. I won't hesitate."

Steph indicated the back door of the lodge. "You're the only doctor we have. We might need you. See if you can put together an aid station."

Emory watched Steph hurry away. It wasn't enough. Caring for the wounded, no matter how necessary, was not going to assuage the terrible anger that roiled in her chest. But doing what she *could* do might keep her from imagining Dana hurt. Dana had to be all right. They had just begun—only hours before she had held her, loved her. Emory refused to believe she would never have another chance.

Matheson shoved Blair toward the sofa. "Sit down."

Blair hesitated. She wouldn't have very many opportunities to get herself out of this, and she didn't have much time. Stark lay slumped on the floor just inside the door. Blair couldn't tell how many times she'd been hit, but a dark pool of blood spread out beneath her body from an obvious bullet wound in her left thigh. She appeared to be unconscious, but Blair wasn't certain. Dana lay face down where she'd fallen after Matheson had clubbed her. Either one of them could be mortally injured, and she wasn't going to stand by and watch them die.

As if reading her thoughts, Matheson said, "If you make a move anywhere except where I tell you to move, I'll shoot one of them."

"She needs attention," Blair said, pointing to Stark. "At least let me see if I can slow down the bleeding."

Matheson didn't answer as he collected Stark's gun, tucked it into the waistband at the small of his back, and sidled next to the front window. With his eyes and his gun still on Blair, he felt for the cord and yanked the drapes closed. Then he stepped over Stark and nudged Dana's shoulder with his boot. When she didn't respond, he shoved and she rolled onto her back with a groan. Matheson flicked a glance at Blair. "Who's this?"

Blair said nothing, and Matheson kicked Dana in the ribs. Blair shot forward as Dana moaned. "Leave her alone."

"I'd stop right there," Matheson said coldly. He pointed the gun at Dana's head. "One more step, and I won't care who she is."

"She's a friend of mine."

"She's not carrying, so she's not an agent." Matheson motioned Blair back to the couch. "Sit *down.*"

Dana opened her eyes, blinked, and lifted her head enough to look around the room. Her expression darkened when she saw Stark. "Christ." She pushed herself to her knees, coughed a few times, and finally focused on Matheson. "I don't think we've met."

He laughed. "Welcome to the party. Who the hell are you?"

"The name's Barnett." She glanced at Blair. "I guess he's not a friend of yours."

"Not exactly."

"Letting a federal agent die isn't a very good idea." Dana got slowly to her feet, swaying slightly. She pressed a hand to her rib cage. "How about I take a look at her?"

Matheson motioned with his gun toward Stark. "I want you over there anyhow. On the floor, next to her. If you want to put your hand over the hole in her leg, be my guest."

Dana inched carefully in Stark's direction, her eyes on Matheson.

Then she knelt and worked her pullover over her head, exposing the white T-shirt she wore underneath. Pressing the balled-up garment against Stark's thigh, she said, "She's bleeding at a pretty good clip. How about if I drag her out onto the porch so someone can get her to a medic." She leveled her gaze at Matheson. "You can watch me through the doorway. If I try to run, you can shoot me."

"Thanks for the permission. She stays."

"I'm the one you want," Blair said. "I'm all you need, and you know it. Let Dana take the agent outside. There's no reason she has to die."

"You might be crazy enough to try coming after me," Matheson said to Blair. "But if you know I'm going to shoot one of your friends if you so much as sneeze wrong, you just might behave. They stay."

Blair glanced at Dana. "I'm sorry about this."

"I'm not." Dana held pressure on Stark's leg but kept her focus on Matheson. "Look, I'm an investigative reporter. You must have an important story to tell. Why don't you tell me, starting with what you want."

Matheson regarded her with interest. "You might be useful, but I'm not sure I'll be here long enough to tell you the story." He smiled and pulled a cell phone from his pocket. "Ms. Powell and I are going for a ride to meet some of *my* friends."

Chapter Twenty-four

Minutes, hours, the arbitrary measures of existence had no relevance for Cam. All that mattered to her was the woman inside the cabin. She, *she* was the touchstone, the focus, the foundation of Cam's life. Until Blair was free, nothing affected her—not the cold, not hunger, not fatigue, not the pain in her bruised ribs or the cramps in her muscles from remaining motionless for so long. When she heard the crunch of footsteps on snow behind her, she didn't turn. She kept her eyes and her weapon trained on the door that separated her from her world.

"Requesting permission to relieve Agent Hara," Renée Savard said stiffly.

Cam glanced at her long enough to see that she carried an assault rifle. "Mac informed you we have a hostage situation?"

"Yes. He said you'd brief me on the details." Renée stared at the cabin. "Egret. Is she injured?"

"Not so far."

Renée drew a shuddering breath. "Mac said Paula was on duty."

"Yes."

"Do we know her status?"

"No." Cam wanted to comfort her, but it wasn't the time. For either of them. "But we think she's injured."

"Gunshot?"

"Probably." Cam spared her another quick glance, taking in the pallor beneath her normally golden skin and her wildly dilated pupils. Her stress level was off the charts. "There's a civilian inside too. Dana Barnett."

"How long are we going to wait?"

"Not long," Cam said grimly. "And I can't afford to have an agent out here who I can't trust to follow my orders."

"I'm all right, Commander."

"And if I tell you that Egret is your priority, your *only* priority?"

Renée gave a short, curt laugh. "Paula would kick my ass if I handled it any other way."

"Take Hara's place. Tell her she will lead the rear team and to check their positions. I want them as close as they can get."

"Yes ma'am." Renée pivoted, then stopped. "He doesn't deserve to leave here alive."

"I didn't hear that. Take your post, Agent. Go."

Silence fell. Sunlight glinted on the pure white snow and Cam blinked to clear her vision in the blinding glare. She agreed with Renée about Matheson's fate, but she couldn't give Renée permission to carry out an action that might later weigh heavily on her conscience—or at the very least end her career. Cam had no such concerns. Matheson had made it personal when he sent a team to assassinate Blair, and she would readily bear the responsibility for delivering justice.

Valerie leaned into the back of the lead Suburban and pulled out a flak vest. Mac had given her a thumbnail sketch of what had transpired when she, Renée, and Felicia arrived. She'd traveled from Manhattan in jeans and boots so all she'd needed to do was exchange her coat for a heavy black sweater she had packed in her luggage. She clipped her holster to her right hip and unlocked the ammunition compartment in the rear of the vehicle. She touched her com link. "Mac, have someone collect all the XM84s from the vehicles."

"Roger."

Straightening, she gripped her vest in one hand and a rifle in the other. When she turned, she found Diane, her arms wrapped tightly around herself, watching her. Despite her heavy, knee-length winter coat, Diane looked frozen. "You shouldn't be out here."

"I heard you were back." Diane glanced down the slope toward the cabins. "I know you need…I imagine you…God, I can't imagine what it is you need to do right now. I know it isn't talking to me, but…"

Valerie quickly strode forward while shifting her rifle beneath the arm which held her vest, and pulled Diane against her. She kissed her, hard, almost desperately. Then she stepped back. "Mac told me you were all right and inside the lodge. I don't have any time, darling. I need you to go back inside. I need you safe."

"I love you," Diane said urgently. "You understand me? I love you. Please, please be careful."

"I love you too. I'll be back as soon as we get our people out." Valerie smiled softly. "Go back inside now. You're cold."

"I'll see you in a little while," Diane said, gripping Valerie's hand. "I *will* see you."

"Yes." Valerie backed away, carefully securing Diane's image in the private place deep inside that comforted her. Then she cleared her mind of love, of fear, of uncertainty, of anything that could distract or deter her, and went in search of Cam.

❖

Cam made the call she knew had to be made.

"Lucinda Washburn."

"Lucinda, it's Cameron Roberts. You need to advise the president's security detail to go to priority one immediately."

"Why?"

"At oh seven thirty this morning Matheson killed an agent, shot another, entered Blair's cabin, and took her hostage. I have no indication that this is a part of a larger operation, but we can't discount it either."

"Hold on." After several seconds of silence, Lucinda returned. "A solitary gunman?"

"Yes."

"What does he want?"

"I don't know yet, but he clearly plans to negotiate for Blair's freedom. I suspect he'll want to talk to the president."

"Is she hurt?"

"No," Cam said gruffly, forcing the image of Matheson's gun against Blair's temple from her mind.

"I can have a strike team from—"

"No. I have teams in place. I don't need more people. Right now he thinks he has the upper hand, and I want to keep it that way."

"She's the president's daughter. We have to respond with force."

"Don't you think I know who she is?" Cam took a deep breath, trying to rein in her temper. "You can't send me anyone more qualified than the people I have here. We're all trained for this. Just make sure that the president is protected."

"I intend to. I want updates. I can't promise you anything else right now. The president and his security adviser will have to be notified at the very least."

"I can promise you this," Cam said. "I'm not letting anyone jeopardize Blair's safety."

"That may not be your call to ma—"

Cam clicked off her phone and shoved it into her pants pocket.

❖

Stark clawed her way to awareness through a thick fog of pain. Her chest burned with every breath and her left leg screamed in agony. The bastard had shot her. Her heart couldn't beat any faster, but a surge of sick apprehension washed through her. *Blair.* She groaned and tried to sit up. She managed to prop herself up a few inches.

"Stay still."

Stark struggled to focus. Dana Barnett leaned over her, her mouth set in a grim line.

"Blair?"

"She's okay," Dana murmured.

Stark's strength deserted her and she collapsed back to the floor. She tried to piece the fragments of images she could recall into a picture that made sense. A gunman had breached their line. Back door. She jerked at the realization that the gunman had to have taken out at least one agent. She groaned and struggled to rise again.

"Don't," Dana insisted. "Don't give him a target."

"What...what does he want?"

"Something I can do for you?" Matheson said from a few feet away.

"She wants to know what you want," Dana said, keeping pressure on Stark's leg as she looked over her shoulder at the man who stood equidistant between her and Blair. If they rushed him simultaneously, he would probably only be able to shoot one of them. However, she couldn't be sure which one it would be, and she didn't want to risk the first daughter being gunned down. She caught Blair's eye and had a feeling Blair was thinking the same thing. "I told you I'm a reporter."

"I recognize your name now. You're good."

"Then now is your chance to say what you want to say."

"First there's a little business transaction that I have to take care of." Matheson punched a number on his cell phone and waited a few seconds. "Phase One completed. I'll await the call."

He hung up, pocketed his phone, and leaned with his back against the stone fireplace, his gaze alternating between Dana and Blair. "Let me start by saying I'm a patriot."

"Yes," Dana said, careful to keep her tone neutral. "I can see that."

❖

"Cameron." Valerie crouched down, her shoulder touching Cam's. She rested her rifle against the boulder that provided them partial cover.

"Hello, Valerie."

"How long has it been?"

"Thirty-two minutes," Cam said without looking at her watch. "Is everyone secured at the lodge?"

"Yes. No secondary force?"

"None that I've seen. I have a feeling he plans to deliver her to whoever wants to use her as a bargaining chip. Otherwise, he would have taken her out already."

"I agree. Up until today, his agenda has been assassination, not kidnapping."

Cam registered the pressure of Valerie's arm against hers and felt an infusion of strength—unsought but freely given. Her next breath came just a little easier. "Any ideas on who's pulling his strings?"

"Foreign interests—probably working with Bin Laden, or allied factions."

Cam's stomach spasmed and she swallowed back a wave of nausea. She agreed. The stakes had been raised. Matheson was probably exactly what he appeared, a deranged but clever domestic terrorist whose alliance with those with far more destructive allegiances had turned him into a lethal adversary. "Recommendation?"

"Two four-man teams, flash-bangs followed by rapid entry."

"We have three hostages at risk." What Cam didn't have to say was that a rescue attempt would likely result in casualties. Even given the five to six seconds of overwhelming disorientation Matheson was likely to experience in the chaos created by a million candlewatt flash of light and a 175 decibel bang, he was certain to open fire. Probably indiscriminately. The assault team would have body armor, but none of the hostages would. "He'll try to take them out."

"If we let him leave here with her, her chance of survival drops drastically. Right now, he's on our turf and he's outgunned."

"He's counting on us not launching a counterattack. He'll kill her if we do, and he knows we know it."

Valerie said nothing. Cam wondered if she would make a different decision if the hostage Matheson was most likely to kill wasn't her lover. She didn't know. How could she? All she knew was what she felt right now. Helpless. Powerless. Afraid.

❖

Blair listened to Matheson talk, her mind rebelling at the insanity of his diatribe. How could anyone believe that mass murder was justifiable for any reason, let alone love of God and country? She had to remind herself that of course he didn't make sense, because he was a madman. The frightening thing was that he didn't look or really even sound crazy, until she absorbed his message of hatred and bigotry. She shivered, not from fear but revulsion.

Dana was amazing, drawing Matheson out with her questions and attention. Somehow she managed to engage him, making him feel as if what he had to say was very important. As if *he* were very important. As Blair watched and listened, she could see Matheson warm to his topic. His voice and face became more animated. He was truly terrifying in his utter sense of righteousness.

As they talked, Blair realized that Matheson's focus, even his body position, shifted more and more toward Dana. She had a feeling that Dana knew it too, and suddenly, she understood exactly what Dana Barnett was doing. Dana was making herself the target.

Blair suddenly feared Dana would try to draw Matheson's fire to give Blair a chance to get away. She couldn't let that happen. And it wasn't just Dana she was worried for. Paula continued to bleed and appeared to have lapsed into unconsciousness again. They were running out of time. Time.

Cam wouldn't wait much longer, Blair was certain of it. Cam would come for her, and when she did, she would be in danger. Too many in danger. Women she loved, men she respected, people risking their lives for her. No more. No more.

She took a breath, emptied her thoughts, prepared herself. She felt calm, at peace. This was right. As it should be. No one should stand between her and evil.

It was her fight, as it always had been. She was not going to let one more person die because of her. She would take him on herself before she let that happen. She eased along the sofa until she was poised on the end closest to him. The distance between them was about six feet. If she pushed off hard and fast and launched a flying kick, she would offer less of a target and she might be able to take him down before he got off more than one shot. If he hit her, the shot would probably be in her leg or shoulder—with luck, nowhere lethal.

Chapter Twenty-five

Cam's cell phone rang. "Roberts."

"We just received a call," Lucinda Washburn reported, "demanding the release of fourteen so-called political prisoners who are slotted to be transported from Afghanistan to a U.S. military holding facility in two days."

"Were you able to triangulate the location of the caller?"

"No, but it wasn't Matheson. Our language analysts all agree this man is Middle Eastern."

"What did he say about Blair?" Cam struggled with the frustration of being out of the loop. She hated relying on bureaucrats and desk jockeys. Lucinda was a great political strategist but she wasn't a field operative.

"He said…" Lucinda's voice cracked and she cleared her throat. "He said we had thirty minutes to agree to his requests. Once we agreed, he would wait twelve hours for us to release the prisoners."

"If you refuse?" A trickle of icy sweat ran down the back of Cam's neck. Despite the freezing temperatures, her hair was soaked with sweat and she had to keep rubbing her forearm across her face to clear her vision.

"Blair will be executed."

Cam knew it was coming but she still felt as if she'd been punched in the gut. "That doesn't make any sense. Matheson walked into a situation with no exit, and without Blair, he doesn't have a chance of getting out of that cabin alive."

"It's possible that Matheson and the individual negotiating for the foreign prisoners have different agendas. They may not be following the same game plan."

"Which makes the situation here all the more volatile."

"We don't have time to provide backup for you, other than the members of the president's advance security team who are already out there. I can call Tom—"

"No, I don't want them involved. I told you, we have the people." Cam squinted through the glare at the cabin. It looked empty, and yet it held everything. Everything. "Let me know if there's any further communication."

"Cam," Lucinda said, her voice losing its tight formality. "The president and I trust you to get her out. Whatever you need to do, get her out. Get them all out."

"I will."

Cam disconnected and said to Valerie, "The president has thirty minutes to agree to a prisoner exchange."

"Will he?"

"No."

Valerie touched Cam's sleeve. "Are you sure?"

"I'm sure." Cam laughed hollowly. "Blair would chew his butt off."

"I would imagine." Valerie tightened her grip on Cam's arm. "Matheson will have to move her. She's his way out of here."

"Yes."

"I want you to relinquish command to me now."

Cam's jaws clenched. "You know I can't—"

"You know it's what should be done." Valerie's gaze was steady and her eyes kind. "Trust me, Cameron, and let me do this for you. For both of you."

"They're my people," Cam whispered, wishing she could will herself into their place.

"I know that, but she's your heart. None of us can think clearly when our hearts are at stake."

"I have to go in."

Valerie smiled. "Of course you do. And you will."

Cam hesitated for what felt like an eternity, agonizing with the decision that would change the course of her life. And because she hesitated, for even a single heartbeat, she said, "Take the lead."

❖

Matheson interrupted his monologue to Dana when the phone in his jacket pocket started to ring. Watching Blair, he smiled as he answered. "Yes? I see. Forty minutes, then. Godspeed, Colonel."

Blair didn't dare risk looking in Dana's direction, and since Matheson's automatic was now pointed squarely at her own chest, she held her position. Sooner or later, he was going to want her to get up. Then she would have a chance, probably her only chance.

"It seems that your father doesn't think you're all that valuable," Matheson said.

Blair grinned with satisfaction. "I guess he said *no* to whatever you wanted."

"Call your girlfriend." Matheson tossed his cell phone to Blair, his expression one of distaste. "I have a message for her."

Blair hoped her hands weren't visibly shaking as she punched in Cam's number.

"Roberts."

"It's Blair, Cam." Blair wanted to say, *It's me, darling, I'm all right. Don't do anything crazy.* But she kept her voice neutral because she wouldn't give Matheson the satisfaction of listening to anything personal between them.

"Are you all right?"

"Yes, but Paula is hu—" She gasped as Matheson wrenched her hair back and yanked the phone from her hand at the same time. He pushed her down onto the sofa and held his gun on her.

"Listen carefully," Matheson said into the phone. "In twenty-five minutes I want one of your armored vehicles in front of this cabin. Don't tell me you can't get it down here, because I know you can."

Blair could barely make out the sound of Cam's voice, but just hearing the strong, steady timbre gave her hope. She strained to catch a few words.

"Too much…snow on…between here…parking lo—"

"You forget, I know what those vehicles are capable of. Twenty-five minutes. Back it up to the cabin with the driver's door level with the porch stairs."

"What abo…agent…get her."

Matheson laughed and glanced across the room at Paula and Dana.

"I don't think she's going to be of any use to either one of us before much longer."

"Let her go," Blair said quickly. "She's only going to slow us down."

Matheson ignored her. "The agent stays. Now you've got twenty-three minutes."

The instant he snapped his phone shut, Blair felt the separation from Cam as if someone had sliced part of her body away with a machete. Cam had sounded stressed and worried, but in command. God, she loved her. She wanted to tell her that again, touch her again. Love her again.

Her heart broke at the thought of Renée out there, not knowing what was happening to Paula. She must be out of her mind with worry. *She* was frantic that Cam was going to come charging in and get herself hurt. She didn't want Cam to come for her, although she knew she would. She couldn't live with losing Cam.

"Get over there next to your friends," Matheson said, taking up position with his back to the fireplace again. From that vantage point, he could easily keep all three of them in his sights.

Blair hurried over and knelt beside Dana. She brushed her hand over Paula's face. Her skin was cool, pale, clammy. When she pressed her fingers to Paula's throat, at first she couldn't find a pulse and a wave of panic crashed through her. Then she felt a faint, thready beat. She looked over her shoulder at Matheson. "She's lost too much blood. We need to get her some help. There's no need for her to die." She took a breath, accepting what she had to do. "Please. Let Dana take her outside. Let them go. I'll stay with you. I'll do whatever you say. You have my word."

Matheson laughed. "If you were a normal woman, I might believe you. But you're not, are you?" He checked his watch. "We don't have that much longer to wait. If she can't last that long, then it must be God's will."

❖

"Emory," Mac said as he stepped into the dining room, which had been designated the aid station, "we might need you in a few minutes.

Felicia will escort you if you have to leave the lodge. Here's a vest. Be sure to put it on and stay with Felicia, no matter what you see or hear."

"What's happening?" Emory braced one hand on the long table in the corner where she had assembled the medical supplies several agents had brought her. Fortunately, Blair's security team traveled with an impressive array of emergency equipment. She had antibiotics, pain medication, and intravenous fluids. Even blood substitute. Everything she needed to stabilize an injured patient, if she got to them quickly enough. The problem was, anyone seriously injured in that first round of gunfire was running out of time. She prayed it wasn't Dana, nearly choking on the guilt because she didn't want Paula or Blair to be injured either.

"Just be ready, okay?" Mac said gently.

Diane appeared in the doorway behind him, her face pale and haunted. "I saw people carrying weapons and other…things…heading toward the cabins. Are you going to get them out now?"

"You're supposed to stay away from the windows," Mac said sharply.

"Those are my friends down there!" Diane hugged herself. "Do you think I can just sit here and pretend nothing's happening?"

"I'm sorry," Mac said. "I have to go. Just stay in the interior of the house. We don't want any more wounded."

"I can't stand this," Diane cried as Mac disappeared. She slumped against the doorway. "I'm going out of my mind just waiting around, doing nothing."

"I'm with you." Emory's hands shook as she sorted through medication vials. "I'd rather be down there with a gun."

"God, me too, and I don't even know which end the bullet comes out." Diane laughed a little wildly. "I'm sorry, I know I should be better at this. I've actually been through this kind of thing before. Except… God, that bastard has Blair. And Paula and Dana…"

"They'll get them out," Emory whispered, the panic she had managed to hold at bay while planning for the injured rushing back.

"Hey!" Diane gripped Emory's shoulders. "You look terrible."

"I'm…I'm all right."

Diane peered at her. "No, you're not. Oh hell, it's Dana, isn't it."

Emory nodded.

"Oh, honey." Diane pulled her close. "What rotten timing. I can't even ask for the details yet."

"Later," Emory said, resting her cheek on Diane's shoulder and closing her eyes. The comfort felt wonderful. "When she's back, I'll tell you all about it."

"You'd better." Diane stroked Emory's hair. "She's so hot she makes my eyes ache."

Emory lifted her head, smiling tremulously. "Valerie is one of the most beautiful women I've ever seen in my life."

Diane's face softened. "She is, isn't she? I never thought I'd be this crazy in love with anyone."

"I know what you mean," Emory whispered. "I just want her back. God, I just want her back."

❖

"Bring the vehicle down," Valerie said into her mic.

Cam tensed as Valerie relayed orders, positioning the strike teams. Next to her, Savard's rapid breathing was punctuated by puffs of frozen air. "You okay?"

"Fine," Savard replied tersely.

"We'll have five seconds at most." As agreed, Valerie had made the decision, and when she had laid out the plan, Cam had concurred. She had given Valerie the lead because she trusted her, and because the only thing she could think about was getting inside that cabin. She couldn't be responsible for anything else. This one time, with everything at stake, she needed to be a player and not the one standing behind the lines directing the action. "I need you right on my shoulder when we take the door, Renée."

"I'll be there. I'm solid. Jesus, I just want to go." Savard shifted in the snow, her hands restless on her assault rifle.

"I know." Cam squeezed Savard's shoulder below the edge of the vest covering her black T-shirt. Neither of them wore coats. Her own shirt was wet under her vest. "So do I."

Under cover of the Suburban slowly grinding through the snow down the steep path from the parking lot above, two agents with XM84 flash-bangs crept alongside it, out of view of the cabin should Matheson look out the front window.

"Alpha team, go." Valerie's voice came through Cam's com link as the vehicle drew opposite Cam and Savard's position.

Cam whispered, "On me, Savard."

And then, finally, with her mind completely clear and every sense focused on only one thing, Cam raced toward the cabin, and Blair.

❖

Matheson edged the drape aside and peered out, grunting in apparent satisfaction. "Our ride is here."

Blair, on her knees by Paula, inched slowly forward until she was between Matheson and the others. "There's no way you're going to get all four of us into that vehicle. I told you I'll go with you—just leave Dana and Paula here."

"You *have* to go with me," Matheson said pleasantly, as if he were discussing plans for lunch. "You're driving." He lifted the automatic. "Your friends are coming. That way, I can be sure you don't try to be a hero. If you try to drive us into a tree, I'll shoot one of them. Barnett— it's your job to get the agent into the vehicle. If you can't manage it, I'll put her down like a wounded animal. Mercy killing."

"You have me." Dana's face clouded with anger. "Besides, I want to come. You owe me the rest of the story, and this is a scoop I don't want to miss. One extra hostage should be enough. For Christ's sake, leave her here."

"It's no wonder we don't let women serve in combat. You're all too busy taking care of each other to concentrate on the fight." Matheson gestured at Paula's unconscious form. "The two of you get her on her feet. When we move out, she's all yours, Barnett. Ms. Powell…you'll be accompanying me."

"Fine," Blair said. She would let him shoot her before she got into that vehicle with him. The farther away she got from Cam and the others, the less chance she would have.

Matheson's cell phone rang, and he smiled. "Saddle up."

Blair straightened and centered herself. The front door was five feet to her right. Matheson faced her off to the other side, just outside her kicking range. She'd have to hope he didn't shoot her the instant she lunged, because she needed that one extra step to reach him.

Matheson pulled his cell phone out of his pocket and flipped it open. "Yes?"

Blair was in midair when the front window shattered and the cabin rocked with an enormous explosion accompanied by a flash of brilliant white light. Her leg connected with something hard, but her mind was too scrambled to determine what it was. She heard gunfire, or maybe it was just the echo of that first blast resounding in her traumatized ears. Pain shot through the right side of her face and down her neck, and she suddenly couldn't breathe. Blinded, dizzy, lungs on fire, Blair arched her back, ignoring the crushing weight on her neck, and thrust both arms behind her. Then, she dropped to her knees and pulled with all her strength.

"Matheson!" Cam shouted, diving into the cabin, her rifle at shoulder height, frantically sweeping the space. Agents crashed through the back door, and the air exploded with yells. She pivoted, her finger tightening on the trigger as her heart stopped. Matheson grabbed Blair from behind, one beefy arm clamped across her throat, and lifted his weapon to her temple. Cam screamed "*No!*"

And then, in one of the most beautiful moves she had ever seen, Blair dropped into a forward shoulder throw, catapulting Matheson over her head and onto the floor in front of her. With an action born of instinct and years of training, Blair gripped his head in both hands and in one swift, fluid rotation of her torso, snapped his neck.

Chapter Twenty-six

C lear! Clear! Clear!"
     The air was charged with the smell of explosives and cloudy with residue. Cam ripped off her protective headgear and goggles and dropped to her knees by Blair's side. Lowering her weapon, she pulled Blair into her arms. "Are you all right?"

"Yes," Blair said breathlessly. "Paula—"

"We know. Emory's on her way. We'll get her to the hospital." Cam cradled Blair's head, her gaze darting over her face. A red welt marred her right temple where Matheson had jammed his weapon. She couldn't quite believe that she was holding her again. She rubbed Blair's arms with both hands, suddenly aware that Blair was shaking uncontrollably. "Did he hurt you? Baby, are you hurt?"

Blair glanced down at the inert form sprawled in front of them. Matheson lay on his back, his hands lax by his sides, his expression one of mild confusion. "No, I'm...I'm all right. But God, Cam, I think I—"

"Come on," Cam said, guiding Blair to her feet. She didn't need to check the body. She'd seen the signature jerk and twitch of his limbs when his spine had been severed. "Let's get out of here."

"I want to stay with Paula."

"As soon as the situation is under control, we'll go to the hospital." Cam brushed Blair's hair with her fingertips. Her hand was trembling. She wanted Blair out of that room, away from the death and the violence. She wanted so desperately to protect her from the ugliness and the hatred, and she couldn't. "I'm sorry. I can't let you leave the grounds yet. He may have a partner close by."

Blair wrapped her arms around Cam's waist and buried her face in the curve of Cam's neck. "I'm so glad to see you."

"God, baby. I love you." Cam stood in the midst of the milling crowd of agents and contract soldiers, rocking Blair, consoling them both. Valerie appeared in the doorway, the sunlight at her back, her face in shadow. Cam could feel her eyes upon them and she nodded her silent thanks. Valerie tipped her head in response. Then Valerie's throaty voice cut effortlessly through the clamor of the adrenaline-charged teams.

"We've got wounded here and potential hostiles still at large, troops. Alpha team—you're evac. Beta team—secure the scene."

As chaos gave way to order, Valerie approached. "Ms. Powell, do you need medical attention?"

Blair eased out of Cam's embrace, but kept her hand on Cam's hip. "No, thank you. Both Paula and Dana were injured."

"She should be looked at," Cam said.

Blair started to protest, but Valerie broke in. "I agree. But as long as it isn't urgent, I suggest you take her somewhere secure, Deputy Director."

Cam wrapped an arm around Blair's shoulders. "You're right. Thanks. If you need me for anything…"

Valerie smiled. "I'll keep you advised, of course."

As Blair and Cam started away, Valerie said softly, "Would you tell Diane I'll be a little longer?"

Blair turned back. "I'll let her know you're all right. And Valerie, thank you for…" She looked around the room. "For this."

"Not necessary," Valerie said, "but you're very welcome."

❖

"All clear," Felicia Davis said to Emory. "You can go in now."

Emory jumped from the Suburban that had pulled in line with the one in front of Blair's cabin and raced over the hard-packed snow to the porch. She leapt up the two steps and pushed through the open door. The main room was filled with men and women bristling with assault weapons. Just a few feet inside the door, Dana knelt by Paula

Stark, both hands pressed to Stark's left thigh while Renée Savard cradled the unconscious woman in her arms. Dana's face was streaked with blood and an egg-sized bruise distorted her left cheek. Her pale shirt was nearly black with blood, and for just a second, Emory was nearly consumed with panic. Then her mind registered that Dana was not seriously injured, and as much as Emory wanted to touch her, she couldn't. Not when Stark needed her more.

"It's okay, sweetie, it's okay," Savard crooned over and over, her lips to Stark's forehead, her face a mask of abject terror.

"We need a stretcher in here," Emory shouted to no one in particular as she crouched down. Dana gave her an anxious smile and Emory quickly smiled back before returning her attention to Paula. Her pulse was easily one-fifty and her skin was cold. "She's in shock." She raised her voice. "I need resuscitation fluid right now."

From beside her a man responded, "Here you go, Doc."

"Cut her jacket and shirt sleeves away," Emory ordered while she tore the plastic wrapping off IV tubing. Then she inserted plastic catheters in the veins in both of Paula's arms and connected the tubing to bags of fluid. "Pump these in. Then hang two more." She looked over her shoulder and saw a collapsible gurney just outside the door. "Do we have MAST trousers?"

"No," one of Tanner's team said. "Sorry, Doc."

Emory shook her head in frustration. "Let's move her, then." She inched closer to Dana. "How much is she bleeding?"

"Not much anymore," Dana said, keeping her voice low. "But she's bled a hell of a lot."

"How badly are you hurt?"

"Thump on the head. I've had worse."

"I want you to ride to the hospital and get checked out. I'm going to be busy with her for a while." Emory feathered her fingers over Dana's cheek, just below the bruise. "I was so worried about you. Don't disappear, all right? God, Dana, I need to see you."

"Just take care of her. I'll find you."

"Good. Don't forget." Then Emory stood. "Let me put a field dressing on that leg and then let's get the hell out of here."

❖

"I'm okay, Dad." Blair cradled the phone in one hand while stripping out of her jeans and sweater in the bedroom of Diane's cabin. "Really, I'm fine… What?"

At the sharp astonishment in Blair's voice, Cam took a step toward her, but Blair waved her away.

"Of course I'm not upset," Blair said adamantly. "I didn't expect you to do anything except what you did. God, Dad. You can't just give in to these fuckers."

Cam didn't care if Blair wanted to be held or not. She needed to hold her. When she put her arms around her, Blair sagged into her.

"I'm sorry," Blair said to her father, her voice shaking. "I'm a little strung out right now. I just want to get a shower. Here's Cam."

Blair broke away from Cam and held out the phone. "Tell him… whatever."

Cam waited until the bathroom door slammed shut and then sat on the edge of the bed. She was exhausted and keyed up at the same time. "Sir, it's Cameron Roberts."

"You're sure she's not hurt?" the president said.

"She's shaken up a bit, but uninjured."

"How bad was it?"

Cam closed her eyes. "Bad. Close call."

"I want a full report."

"Yes sir. Of course."

"You told Lucinda the threat was neutralized?"

Cam hesitated. She'd only told Lucinda in a quick phone call that Blair had been recovered, that they had injuries, and that Matheson was no longer a threat. She hadn't provided any details. She wasn't sure how much she wanted to tell the president about what had happened in that cabin.

As if reading her thoughts, Andrew Powell said, "I'm her father, Cam. This is between you and me."

"Blair killed him, hand to hand."

The president sighed. "Well. How is she taking it?"

"I don't know." Cam glanced toward the bathroom. Not being able to see her, even for a few seconds, was driving her crazy. "If it's all right with you, sir, I'd like to finish my report later."

"Take care of her."

"Yes sir. I will."

Cam dropped the phone on the bedside table, unstrapped her weapon, and stripped down. She wanted to take the weapon with her into the bathroom, but the last thing Blair needed right now was to feel unsafe. She compromised by placing it on the chair closest to the bathroom door. She knocked, tried the handle, and finding the door unlocked, slipped inside. The shower was running, but Blair stood in front of the vanity, her hands clutching the edge, her head down. Her hair fell forward to cover her face, but it was easy to tell that she was crying. Cam cradled her from behind. "It's okay, baby."

Blair turned and wrapped her arms tightly around Cam's shoulders, pressing her face to Cam's neck. "It was over so fast. I didn't think about it. He didn't care if Paula died. I had to stop him."

"Are you sorry?"

"No," Blair said after a few seconds. She raised her head and searched Cam's face. "Should I be?"

Cam smiled wryly. "No, baby. You shouldn't be. He murdered one of Tanner's men, he shot Stark and left her to die. He most certainly would have killed you and Dana once he realized there would be no negotiations. And that was just today."

Blair smiled weakly. "Have you ever…with your bare hands?"

"No. With a weapon." Cam sighed. "And I've given the order, when I would much preferred to have done it with my own hands." She stroked Blair's cheek. "You were amazing. You saved yourself, you saved Dana and Paula. You did exactly what needed to be done." She kissed her. "I'm proud of you."

"You're shaking," Blair murmured.

Cam squeezed her eyes tightly closed, holding back the tears that rose out of nowhere. "I just need to hold you."

Blair caressed Cam's back, smoothed her hand over her hair. "I'm okay. I'm right here."

"Christ, I was scared."

"I knew you would come," Blair whispered. "Don't cry, darling. I'm never leaving you."

Cam swiped her face on her arm. "I just want to spend the rest of the day with you in my arms, but we need to get to the hospital."

"How about taking a shower with me first?"

"I'll take a shower with you. Hell, I'll even go shopping with you."
Cam kissed her, hard. "I'm not letting you out of my sight. Ever."

"I won't complain." Blair laughed. "How things change."

Cam held open the shower door. "Love will do that to you."

❖

Dana pressed a cellophane-wrapped sandwich she'd picked up in
the hospital cafeteria into Renée's hand. She set a cup of coffee on the
end table next to her and dropped into a surprisingly comfortable chair
close by. "I know you don't want to eat, but you should. It's been a long
day. It's probably going to be a longer night."

Renée turned the sandwich around in her hands as if she'd never
seen one before. She still wore her black BDUs and T-shirt, and
she looked wild and dangerous. "She's been in there for almost five
hours."

"The trauma resident told Emory a branch of the femoral artery
was nicked. They have to repair that. That kind of stuff takes a while."

"They said the nerve was okay, didn't they?" Renée asked for the
third time. "Her leg…if her leg…if she can't…"

Dana had never seen anyone faint while sitting down, but she
thought Renée was about to. Her normally vibrant golden skin was
a lusterless, washed-out beige, and her eyes were unfocused. Dana
quickly knelt in front of her and cupped the back of her neck. "Here,
put your head down for a second."

"Sorry," Renée whispered. "Sorry."

"It's okay," Dana murmured, rubbing her shoulder. "It's been a
really crappy day."

Renée laughed weakly and slowly raised her head. Her eyes
glistened with tears. "Yeah. Really." She brushed her cheeks. "She
loves her fucking job. If she can't do it anymore, I think it will break
her heart."

Dana smoothed her hands over Renée's shoulders, then squeezed.
"That kind of decision is way down the road. I think this country needs
people like her right now, and the government doesn't let go easy.
They'll probably rehab her until her ass falls off, but they'll get her
back to work."

"Yeah. I've been there. Rehab's a bitch." Renée looked past Dana's shoulder and stiffened. "Emory! Is there any word?"

"One of the nurses just stuck her head out of the OR. They're almost done. She's stable."

"Do they know anything about her leg yet?"

"It's too soon to tell, but arterial repairs are usually straight-forward." Emory rested her hand on Dana's shoulder as Dana stood up. "I won't say don't worry, because that's impossible. But I think we have reason to be optimistic."

Renée took a shaky breath. "Thanks for everything."

Emory leaned into Dana. "I think Dana is the one to thank. Keeping pressure on the wound all that time made a huge difference."

Dana blushed, liking the way Emory touched her in public. She wished they could be alone. With everything that had been going on, they had barely had a chance to see each other since the counterassault on the cabin. Still, whenever Emory saw her, her gaze lingered on Dana's, and her mouth curved into a small smile. Even the slightest glance made Dana quiver.

Her thoughts were about to wander down decidedly inopportune avenues, considering where they were and how long they were likely to be there, when Blair Powell and Cameron Roberts entered the small waiting area. The president's daughter looked remarkably fresh and composed in jeans and a plain dark blouse. The deputy director wore a jacket and pants and an unreadable expression. *Worried,* Dana thought. She doubted Cameron Roberts liked Blair venturing out in public, which probably explained the presence of a cadre of agents close behind them. Dana nodded toward Blair. "Ms. Powell's the one to thank. She saved our asses."

Renée jumped up as Blair hurried over.

"Hey," Blair said, hugging her. "How are you doing?"

"Okay," Renée said. "How about you?"

Blair's expression clouded. "I'm so damn sorry about Paula, Renée."

Renée frowned. "If it weren't for you, she might be dead."

"If it weren't for me," Blair said bitterly, "she wouldn't be in the operating room right now."

"Blair," Cam said gently.

"It's true, Cameron, and there's no way to pretty it up," Blair said sharply. "Damn it. They were after me."

"Yes, they were," Cam said in a reasonable tone, although the look in her eyes was hot and angry. "They were after you, personally, which is bad enough. But by trying to use you as leverage against the president, they were also after all of us, and all of those that we as a nation protect, not just here, but everywhere. Matheson and those working with him were trying to destroy something far greater than you." She took Blair's hand. "And I can guarantee that Paula Stark or any one of us, *including* you, would gladly go down fighting to prevent that from happening."

Every agent in the room nodded and Blair just shook her head before kissing Cam's cheek. "I love you, you know that?" She looked around the room. "All of you."

"Can I quote you on that?" Dana asked.

"Yes," Blair and Cam replied together.

CHAPTER TWENTY-SEVEN

Diane turned away from the window, sensing a presence despite the utter silence in the room.

Valerie stood just inside the bedroom door, as if she were waiting for permission to come any farther. Diane hadn't heard the door open or close, which wasn't unusual. Valerie appeared and disappeared as if her existence were merely a ripple on the surface of other people's lives.

Diane wondered when Valerie would trust what was between them and believe that there was nothing about her—not her past, not her present, and not what she might have to do in the future—that would force Diane to turn from her. Slowly, she closed the blinds, then crossed the lamplit room until she was standing in front of Valerie. She took both of her hands, marveling at the soft, subtle strength in her long fingers. With her hair tied back in a simple ponytail, without makeup, in the jeans she so very rarely wore and heavy boots, she looked nothing like the sophisticated, elegant woman she usually presented to the world.

"I like you like this," Diane mused, tracing her fingertip along the edge of Valerie's jaw. "You're gorgeous in anything you wear. Or when you wear nothing at all." She laughed and draped her arms loosely around Valerie's neck. "But just like this, you look so strong. Simply beautiful."

Valerie closed her eyes briefly. "I've spent most of my life trying not to be seen. Or at least to be sure that others only saw what I wanted them to see. I'm not sure that what you see is real."

"Oh, believe me," Diane murmured, insinuating her body against Valerie's. "It's real. You are real. What's between us is real."

"I'm very much in love with you," Valerie said quietly.

"Even if I'm not heroic?"

Frowning, Valerie glided them across the room to the bed and pulled Diane down beside her so they were half lying, half sitting, facing each other. "Where did that come from?"

"I'm surrounded by accomplished women. Brave. Valorous. Warrior women." Diane shrugged and stared at a spot on the bed between them. "I'm none of those things. I'm frivolous and fainthearted and—"

"Stop." Valerie silenced her with a kiss. "Bravery isn't about carrying a gun or even being willing to fight. It's about being willing to fight, maybe even die, *for* something. I know you would die for Blair. For any of your friends."

"For you." Diane pulled Valerie closer until their legs entwined. They kissed, and she smelled the lingering hints of battle. She held Valerie tighter, aware that she might not have come back. Accepting that this moment, every moment, was precious. "I love you."

Valerie rested her forehead against Diane's and sighed. "I'm so tired. So tired of never being able to stop. Of never feeling safe."

"Come to bed with me. Let me hold you. Let me keep you safe tonight."

"I will." Valerie pulled away. "But I have to see Cameron first. There are things I need to tell her. They're on their way back from the hospital now. I told them to keep your cabin."

"Fine. Go see her. But then I want you back."

"As soon as I can."

Diane didn't want to let her go. Valerie's eyes were rimmed with shadow, and the pain of too many lonely years shimmered in them. "I'll be here. I want to be here. No matter what comes."

"I want that too." Valerie cradled Diane's hand against her cheek. "More than I have ever wanted anything or anyone."

Diane smiled. "Well, that's a good start."

Laughing, looking lighthearted and suddenly years younger, Valerie rolled away and got to her feet. She pointed, shaking her finger. "Stay right there. Better yet, take off your clothes and get in bed. I'll be right back."

"Go," Diane chided as Valerie backed up slowly, her gaze hungry. Diane was afraid if Valerie didn't leave quickly, she'd go after her, and if she touched her, she might not let her go. "You owe me a night of impossible pleasure, and I plan to collect."

"Impossible?" Valerie shook her head. "That word does not apply to us."

Then Valerie was gone, as quickly and quietly as she had entered. She might be used to passing through other people's lives without leaving a trace, but her presence was indelibly marked on Diane's heart.

With slow anticipation, Diane undressed.

❖

Emory let herself into the cabin as quietly as she could. She'd sent Dana back to the lodge with some of the others hours before, after she'd taken a good look at her and realized that Dana was about to fall down. She'd made Dana promise to go to bed, and hopefully, she was sound asleep right now. She undressed in the living room and tiptoed naked across the darkened bedroom. When she stood by the side of the bed listening to Dana's regular breathing, she thought it was the sweetest sound she'd ever heard. Carefully, she eased under the covers.

"Emory?" Dana asked sleepily.

"Hi," Emory whispered, snuggling close. When she draped her arm around Dana's middle, Dana drew a sharp breath and tensed.

"What is it?" Emory sat up. "Are you hurt? God, Dana—are you hurt?"

"No," Dana said, sounding wide awake now.

"Let me turn on the light and look at you."

"I'm okay," Dana said, stopping Emory with a hand on her arm. "My ribs got banged up this morning, and I'm a little stiff. It's nothing serious."

Emory ran her fingers through Dana's hair. "Are you sure?"

"Promise. We just have to go easy for a few days."

"Damn," Emory murmured, relaxing into Dana's arms again. "And here I had such plans for you."

"They'll keep, won't they?"

Emory heard uncertainty in Dana's voice and kissed the edge of her jaw. "Didn't we say this morning—God, was it only this morning? Didn't we say that being together last night was a beginning? Today, when I thought something might have happened to you…" Emory's voice wavered and she had to take a deep breath. "I want you in my life. I want us to find out what that means."

"I want that too." Dana kissed her forehead, then her lips. "I'm away a lot."

"I work a lot."

"I don't fool around."

"That's too bad." She danced her fingers down the center of Dana's chest, over her abdomen, then lower. "Because I do."

"Let me revise that," Dana whispered. "I only fool around with you."

"May I quote you?" Emory asked, gently stroking.

"Yes." Dana groaned. "Can you…please…oh, God. Can you just keep doing that forever?"

Emory laughed softly. "Well, that's a start."

❖

"Drink?" Cam asked as she poured another two fingers of scotch into her glass.

"No, thank you," Valerie said, quickly scanning the room. "Blair?"

Cam nodded toward the closed bedroom door as she returned to the sofa. "Asleep. As soon as we got back from the hospital she crashed."

"No wonder. I got word that Stark is out of surgery."

Cam sat heavily, stretched her legs out, and let her head drop onto the back of the sofa. She had changed into jeans and a sweatshirt after Blair had fallen asleep, and waited, knowing that Valerie would eventually arrive. "All things considered, she's lucky. The round tore up some muscle but missed the bone and the nerve. If it hadn't nicked the artery, she probably wouldn't even have gone down. The blood loss is what took her out."

"Then she should do well."

"With a little more of that luck." Cam grimaced, thinking of the man they had lost. Of almost losing Stark. Of Dana. And God, of Blair. She gestured to the sofa. "Sit down. You must be beat, because I sure as hell am."

"Our situations are a little bit different." Valerie settled on the couch a few inches from Cam. "I thought you'd want a report tonight."

"I do." Cam sipped her scotch. "I'll trade you what I got from Lucinda if you tell me you got Matheson's partner."

Valerie tilted her head, half smiling. "Which one?"

"Not the one that was making the phone demands to DC. The one Matheson was counting on to get him out of here today."

"I wondered if you'd figured that out."

Cam grinned wearily. "I'm tired, but I think my brain is still functioning."

"No one would blame you for being off your game today, but you weren't."

"Yes, I was, and you know it. I owe you…we all owe you…for telling me so."

"I didn't want control of the operation because I didn't trust your judgment, Cameron." Valerie shot a look toward the bedroom door and lowered her voice further. "If something went wrong, I wanted—"

"I know what you wanted." Cam tapped Valerie's arm, a light caress, then drew her hand away. "You wanted the casualties to be on your head, not mine. Especially if one of them was Blair."

"Yes."

"Thank you."

"You're welcome." Valerie angled sideways on the sofa and her leg lightly brushed Cam's thigh. "We're almost even."

Cam shook her head. "Let's just say we've each saved each other's lives more than once. Hopefully we won't have to do it again."

"Hopefully," Valerie said pensively.

"So tell me."

"When Greg was flying a grid over the area in the chopper, he spotted a snowmobile trail cutting through the forest about five miles down the mountain. It didn't intersect with the main road, but it ran close enough in spots that a heavy off-road vehicle could have reached it."

"A big SUV like the Suburban," Cam said.

"Yes. He had the pilot bring the helicopter down where the trail came closest to the road and it looked like the trees were thinner. He found an old fire trail and followed it. Guess what he found."

Cam drained her scotch and set the glass carefully on the table beside her. "An abandoned snowmobile?"

"Precisely."

"Matheson knew we would follow him if he managed to get out of here with Blair in the SUV," Cam said tonelessly. "But all he needed was to be a minute ahead of us—then he pulls off road, reaches the trail where his partner is waiting, transfers to the snowmobile, and disappears into the forest. We wouldn't be able to see them from the air and we wouldn't have the equipment to track them on the ground."

Valerie shrugged. "Simple, but elegant. The best plans always are. I've got people out there now following the snowmobile tracks, but I doubt they'll find anything."

"He didn't expect us to risk the hostages by engaging him in the cabin." Cam stood abruptly, her chest hot with anger. Matheson would have executed the hostages in the forest, she was certain of that. "He thought he could put Blair in that vehicle and drive away, and we'd let him."

"He was counting on us being cautious because of who Blair is."

Cam grinned with dark pleasure. "He underestimated her, didn't he?"

"He did. How is she?"

"Exhausted." Cam braced an arm on the fireplace and watched flames lick at the logs. "She wasn't supposed to have to do this herself. That's why we're here, to spare her this."

"Cameron," Valerie said softly. She went to Cam and rested both hands on her shoulders. "What's important is that she survived. And she has you to remind her that what she did was right, on every level."

"Lucinda couldn't get a trace on the caller." Cam sighed as Valerie lightly massaged her shoulders. "When he was advised there would be no prisoner exchange, he said this was only the first strike. Then he hung up."

"We've heard that before. We know this is only the beginning."

"I need you on the team, now more than ever." Cam turned and Valerie dropped her hands. "I've got the best people there are, but you...you know me, and I need that."

"The agency teaches us to believe that the greatest danger is allowing others to know us." Valerie cupped Cam's jaw and kissed her fleetingly. "That was for showing me how very wrong they were. Thank you."

"You're welcome," Cam said softly as Valerie stepped away. Cam squared her shoulders. "Let the others know we'll be briefing at oh six hundred."

"I'll do that. Good night."

❖

"Was that Valerie?" Blair asked when Cam came into the bedroom.

"Yes. Giving report." Cam kicked off her boots and undressed. She climbed into bed and drew Blair into her arms. "I'm sorry if we woke you."

"No, I was awake." Blair tucked her head beneath Cam's chin. "Is everything all right now?"

"We're secure."

"Are we going to be able to find Matheson's accomplices?"

"Eventually," Cam said with certainty.

"And until then?"

"We go on with our lives, just as we planned."

Blair sighed. "My father shouldn't come out here right now, should he?"

"Ah, baby," Cam murmured. "I'm sorry."

"And Paula is going to be in the hospital for another week at least." Blair inched closer until she was lying on top of Cam. She curled her arms around Cam's shoulders and nuzzled her neck. "I'm not getting married without Paula there."

"We'll reschedule." When Blair stiffened, Cam caught her chin and raised her head, forcing Blair to look at her. "Postpone. Not cancel. You can't get out of it this easily."

Blair laughed. "And here I thought I was going to get rid of you."

"Never." Cam grasped Blair's shoulders and rolled them over, settling her hips between Blair's legs. She kissed her, sinking into the heat of her mouth and the soft welcome of her body. She whispered against her lips, "I love you, and no one and nothing will come between us. I intend to say that to everyone who will listen."

"They…whoever *they* are…probably think they'll frighten us into hiding. Not just how we feel about one another, but from them. I won't hide."

"No, we won't hide." Cam spread her fingers through Blair's hair, holding her as she kissed down her neck. When Blair's legs came around hers, pulling her in tighter, she felt the familiar surge of arousal that never failed to amaze her. What they shared was more than love, it was life, and no one would take that from them. "Are you too tired?"

Blair found Cam's hand and brought it to her breast. She pressed Cam's fingers against her heart. "I need you, in here. Make love to me in here. You're the only one who can."

With passion and reverence, power and joy, Cam took what was given and gave all that she had.

CHAPTER TWENTY-EIGHT

One Month Later

L et me go around and get the door," Renée said as the Suburban
pulled to a stop on the circular drive in front of the sweeping
wood and glass house on the edge of the ocean. "Use your cane, all
right?"

"I've got it right here," Paula replied, waiting dutifully while
Renée jumped out and sprinted around the vehicle to open her door. She
really didn't need the help any longer, but Renée needed to do it. She'd
felt the same way when Renée had been shot, helpless and scared. So
she didn't protest when Renée leaned in to take her arm and guide her
onto the flagstone walkway leading up to Tanner and Adrienne's home
on Whitley Island.

"Just let me know if you start feeling tired," Renée said, "and
we'll go someplace and sit for a while."

"Right. I will."

Renée hooked her arm through Paula's as they made their way
past terraced gardens that were covered now with snow and the empty
fountains that in summer filled the air with cascading rainbows. "I'm
hovering, aren't I?"

"Nope." Paula nodded to the agents who flanked the staircase
leading up to the wide veranda, checking IDs and guest lists. She
blushed when several casually saluted her. The notoriety that came with
having been shot in the line of duty was embarrassing, especially when
she hadn't even been able to neutralize the threat to her protectee. She
certainly did not feel heroic.

"You did your job, sweetie," Renée murmured. "You made everyone proud."

"It's scary the way you can read my mind."

Renée kissed her cheek. "It's only because I love you."

"That's good." Paula laughed and hooked an arm around Renée's waist. "Because I'd hate to think that anybody else would know what I was thinking—especially when you look so spectacular in that dress."

"Is that a line?"

Paula waited while the agent at the door held it open for them, and once they were inside the great room, which was already alive with activity and the buzz of conversation, answered, "Absolutely. The doctor said no restrictions except heavy lifting. And you're not heavy."

Renée laughed and waved to Emory and Dana. "You've got two weeks until you start serious rehab. In the meantime, I guess we can work a little on your flexibility."

"Sounds like just the therapy I need."

❖

"It's hard to believe it's only been a month since that nightmare," Emory said when Paula and Renée moved off to speak to the hostesses. Her gaze swept over Dana, her lids slowly lowering as her lips curved playfully. "Although I *am* aware it's been almost a month since the last time I saw you. Painfully aware."

"Longest month of my life," Dana muttered, concentrating on the feel of Emory's hand in hers. They hadn't touched in twenty-eight days. Twenty-eight endless days and restless nights. She wished they were anywhere else right now, doing anything other than waiting for the first daughter to get married. She was still officially on this story, although she didn't seem to be able to pay attention to anyone but Emory. God, but Emory smelled so good, and her dress—a shade of blue the exact color of the Mediterranean Sea—accentuated all her curves and revealed just enough skin as it dipped low over her chest and back to make Dana's palms tingle. "It's so damn good to see you. I've been living on the sound of your voice over the phone, and as fun as that is sometimes, it's not enough. I'm dying to touch you."

"I'm sorry I couldn't get away sooner. Knowing that you arrived last night to interview Blair and I couldn't get here until this morning has been driving me crazy." Emory leaned closer and whispered, "I want to kiss you. Actually, I want to get you out of that very elegant suit and make love to you for a week."

"Only a week?"

"That's round one."

Dana wondered how she was going to manage civil conversation for the next five hours while she was completely aroused. "I'm due some time off. I never collected on my leave after I got back from overseas the last time. Clive has had me chained to my desk."

"Your reports on terrorism and what it means for us, all of us, have been amazing. I'm glad the White House didn't demand a blackout on all of it." Emory scanned the crowd waiting for the signal to move into the solarium where the ceremony would be held, noting the large number of security guards. "You handled what happened to Blair very sensitively."

"Even if I didn't know her personally, I wouldn't have reported the details of what happened out there anyhow." Dana shrugged. "I don't have to give some other bunch of crazies any ideas in order to report what really matters. While Lucinda Washburn and my editor were fussing at each other over First Amendment rights versus national security, I just wrote my story and let them worry about the spin."

"I loved reading your articles. It made me feel closer to you."

"Can you get away?" Dana asked, knowing she sounded desperate. "I really need—"

"Yes. That's why I've been so busy. We had funding reports due, and I needed to get my senior people started on an important leg of our current project. Now I can take a break." Emory squeezed Dana's hand. "I need time with you too. Will you...will you be going back overseas?"

"I don't know. It depends on how long that dustup over there lasts. Maybe." Dana knew it wasn't easy for people in her line of work to maintain a relationship, and she wanted to so badly. "I know it's soon and I know my lifestyle isn't ideal, but—"

"It's not too soon. And I understand about your job." Emory kissed her cheek. "I'm not always available either. But you matter—*we* matter—we'll find a way to make it work."

Dana kissed her, a soft kiss of promise. "We will."

"I'm surprised you're still doing this part of the story," Emory said, gesturing to the crowd.

"If it had been anyone else's wedding, I would've found a way to get out of it. But I wanted to see you, and I wanted to be here for Blair and Cam, and"—she gestured toward the door as the president of the United States walked in with Lucinda Washburn on his arm—"this is the story of the hour."

❖

"Nervous?" Diane zipped up the back of Blair's cream Armani dress and rested both hands on Blair's shoulders, studying her in the mirror in front of them. The squared bodice highlighted Blair's smooth, strong shoulders and the subtle ruching accentuated the flowing lines of her body. "This dress is fabulous. You're a knockout."

Blair tipped her head back against Diane's shoulder and sighed. "I'm not really nervous. Excited, mostly."

"Tanner has done a great job keeping the press from bugging us this week, and having Dana stay on as the official reporter has really helped."

"It's the first time I've ever been happy to have a reporter in my pocket," Blair said with a laugh. "Is everything okay with you? I haven't seen much of Valerie this week."

"She's here, but she's keeping a low profile, mostly to keep me happy. I know Cam said that with her handler gone and Matheson dead, there's probably no one in the agency interested in her any longer, but I still don't want her picture in the newspapers."

Blair slid in the diamond drop earrings that Cam had given her as an early birthday present. "You're getting pretty good at the secret agent stuff."

Diane laughed and shook her head. "I know. Whoever would have thought."

"But you're okay?" Blair turned and took Diane's hands. "You're happy?"

"More than I ever imagined." Diane gave Blair's hands a shake. "Especially since Cam got to you before I could convince you what a great catch I am."

Blair kissed her cheek, then hugged her. "I love you."

"Hair! Makeup!" Diane exclaimed in horror, but she hugged Blair back. "I love you too."

A knock sounded on the door followed by a male voice inquiring, "Blair?"

Diane stepped away. "That's my cue to go find my lover. I'll see you downstairs."

"Don't get lost. I'm not doing this without you right next to me."

"That's where I'll be, anytime you need me."

Blair called, "Come in."

The door opened and the president stepped inside. "Hi, Diane."

"Mr. President, great to see you." Diane slipped past him and disappeared outside.

"Hi, Daddy," Blair said.

"Hi, honey. All set?"

She took his hand. "Yes."

❖

"Let me do that," Marcea said, fastening the small emblem of the seal of the United States that the president had presented to Cam for meritorious service to the lapel of her charcoal gray morning coat. Then she smoothed her hands over Cam's shoulders and down her sleeves. "You look very dashing."

"No one will be looking at me," Cam said. At least she hoped that was the case.

"You're every bit as beautiful as Blair."

Cam laughed. "Spoken like a mother."

"Which I am," Marcea said affectionately. "This is a very brave thing you are doing. I'm very proud of you."

"Loving Blair is the smartest thing I've ever done in my life," Cam said. "Convincing her to have me was the hard part. Everything after that is easy."

"I know that what happened in Colorado could happen again. But we can't live in fear, can we." Marcea kissed Cam's cheek. "Let your friends help you both take care of each other."

"I will." Cam held out her arm to her mother. "If I can be half as wise and brave as you, we'll be fine."

"Then I won't worry about you at all. Ready?"

"I am."

❖

Blair stepped into the hall with her father just as Cam and Marcea came out of the room opposite.

"Sir." Cam nodded to the president.

"Cameron."

"Hello, darling," Blair said softly.

"Hi, baby," Cam murmured, stepping close as the president and her mother turned away to say hello.

"Any second thoughts?" Blair asked.

"Not a one." Cam wanted to kiss her, but she held back. "You look beautiful."

"So do you." Blair was surprised to hear her voice shaking. "Just to be clear, I want to spend the rest of my life with you."

"I'm yours, forever. Count on it."

"I do."

"I do too."

Blair joined her father. "I'll see you downstairs, then, and we can say it again for the whole world to hear."

"Anything you say, Ms. Powell," Cam called after her as Blair's laughter filled her heart.

About the Author

Radclyffe is a retired surgeon and full time award-winning author-publisher with over thirty lesbian novels and anthologies in print, including the Lambda Literary winners *Erotic Interludes 2: Stolen Moments* ed. with Stacia Seaman and *Distant Shores, Silent Thunder*. Her novels *Justice Served, Turn Back Time*, and *When Dreams Tremble* were Lambda Literary Award finalists. She has selections in multiple anthologies including *Wild Nights, Fantasy, Best Lesbian Erotica 2006, 2007*, and *2008, After Midnight, Caught Looking: Erotic Tales of Voyeurs and Exhibitionists, First-Timers, Ultimate Undies: Erotic Stories About Lingerie and Underwear, A is for Amour, H is for Hardcore, L is for Leather,* and *Rubber Sex*. She is the recipient of the 2003 and 2004 Alice B. Readers' awards for her body of work and is also the president of Bold Strokes Books, one of the world's largest independent LGBT publishing companies.

Her forthcoming works include *Night Call* (October 2008) and *Justice for All* (2009).

Books Available From Bold Strokes Books

Finding Home by Georgia Beers. Take two polar-opposite women with an attraction for one another they're trying desperately to ignore, throw in a far-too-observant dog, and then sit back and enjoy the romance. (978-1-60282-019-7)

Word of Honor by Radclyffe. All Secret Service Agent Cameron Roberts and First Daughter Blair Powell want is a small intimate wedding, but the paparazzi and a domestic terrorist have other plans. (978-1-60282-018-0)

Hotel Liaison by JLee Meyer. Two women searching through a secret past discover that their brief hotel liaison is only the beginning. Will they risk their careers—and their hearts—to follow through on their desires? (978-1-60282-017-3)

Love on Location by Lisa Girolami. Hollywood film producer Kate Nyland and artist Dawn Brock discover that love doesn't always follow the script. (978-1-60282-016-6)

Edge of Darkness by Jove Belle. Investigator Diana Collins charges at life with an irreverent comment and a right hook, but even those may not protect her heart from a charming villain. (978-1-60282-015-9)

Thirteen Hours by Meghan O'Brien. Workaholic Dana Watts's life takes a sudden turn when an unexpected interruption arrives in the form of the most beautiful breasts she has ever seen—stripper Laurel Stanley's. (978-1-60282-014-2)

In Deep Waters 2 by Radclyffe and Karin Kallmaker. All bets are off when two award winning-authors deal the cards of love and passion… and every hand is a winner. (978-1-60282-013-5)

Pink by Jennifer Harris. An irrepressible heroine frolics, frets, and navigates through the "what ifs" of her life: all the unexpected turns of fortune, fame, and karma. (978-1-60282-043-2)

Deal with the Devil by Ali Vali. New Orleans crime boss Cain Casey brings her fury down on the men who threatened her family, and blood and bullets fly. (978-1-60282-012-8)

Naked Heart by Jennifer Fulton. When a sexy ex-CIA agent sets out to seduce and entrap a powerful CEO, there's more to this plan than meets the eye…or the flogger. (978-1-60282-011-1)

Heart of the Matter by KI Thompson. TV newscaster Kate Foster is Professor Ellen Webster's dream girl, but Kate doesn't know Ellen exists…until an accident changes everything. (978-1-60282-010-4)

Heartland by Julie Cannon. When political strategist Rachel Stanton and dude ranch owner Shivley McCoy collide on an empty country road, fate intervenes. (978-1-60282-009-8)

Shadow of the Knife by Jane Fletcher. Militia Rookie Ellen Mittal has no idea just how complex and dangerous her life is about to become. A Celaeno series adventure romance. (978-1-60282-008-1)

To Protect and Serve by VK Powell. Lieutenant Alex Troy is caught in the paradox of her life—to hold steadfast to her professional oath or to protect the woman she loves. (978-1-60282-007-4)

Deeper by Ronica Black. Former homicide detective Erin McKenzie and her fiancée Elizabeth Adams couldn't be happier—until the not-so-distant past comes knocking at the door. (978-1-60282-006-7)

The Lonely Hearts Club by Radclyffe. Take three friends, add two ex-lovers and several new ones, and the result is a recipe for explosive rivalries and incendiary romance. (978-1-60282-005-0)

Venus Besieged by Andrews & Austin. Teague Richfield heads for Sedona and the sensual arms of psychic astrologer Callie Rivers for a much-needed romantic reunion. (978-1-60282-004-3)

Branded Ann by Merry Shannon. Pirate Branded Ann raids a merchant vessel to obtain a treasure map and gets more than she bargained for with the widow Violet. (978-1-60282-003-6)

American Goth by JD Glass. Trapped by an unsuspected inheritance and guided only by the guardian who holds the secret to her future, Samantha Cray fights to fulfill her destiny. (978-1-60282-002-9)

Learning Curve by Rachel Spangler. Ashton Clarke is perfectly content with her life until she meets the intriguing Professor Carrie Fletcher, who isn't looking for a relationship with anyone. (978-1-60282-001-2)

Place of Exile by Rose Beecham. Sheriff's detective Jude Devine struggles with ghosts of her past and an ex-lover who still haunts her dreams. (978-1-933110-98-1)

Fully Involved by Erin Dutton. A love that has smoldered for years ignites when two women and one little boy come together in the aftermath of tragedy. (978-1-933110-99-8)

Heart 2 Heart by Julie Cannon. Suffering from a devastating personal loss, Kyle Bain meets Lane Connor, and the chance for happiness suddenly seems possible. (978-1-60282-000-5)

Queens of Tristaine by Cate Culpepper. When a deadly plague stalks the Amazons of Tristaine, two warrior lovers must return to the place of their nightmares to find a cure. (978-1-933110-97-4)

The Crown of Valencia by Catherine Friend. Ex-lovers can really mess up your life…even, as Kate discovers, if they've traveled back to the eleventh century! (978-1-933110-96-7)

Mine by Georgia Beers. What happens when you've already given your heart and love finds you again? Courtney McAllister is about to find out. (978-1-933110-95-0)

House of Clouds by KI Thompson. A sweeping saga of an impassioned romance between a Northern spy and a Southern sympathizer, set amidst the upheaval of a nation under siege. (978-1-933110-94-3)

Winds of Fortune by Radclyffe. Provincetown local Deo Camara agrees to rehab Dr. Bonita Burgoyne's historic home, but she never said anything about mending her heart. (978-1-933110-93-6)

Focus of Desire by Kim Baldwin. Isabel Sterling is surprised when she wins a photography contest, but no more than photographer Natasha Kashnikova. Their promo tour becomes a ticket to romance. (978-1-933110-92-9)

Blind Leap by Diane and Jacob Anderson-Minshall. A Golden Gate Bridge suicide becomes suspect when a filmmaker's camera shows a different story. Yoshi Yakamota and the Blind Eye Detective Agency uncover evidence that could be worth killing for. (978-1-933110-91-2)

Wall of Silence, 2nd ed. by Gabrielle Goldsby. Life takes a dangerous turn when jaded police detective Foster Everett meets Riley Medeiros, a woman who isn't afraid to discover the truth no matter the cost. (978-1-933110-90-5)

Mistress of the Runes by Andrews & Austin. Passion ignites between two women with ties to ancient secrets, contemporary mysteries, and a shared quest for the meaning of life. (978-1-933110-89-9)

Vulture's Kiss by Justine Saracen. Archeologist Valerie Foret, heir to a terrifying task, returns in a powerful desert adventure set in Egypt and Jerusalem. (978-1-933110-87-5)

Sheridan's Fate by Gun Brooke. A dynamic, erotic romance between physiotherapist Lark Mitchell and businesswoman Sheridan Ward set in the scorching hot days and humid, steamy nights of San Antonio. (978-1-933110-88-2)

Rising Storm by JLee Meyer. The sequel to *First Instinct* takes our heroines on a dangerous journey instead of the honeymoon they'd planned. (978-1-933110-86-8)

Not Single Enough by Grace Lennox. A funny, sexy modern romance about two lonely women who bond over the unexpected and fall in love along the way. (978-1-933110-85-1)

Such a Pretty Face by Gabrielle Goldsby. A sexy, sometimes humorous, sometimes biting contemporary romance that gently exposes the damage to heart and soul when we fail to look beneath the surface for what truly matters. (978-1-933110-84-4)

Second Season by Ali Vali. A romance set in New Orleans amidst betrayal, Hurricane Katrina, and the new beginnings hardship and heartbreak sometimes make possible. (978-1-933110-83-7)

Hearts Aflame by Ronica Black. A poignant, erotic romance between a hard-driving businesswoman and a solitary vet. Packed with adventure and set in the harsh beauty of the Arizona countryside. (978-1-933110-82-0)

Red Light by JD Glass. Tori forges her path as an EMT in the New York City 911 system while discovering what matters most to herself and the woman she loves. (978-1-933110-81-3)

Honor Under Siege by Radclyffe. Secret Service agent Cameron Roberts struggles to protect her lover while searching for a traitor who just may be another woman with a claim on her heart. (978-1-933110-80-6)

Dark Valentine by Jennifer Fulton. Danger and desire fuel a high-stakes cat-and-mouse game when an attorney and an endangered witness team up to thwart a killer. (978-1-933110-79-0)